100 YEARS *of* THE GREAT GATSBY

LANDMARKS

The series commemorates and celebrates texts, events and personalities that have shaped societies, cultures and communities in India. The volumes bring together personal narratives and scholarly explorations as they reconsider and reread histories and cultures.

100 YEARS *of* THE GREAT GATSBY

Responses: Local and Global

Edited by
Sanjukta Dasgupta

Orient BlackSwan

100 YEARS OF *THE GREAT GATSBY*

ORIENT BLACKSWAN PRIVATE LIMITED

Registered Office
3-6-752 Himayatnagar, Hyderabad 500 029, Telangana, India
Email: centraloffice@orientblackswan.com

Other Offices
Bengaluru, Chennai, Guwahati, Hyderabad,
Kolkata, Mumbai, New Delhi, Noida, Patna

First published 2026

ISBN 978-93-6973-046-9

041915

Typeset in Minion Pro 11/13.2 *by*
LiteBook Prepress Services, Chennai 600 069

Printed in India at
Manipal Technologies Limited., Manipal

Published by
Orient Blackswan Private Limited
3-6-752 Himayatnagar, Hyderabad 500 029, Telangana India
Email: info@orientblackswan.com

Contents

Introduction

Sanjukta Dasgupta

Remember my words, I may again return,
I love you, I depart from materials,
I am as one disembodied, triumphant, dead.

Walt Whitman, 'So Long'

I

This concluding couplet of Walt Whitman's poem 'So Long' probably is not inappropriate as an epigraph to this introductory essay on the celebrated American writer Francis Scott Key Fitzgerald's (1896–1940) phenomenal novel *The Great Gatsby* first published on 10 April 1925. One hundred years later, in 2025, we notice that in its centennial year, the novel instead of being relegated to the back shelves of libraries, has probably gained in relevance in this second millennium. *The Great Gatsby* cannot be compartmentalised as a venerable 'old' book about old times, summed up as an early-twentieth century American classic, about those good old days of reckless permissiveness, the burgeoning of the American nouveau riche class, the resultant exponential impact of dysfunctional relationships leading to trauma and tragedy.

In this centennial year since its first publication on 10 April 1925, we notice that the uniqueness of *The Great Gatsby* lies in the fact that time has not been able to gnaw at its vitals, it is still pertinent sometimes even more relatable in this era of cultural globalisation, open market economy, capitalist patriarchy and neo-liberal policies than just another archival material, a historical script of post-First World War America. Scott Fitzgerald's novel is not fossil fiction. *The Great Gatsby* is still being read, discussed, filmed and included in university courses, as it is relatable even in the twenty-first century.

After the recognition and success of his first three fictional works, *This Side of Paradise* (1920), *The Beautiful and the Damned* (1922) and *The Diamond as Big as the Ritz* (1922), Fitzgerald published *The Great Gatsby* in 1925. In the meantime, he wrote some significant short stories that seemed to experiment with the content that would eventually constitute an integral part of his outstanding novel *The Great Gatsby*, though certain literary critics consider his first novel or even his last unfinished novel *The Last Tycoon* to have been his best work.

Fitzgerald was never at ease with the title of his fourth novel, even days before it went off for printing. The title *The Great Gatsby*, with its alliterative appeal was not the author's favourite or first choice. Fitzgerald's suggested titles were *Trimalchio* and *Trimalchio in West Egg*, *On the Road to West Egg*, *Under the Red, White, Blue*, *Among Ash Heaps and Millionaires*, *The Gold-Hatted Gatsby* and *The High Bouncing Lover*. Max Perkins, the editor of Charles Scribner's publishing house, turned down the suggestions and preferred *The Great Gatsby* as the title of Fitzgerald's fourth book. Fitzgerald, himself, wrote the epigraph of the novel, under the pen name Thomas Parke D'Invilliers, wherein his own choice of title is perhaps indicated—'Then wear the gold hat, if that will move her; If you can bounce high, bounce for her too, Till she cry "Lover, gold-hatted, high-bouncing lover, / I must have you!"'

Interestingly, there are certain tangential thematic similarities between Fitzgerald's fictional representation of the life of Gatsby, first published in 1925, and Jordan Belfort's memoir *The Wolf of Wall Street* published in 2007. The spectacular roller-coaster life of Belfort as a stockbroker, gained international acclaim and awards when the film version with the same title, *The Wolf of Wall Street*, directed by Martin Scorsese was released in 2013. Quite remarkably a more glamorous film version of *The Great Gatsby*, was released in that same year, 2013. In the film versions of the novel and the memoir, *The Great Gatsby* and *The Wolf of Wall Street* respectively, the role of the protagonist was played by Hollywood's superstar

Leonardo De Caprio. In both cases the casting seemed to have been perfect.

Several of Fitzgerald's short stories, published in 1920, bear the first evidences of the *Gatsby* content that probably was crystallising in the author's mind. In her introduction to Fitzgerald's short stories Sarah Churchwell observed, 'In many ways Fitzgerald's stories amplify the novels, surrounding his more symphonic works almost chorally playing out variations on characteristic motifs. But his stories are not thematically similar to the novels, they also contain a great deal of the delicate, exquisite magic of Fitzgerald's poetic prose—the superlative artistry he could conjure, which Hemingway enviously compared to "the dust on a butterfly's wings"' (in Fitzgerald 2010, vii). Churchwell further commented, 'to a certain extent, Fitzgerald used his stories as notebooks or even workshops, experimenting with various approaches to his current ideas and themes. The stories from *All the Sad Young Men* such as "Winter Dreams", "The Last of the Belles", "The Sensible Thing", "The Rich Boy" and "Absolution", anticipate and echo the entwined themes of dreams and disenchantment, romance and class consciousness in *The Great Gatsby*' (viii).

So in *Flappers and Philosophers*, a volume of short stories published in 1920, Fitzgerald was already mulling the idea of creating a Gatsby figure and folks of his ilk, who were envisaged as being so affluent that they had ceased taking interest in the world beyond their own social circles and business worlds. So in the short story titled 'The Rich Boy', the authorial voice intervened, explaining in lucid terms, that the rich were more vulnerable than those who aspired to emulate them. Scott Donaldson, one of Fitzgerald's biographers, had commented, 'His young men either live in an eternal romantic dream, nursing the sorrow of their unrequited love for the magical girl in the distance, or they actually capture her and are inevitably disillusioned. It's a no-win situation for the girl, either way. For the young men, however, the sorrow-dream is preferable' (1983, 110). Biographer Meyers had remarked that in the novel Fitzgerald continues to use fiction to tell his story, 'reflecting on the superior and brutal qualities of the rich and on the impossibility of becoming one of them—but

[*Gatsby*] is now truly *invented* fiction, not something carelessly cobbled' (1994, 139).

As pointed out by Sarah Churchwell, Fitzgerald had written to his publisher Max Perkins about his resolution to write a novel that would bear the evidence of unprecedented narratorial excellence that would stand the test of time. He wrote that his next writing venture, that is *The Great Gatsby*, would be 'a consciously artistic achievement', one that he explicitly contrasted with his 'trashy fiction': 'so in my new novel I'm thrown purely directly on purely creative work—not trashy imaginings as in my stories but the sustained imagination of a sincere and radiant world' (Churchwell in Fitzgerald 2010, xii).

Yet when *The Great Gatsby* was first published, much to the disappointment of the author, the book failed to emerge as an outstanding bestseller. The sale of about twenty-five thousand copies, far less than his first two novels, did not match his expectations and barely paid off his advance. Two weeks after the book was published, he admitted to Perkins that he was trapped by his own extravagance. He mentioned the old conflict between art and money, and said he might have to sacrifice his career and sell out to the movies if *Gatsby* does not support him (Meyers 1994, 147).

By 1980, *The Great Gatsby* (which had been dropped from the Modern Library publishing house for lack of interest during the 1930s) was selling at the rate of three hundred thousand copies a year and the total sales of Fitzgerald's books had reached eight million.

In fact, it is quite remarkable to ponder that at the time when Fitzgerald and Hemingway were writing and publishing their novels such as *This Side of Paradise, The Great Gatsby, The Sun also Rises* and *A Farewell to Arms,* Rabindranath Tagore was writing and publishing the intensely romantic *Shesher Kabita* ('The Final Poem') in 1929, and again *Char Adhay* in 1936, a romantic critique of the armed resistance against British rule. Significantly, Sarat Chandra Chattopadhyay published his novel *Pather Dabi*, in support of armed resistance, in 1926. The most significant publication around this period, however, was Tagore's self-translation of his play *Raktakarabi* as *Red Oleanders*. The play underpinned issues of personal freedom, exploitation and oppression of the disadvantaged, the carcinogenic networks of capitalism and its targets profit and power.

In *The Great Gatsby*, Fitzgerald addressed similar issues focussing on human vulnerabilities, how lust for wealth, profit and power can dehumanise and destroy individuals, who are besotted with the narcotic impact of capitalism. There are multiple evidences that these stalwarts of the Bengali literary environment, contemporaries of Fitzgerald and Hemingway, were familiar with the writings of the American writers of their times. However, as this is a centennial volume on Fitzgerald's novel, *The Great Gatsby*, I will not delve further into the sameness and differences that contribute to their global and local historical contexts, including British colonialism and its aftermath.

In 1925, the year *The Great Gatsby* was published, Theodore Dreiser published *An American Tragedy*, Dos Passos published *Manhattan Transfer* and Hemingway published *In Our Time*. In its essence Fitzgerald's *The Great Gatsby* maybe read as a caveat directed against dizzying heights of self-destructive aspirational goals that defy reason. Unharnessed targets geared towards acquisition of wealth without wisdom and reflection, can inevitably lead to disastrous results. The stratification of economic class divisions, the social hierarchy in capitalist America, cannot be made to be the representative graph, the exceptionalism of a single *have-not* entrepreneur evolving into an unhappy *have-all*. Jay Gatsby remains unique and exceptional, not a stereotype of the Jazz Age.

Jay Gatsby's ascending curve stops at the fringes of the elusive dream of American capitalism. It is not a simple dream. The American Dream has many overt and covert layers. The tinted seductive dream that material success secures happiness—larger the mansion, more the happiness—has been adroitly torn into tatters by Fitzgerald in his tragic novel. The burgeoning class of the nouveau riche is symbolised by the architectural extravagance of Gatsby's mansion, 'it was a factual imitation of some Hotel de Ville in Normandy, with a tower on one side, spanking new under a thin beard of raw ivy, and a marble swimming pool, and more than forty acres of lawn and garden. It was Gatsby's mansion' (Fitzgerald 1950, 13). Fitzgerald also emphasised how affluence and a life of privilege could have a negative impact on the psyche of a person, as in the case of Tom Buchanan, the husband of Daisy.

Nick Carraway, the narrator in Fitzgerald's *The Great Gatsby*, describes Tom Buchanan with incisive precision, 'Two shining arrogant eyes had established dominance over his face and gave him the appearance of always leaning aggressively forward. Not even the effeminate swank of his riding clothes could hide the enormous power of that body—he seemed to fill those glistening boots until he strained the top lacing, and you could see a great pack of muscle shifting when his shoulder moved under his thin coat, It was a body capable of enormous leverage—a cruel body.' (Fitzgerald 1950, 13)

The Great Gatsby was a warning signal in post-First World War, Jazz Age affluent, white America, in the 1920s. Fitzgerald warned that infatuation embedded in unreason, the deceptions underpinning material wealth, power, glitz, glamour, more the merrier rave parties, and the defiance of middle-class social norms and ethics could lead to the destruction of innate human values of love and happiness. Readers are made to notice how, ironically, wild exhibitionism of bacchanalian revelry could grind to a halt in a second, as a bullet seeking vengeance ushers in the tragic end of the fantasist, the *great* Gatsby. Gatsby's father, a man of obvious modest means, attends the funeral of his wealthy and extravagant son. Despite proving himself as an iconic successful American dreamer, Gatsby dies as a victim of the changing times of America's socio-economic profile of the nineteen twenties.

Gatsby, the rich, simple, passionate and sincere bootlegger, could not isolate dreams of success from the absurdities of illusions, hallucinations and nightmares. The drug of dreams permeated his critical intelligence. Fitzgerald underscores how the American Cream could be simultaneously alluring and lethal. Gatsby's obsessive love for Daisy made him blind to her faults and eccentricities. Gatsby's infatuation and one-track mind may remind readers of Heathcliff, Emily Bronte's enigmatic and romantic, tall, dark and handsome hero in *The Wuthering Heights*. Despite the obvious differences in context, from location to historicity in terms of space and time, the surprising commonalities between the nouveau-riche Gatsby and the avaricious Heathcliff cannot escape attention.

Fitzgerald, who referred to himself as a cynical idealist, had a lover's quarrel with affluence and material success. *The Great Gatsby* was intended as an alarm bell; it brought to the forefront, the shock and awe, the destructive dehumanisation that excessive wealth and unbridled hedonistic revelry created. According to Fitgerald's first biographer Arthur Mizener, both Fitzgerald and his wife Zelda, defied all social norms and led an incredible life of wild euphoria. Arthur Mizener, wrote about Fitzgerald and Zelda,

> They rode down Fifth Avenue on top of taxis because it was hot or dove into the fountain at Union Square or tried to undress at the Scandals, or, in sheer delight at the splendor of New York, jumped, dead sober, into the Pulitzer fountain in front of the Plaza. Fitzgerald got in fights with waiters and Zelda danced on people's dinner tables. (1951, 128)

Richard Gray in his appraisal of Scott Fitzgerald as a writer commented, 'Of all American writers concerned with the inventions of modernism, F. Scott Fitzgerald (1896–1940) was the most autobiographical. Finding in the compulsions of his life the contours of his fiction, he sustained for his generation the great American romance of the self. It was a romance, however, that was alive to the dissonances and disjunctions of the modern age and that was refracted through Fitzgerald's own sense of the porous, plural nature of his personality. "Sometimes", Fitzgerald once said, "I don't know whether I'm real or whether I'm a character in one of my own novels"' (Gray 2011, 203). Also, it is significant to notice that in *The Great Gatsby* Fitzgerald moves away from the third person narratorial style used in his earlier novels. The role of Nick Carraway as the narrator, the observer- participant whose interventionist comments, doubts, admiration and dilemma become an integral part of the Gatsby narrative, thereby undoubtedly instilling in the narrative, a sense of dramatic immediacy. Referring to the role of Nick Carraway as observer and commentator, Thomas Hanzo argued in his essay, '*The Theme and the Narrator of* The Great Gatsby', that, '*The Great Gatsby* is not a melodrama about Jay Gatsby, but a definition of the senses in which Nick understands the word "great". Its subject is an American morality. It is explored historically through the conflict between the surviving Puritan morality of the West and the post-war hedonism of the East; topically, through characteristic manifestations of American money values; formally and most significantly, through the personal history of a young American provincial whose moral intelligence is the proper source of our understanding and whose career, in the passage from innocence to revaluation, dramatizes the possibility and mode of a moral sanction in contemporary America' (1956, 190).

Furthermore, Fitzgerald's biographer Scott Donaldson deciphers Daisy's role in the novel, modelled on Fitzgerald's real-life infatuation with Ginevra King. Daisy was undoubtedly attracted to Gatsby's glamorous parvenu identity, that flaunts ostentatious wealth as power, but she was not ready to leave her familiar comfort zone of elitism and recognised social status. Donaldson also stressed on the elements of pretence and affectation in the mesmeric 'exhilarating ripple' of Daisy's voice. In an outstanding comment, almost unexpected from the infatuated romantic Gatsby, Donaldson points out that Gatsby explains to Nick that Daisy's voice resonated with the jingle of money and Nick the perceptive narrator of the Gatsby story, readily agrees, 'Her voice is full of money … That was it. I'd never understood before. It was full of money— that was the inexhaustible charm that rose and fell in it, the jingle of it, the cymbals' song of it. ... High in a white palace the king's daughter, the golden girl' (Fitzgerald, 126).

In fact, lack of wealth, affluence, not being richer than others, seemed to cause a lifelong low self-esteem in Fitzgerald's psyche. In a letter to John O'Hara, Fitzgerald wrote with remarkable candidness, 'I am half black Irish and half old American stock with the usual exaggerated ancestral pretensions … So being born in that atmosphere of crack, wisecrack and counter crack I developed a two-cylinder inferiority complex. So if I were elected King of Scotland tomorrow after graduating from Eton, Magdalene to Guards, with an embryonic history which tied me to the Plantagenets, I would still be a parvenu' (Donaldson 1983, 2–3).

Intriguingly, Fitzgerald's *The Great Gatsby* (1925) set in New York is perhaps matched by Ernest Hemingway's *The Sun Also Rises* (1926) set in Paris, a novel that is an incisive commentary on the fractured hollow survivors in the aftermath of the First World War, which changed the Global North forever. Perhaps this is one of the crucial reasons why even in the twenty-first century, the carefully crafted aspirational track, from Jimmy Gatz to the Great Gatsby, a tragic journey, that in its bid to translate the American dream into reality, ironically scripts the life of an average American citizen, who is neither a hero nor a villain, and yet meets a violent end, due to circumstantial factors.

Fitzgerald's excellence as a story teller reaches new heights as he brings in Gatsby's father to attend his son's funeral. Gatsby's father, Henry C. Gatz, insists that he wants to be present at his son's funeral, having read about Gatsby's death in the Chicago newspapers. When Nick Carraway meets Gatsby's father he notices, '...a solemn old man, very helpless and dismayed, bundled up in a long cheap ulster against the warm September day' (Fitzgerald, 173).

The most fascinating part of this encounter between the narrator Nick and Gatsby's father is when the elderly man, who is completely overawed by the luxurious mansion his son had built, shared with Nick, a timetable, a daily routine that Gatsby had drawn up, scribbled on the back-cover of a self-help book, *Hopalong Cassidy.* In fact, as in the early-twentieth century, self-help books are sought after even in the digital universe today, as these books are regarded as gospels by those in pursuit of material success. Here is the excerpt from a sequence, where we find Gatsby's father showing Nick how Gatsby as a young boy had self-imposed a rigorous schedule in order to train himself as an aspirant in order to secure the American Dream. Henry Gatz tells Nick,

> Look here, this is a book he had when he was a boy. It just shows you.' He opened it at the back cover and turned it around for me to see. On the last fly-leaf was printed the word SCHEDULE, and the date September 12, 1906....
> Rise from bed 6.00 am.
> Dumbbell exercise and wall-scaling...... 6.15–6.30 am
> Study Electricity etc 7.15–8.15 am
> Work 8.30–4.30 pm.
> Baseball and sports 4.30–5.00 pm
> Practice elocution, poise and how to attain it 5.00–6.00 pm
> Study needed inventions. 7.00–9.00 pm
>
> GENERAL RESOLVES
> No wasting time at Shafters or [a name, indecipherable] —
> No more smokeing or chewing.
> Bath every other day
> Read one improving book or magazine per week
> Save $5.00 [crossed out] $3.00 per week
> Be better to parents (Fitzgerald, 180)

In the twenty-first century, this journey of Gatsby can now be traced to the ambitions of high-skilled immigrant professionals in search of the dream of material success, implying the acquisition of moveable and immovable property. They often remain in an inexplicable search for home, despite the acquisition of a grand dream-house. In this context, one may even recall Arthur Miller's tragic play *The Death of a Salesman* (1949) which underscored how the American dream of material success could destroy a middle-class home and its family members. The challenges of free enterprise and survival of the fittest in capitalism's three-point register, achievers, losers and survivors, embed inhuman expectations in a post-truth, post-ethics ecosystem that often triggers dehumanisation as the banality of evil is internalised into the veins of the system, itself.

Perhaps this could have been the reason why the second chapter of *The Great Gatsby* is so brutally morbid. We are coerced into noticing the eerie, haunting lines of the first page of the second chapter of the novel, that upsets the stereotypical twentieth-century fairy tale of love, conflict, confrontation, containment, marriage and they-lived-happily-ever-after formula. *The Great Gatsby* is not simply a rags-to-riches story. The following lines in chapter two tell us that Fitzgerald's novel is deeply complex, gesturing towards existential dilemma— 'This is a valley of ashes—a fantastic farm where ashes grow like wheat into ridges and hills and grotesque gardens where ashes take the forms of houses and chimneys and rising smoke and finally, with a transcendent effort, of men who move dimly and already crumbling through the powdery air' (Fitzgerald 1950, 19).

These lines create a morbid visual impact of an arid wasteland peopled by individuals who were overwhelmingly stressed, unable to understand the world in which they were all trapped. Those who peopled this environment were all spectres, hollow individuals. '[T]he ash-grey men swarm up with leaden spades and stir up an impenetrable cloud which screens their obscure operations from your sight' (Fitzgerald 1950, 19).

Again, in contrast to this environment of sterility, the erstwhile hyper-masculine football hero Tom Buchanan's braggadocio exudes the arrogance of ignorance as he refers to Europe, the Old World, in acerbic terms, that presents the typical cultural contention between the Old World of Europe and the New World of American capitalism and euphoric democracy—

> God damn the continent of Europe. ... The negroid streak creeps northward to defile the Nordic race ... I think it's a shame that England and America didn't let Germany conquer Europe. It's the only thing that would have saved the fleet of tottering old wrecks. My reactions were all philistine, anti-socialistic, provincial and racially snobbish. I believe at last in the white man's burden. (Fitzgerald quoted in Meyers 1994, 89)

Significantly, I could not find the above excerpt in the Penguin first edition of 1925, the second edition published in 1950 and a recent edition published by Penguin Random House in 2024. In Meyers notes, I noticed that he had cited that all the excerpts are from *The Great Gatsby* (Authorised Text) by F. Scott Fitzgerald, copyright 1925 by Charles Scribner's Sons.

This is the reason why I have included this passage from Meyers' biography. It is undoubtedly important to address the novel as it was published in 1925. Critics have accused Fitzgerald of being a racist and a white supremacist as there are no immigrant non-white representatives in his novel. We cannot elide the fact that the 1920s was also about the Harlem Renaissance as well as the First World War, in which around thirty thousand African Americans had died, mostly due to illnesses and not combat.

We should not read Tom Buchanan's statements about racial superiority as Fitzgerald's convictions. Instead, we may read those sections as the corrosive impact of wealth and resultant arrogant power that destroys the human responses of empathy and inclusiveness. The new generations of capitalist American aristocrats of the 1920s with their reckless lifestyles have been documented by Fitzgerald with unprecedented mastery, through the use of language, vibrant, nuanced, ironic, sarcastic, with dry wit and humour that set his narrative style apart from his contemporaries, such as Doss Passos and Ernest Hemingway, among others.

In all fairness, let us say, pun unintended, Fitzgerald made Tom Buchanan ask his friends whether they had read a book titled, 'The Rise of the Colored Empires'. His comment thereafter exudes negrophobia. This is remarkably the rhetoric of the twenty-first-century far right ideology that considers diversity, ethnic minorities and all poor people of the world a threat, citing statistics and census. So Buchanan says, 'Well, it's a fine book, and everybody ought to read it. The idea is if we don't look out the white race will be—will be utterly submerged. It's all scientific stuff; it's been proved.... It's up to us, who are the dominant race, to watch out or these other races will have control of things...' (Fitzgerald 1950, 19).

The comment of the narratorial voice in the following page quite directly distances the author from the speaker Tom, who validates his role as a typical stereotype of the Jazz Age—'There was something pathetic in his concentration, as if his complacency, more acute than of old, was not enough to him any more' (Fitzgerald 1950, 20).

In fact, Fitzgerald sums up the hedonistic irresponsibility of the burgeoning rich class of the American nineteen twenties through the narrator Nick as he commented, 'They were careless people, Tom and Daisy—they smashed up things and creatures and then retreated back into their money their vast carelessness, or whatever it was that kept them together, and let other people clean up the mess' (Fitzgerald 1950,186). The two essays by Sachidananda Mohanty and Amritijit Singh and his co-author Richard Courage included in this centennial volume address the issues raised here, with scholarly insight.

Interestingly, T. S. Eliot, whose *The Waste Land* had in all probability influenced the imagism in Fitzgerald's desolate valley of ashes, remarked about *The Great Gatsby* that it was the only new novel, English or American, that had interested him in many years—'the first step that American fiction has taken since Henry James' (Meyers 1994, 147). Also, the American novelist Edmund Wilson (1895–1972) had contrasted his own 1929 published novel, *I Thought of Daisy* (their fictional heroines had the same name), to Fitzgerald's best work of fiction. For the first time, though privately, he acknowledged Fitzgerald's superiority, and placed his achievement on a national rather than on a merely personal level: '[Gatsby is] one of the best novels that any American of his age has done' (Meyers 1994, 146).

Fitzgerald's critics inform us that he was deeply impressed by Conrad's narrative style and consciously emulated Conrad's use of evocative symbolism through literary devices such as the green light on Daisy's dock, the eyes of Dr T. J. Eckleburg and the role of the narrator Nick Carraway emulating Conrad's Marlow *in The Heart of Darkness* and *Lord Jim*. Moreover, in a riveting article about Gatsby's desire to rise out of his hereditary roots, Adam Meehan had observed, 'Put in this broader context, we can read Gatsby's renouncing of his biological family as a denial of his racially adulterated lineage and his desire to marry Daisy as an attempt to enter/create a family that would regenerate his socially-projected ancestry as figuratively white. Ultimately, this reading offers us a unique way of reconciling the symbolic duality of Gatsby's autopoietic process and America's fantasized (and racially whitewashed) mythopoeic past' (2014, 79).

Furthermore, Meehan refers to Slavog Zizeg's interpretation of the sinking of the *Titanic* as evidence of 'material leftover' as he argued, 'While Žižek's *Titanic* serves 'as a condensed, metaphorical representation of the approaching catastrophe of European civilization itself' (2014, 70), Fitzgerald's valley of ashes can be said to serve the same function in relation to American civilization as manifested in the views of Tom and other nativists of the time'.

Also, in Fitzgerald's novel, as in most of his other writings, the semi-autobiographical style of narration is apparent. Critics have located real-life models who have contributed to the characters in the novel. Daisy Fay has the surname of the Catholic priest Sigourney Webster Fay and her erratic character is based partly on the Chicago debutante Ginevra King and partly on Zelda. In the novel, as Tom reclaimed Daisy from Gatsby, in real life Fitzgerald had reclaimed Zelda from Jozan. Nick's girlfriend Jordan Baker was based on Ginevra's close friend Edith Cummings and Tom Buchanan was modelled on Fitzgerald's friend Tom Hitchcock, an affluent polo player.

Fitzgerald's friend Alice Toklas, summarised Fitzgerald's life in two perceptive sentences. She called him 'the most sensitive ... the most distinguished—the most gifted and intelligent of all his contemporaries. And the most lovable—he is one of those great tragic American figures' (Meyers 1994, 402).

Moreover, in his essay *The Crack-Up* published in 1931, Fitzgerald candidly admitted that he was overtaken by an excruciating period of psychic stress and depression, that never quite left him. In the essay he also mentions that he could not live up to the standards of romantic ideology that had initially attracted him as a young student at Princeton—'The old dream of being an entire man in the Goethe-Byron-Shaw tradition, with an opulent American touch, a sort of combination of J. P. Morgan, Topham Beauclerk, and St Francis of Assisi, has been relegated to the junk heap...' (Fitzgerald 1931, 13)

II

From around the 1960s, American literature was introduced as an optional course in the English Masters level of many

Indian universities. Thereafter, American literature was introduced as an optional course in the undergraduate English Honours level of many Indian universities as well. Along with Mark Twain, Melville, Hawthorne, Walt Whitman, the two early-twentieth-century contemporary writers, Scott Fitzgerald and Ernest Hemingway, captured the attention and admiration of the students. Thereafter PhD dissertations on these two writers became so common that supervisors had to advice their research scholars to work on any other American writer but Fitzgerald and Hemingway. In his book *Critical Approaches to Scott Fitzgerald and Ernest Hemingway* (2012), Sourin Ghosh wrote in his introduction, ' My object is not to produce academic trivia. I have read Fitzgerald and Hemingway comprehensively, together with some other critics, and the line of approach and treatment is mine own. By good criticism I mean critical analysis based on a close textual study, depth of understanding and clarity of presentation...' (vi). He further adds a rather scathing comment, that I find intriguing. Guha stated, '...what goes by the name of original research by Indian scholars in American literature amounts to funny absurdities or unintelligible vagueness' (2012, vi).

More remarkably in 1997, Prestige Books published *F. Scott Fitzgerald: A Centennial Tribute* with the subtitle, '*The Multifaceted Scott*'. The book was edited by Somdatta Mandal. In her introduction, Mandal referred to the centennial celebrations in the USA as well as India. Mandal noted, 'In India, the American Studies Research Centre at Hyderabad celebrated Fitzgerald's centenary by holding a two-day seminar in September, 1996' (1997, 21). She also mentioned that a twenty-three-cent commemorative stamp of Fitzgerald was released on 24 September 1996 by the US Postal Service. '... This stamp features a real handsome Fitzgerald at age 23 or 24 at the peak of his career, in front of a harbour. *At the lower right hand corner of the stamp is a streak of green light, a reference to* The Great Gatsby *symbolizing Gatsby's love for Daisy Buchanan*' (23, italics mine) .

Moreover, in Mandal's commemorative volume, M Sivaramakrishnan's essay, 'Some Indic Pathways to Fitzgerald's

"Paradise"', critiques *The Great Gatsby* and refers to the American obsession with *kama* (desire) and *artha* (money) and the interplay of mystic illusions created by *leela* and *maya*, as a result of which the troubled protagonist is engaged in a futile quest for transcendence and freedom. In my own essay, included in Mandal's centenary volume, titled 'The Crack-Up: Scott Fitzgerald, Ernest Hemingway and the Lost Generation', I had observed, 'Scott Fitzgerald can be looked upon as a social historian of his times for his fiction is undoubtedly the meticulous record of an extraordinary period in American social history' (1997, 34). In fact, in the autobiographical memoir *The Crack-Up,* Fitzgerald had remarked with wry humour, 'all the stories that came to my head had a touch of disaster in them- the lovely, young creatures in my novels went to ruin, the diamond mountains in my short stories blew up, my millionaires were as beautiful and damned as Thomas Hardy's peasants' (1936, 34).

In their article on time and place in Fitzgerald's fiction, Tony Magistrale and Mary Jane Dickerson stated, 'The novel's evolution, its textual history, reveals the genesis of an intertextual dimension, a dialogue between a monologistic and unified mythic past and a materially debased and chaotic present? that allows Fitzgerald to suggest the complexity of the American experience. In doing so, he observes and questions American conceptions of history and self within shifting, social contexts' (1989, 118). Magistrale and Dickerson also state that Bakhtinian chromotropes are replete in *The Great Gatsby.* They state, 'of the best examples of a Bakhtinian chronotope in Gatsby occurs while a drunken Nick is still inside the New York apartment where Tom Buchanan has just broken Myrtle's nose. In this scene, Nick occupies a role similar to the one which Bakhtin assigns the reader: he is at once enmeshed in the dialogue and physical actions that take place among the characters, and yet at the same time he occupies a space apart from them' (120).

In her essay on 'Individual Responsibility' Susan Resneck Parr had also argued, 'Specifically, much of the brilliance of *The Great Gatsby* lies in its revelation of the disparities between America's myths and her social realities while it simultaneously dramatizes the continuing potency of those myths. Both Gatsby and Daisy's stories, for example, reveal how compelling the American dream has remained, despite the fact that the dream, as it has been given material life, has betrayed its original moral premises. Certainly both Gatsby and Daisy have been victimized by their disregard of *the moral implications of their choice*' (1985, 665; italics mine).

In fact in his essay, 'Echoes in the Jazz Age November 1931', included in *The Crack-Up*, Fitzgerald had summed up the era like a social commentator, as he wrote, 'Contrary to popular opinion, the movies of the Jazz Age had no effect upon its morals. The social attitude of the producers was timid, behind the times and banal—for example, no picture mirrored even faintly the younger generation until 1923, when magazines had already been started to celebrate it and it had long ceased to be news ...' (7).

Moreover, in his introduction to Fitzgerald's 1933 novel *Tender is the Night*, Malcolm Cowley made an insightful comment, 'Perhaps, as Fitzgerald had first planned, it was the standards of the leisure class that corrupted him; perhaps it was the chaos of curing a psychotic wife, who gains strength as he loses it by a mysterious transfer of vitality; perhaps it was a form of emotional exhaustion, a giving himself so generously that he went beyond his resources, 'like a man overdrawing on his bank', as Fitzgerald would later say of his own crack-up ...' (xviii).

The Essays

The twelve scholarly essays included in this commemorative volume by experts of American literature address and argue about the diverse challenging features of *The Great Gatsby*, that still intrigue readers and literary critics, though a hundred years have gone by, since the novel was first published in April, 1924.

Opening up new vistas of perception, Sachidananda Mohanty's essay foregrounds the lost narratives comprising the economic recession and the Jazz Age, the racial conflicts, the phobia of the American white race against the black, the birth of the Soviet Union, socialism and the Bolshevik Revolution.

Mohanty emphasises the need to revisit the historical sites and contexts in order to locate the elisions, slippages and absences in Fitzgerald's grand narrative. This probably may stir a debate about the selection and rejection process of a creative writer, who often ignore contemporary political and social history as the focus of the fictional narrative is different. *The Great Gatsby* may be regarded. thus, as a narrative of the interplay of Eros, Thanatos and Mammon, in post-First World War, young, capitalist America.

Somdatta Mandal's essay journeys through diverse locations around the world, in order to track the impact of Fitzgerald's classic narrative and its protagonist as a symbol and metaphor of America in the 1920s. Describing the allusions to *The Great Gatsby* in novels as diverse as one set in communist China and the other in Iran, the essay's study of Marxist and Islamic fundamentalism's reception of the American classic and its charismatic protagonists, Jay Gatsby and his beloved Daisy, is undoubtedly intriguing. Diverse cultures, religions and locations appropriation of this path-breaking American classic, underscore the relevance of cultural self-fashioning, differences and local social prejudices in the process of interpretation of Fitzgerald's novel.

Manju Jaidka's essay 'Roots and Wings' is a critically informed pedagogic assessment of the American classic. Jaidka refers to the spatio-temporal parameters that are integral to the ramifications of a fictional narrative that encompasses history, society, lived experiences and interpellations that manifest a layered text. The references to Soja's categories of the firstspace, secondspace and thirdspace expand the nuances of contextualisation, that remain mostly covert in this narrative of love at the time of social and cultural paradigm shifts in white America of the 1920s.

In her perceptive study of failed relationships, Tania Chakravertty delves into the differences that configure the elite classes. Chakraverrty states that Fitzgerald has incisively critiqued the cultural difference between those who have been born into wealth and the nouveau riche. The novel underscores how the lack of inbred sophistication among the newly rich, make the privileged leisured classes regard them with an air of superciliousness. This is where Jay Gatsby fails despite his acquisition of immense wealth. The representatives of the middle classes and working classes, Nick Carraway, George Wilson and his wife Myrtle among other subsidiary characters, lack the charisma and power that possession of material wealth instil in the vocabulary and body language of Gatsby and the Buchanans. The essay carefully explores the role of young women in the 1920s from a feminist perspective but does not limit itself to a reductionist feminist reading.

Avishek Parui's essay links the Jazz Age and the impact of economic globalisation in India in the twenty-first century. Parui locates the compulsions of capitalist structures that severely destabilise the communitarian spirit in order to assert the megalomania that nestles within the irrational dreams and desires for the acquisition of unlimited power and profit. Parui refers to Karl Marx and fictional capital as he elaborates on the rollercoaster ride that Gatsby undertakes in his personal life and the surreptitious underworld of making unaccounted profits and compares the Jazz Age with twenty-first century India, where crony capitalism, corporations and venture capitalists impact not just the economy but the emotional capital that is not only shaken and fractured but disintegrates. Parui compares Fitzgerald's novel, that is located on the fringes of the Great Depression and the eventual New Deal, with Emily Brontë's *Wuthering Heights* where we notice how the orphan and pauper Heathcliff transforms into an avaricious man of wealth and property. Parui argues how the curve of memory and masculinity predominates the spiralling economy that pumps and dumps the fortunes of those who are unable to sustain and stabilise their material fortunes and their personal lives. Heathcliff, in 1837, Jay Gatsby, in 1925, and the 2007 memoir of Jordan Belfort, *The Wolf of Wall Street*, seem to define not just a rags-to-riches arc, but an arc that boomerangs.

Madhuchhanda Ray Choudhury focusses on lurking Gothic elements in Fitzgerald's twentieth-century American novel. As some essays have referred to the nineteenth-century classic *Wuthering Heights* and its protagonist Heathcliff,

Ray Choudhury draws inferences from Stoker's Count Dracula and Byron's Manfred. The barrenness of the valley of ashes decisively dismisses the American Dream as illusory, misleading and deceptive. The self-made man, lacking in sophistication, gentility and etiquette is a recurring theme in fictional narratives of many cultures. The haunting Gothic elements in Fitzgerald's novel creates Gatsby as a presence who remains an outsider, lacking in that sense of belonging that is part of coteries of friendship, entertainment and relationships. Gatsby and his grand mansion are physically present and yet their being out of place, creates that spectral presence that defines the environment of West Egg and East Egg, inhabited by hollow men and women.

The engaged re-reading of *The Great Gatsby* by Amritjit Singh and Richard Courage open up new windows of perception by prioritising the problematics of race, class and colour integral to the social history of America in the early-twentieth century. The emergence of Harlem as the capital of Negro America and the decadent Jazz Age capitalist New York, with the rich elitists of East Egg vying with the burgeoning nouveau riche and the white urban poor tucked in the fringes of West Egg and the valley of ashes located in between is a penetrating comment by Fitzgerald that Singh and Courage, the two American scholars and experts in the field of African American studies have astutely identified. The reference to the negrophobia of white Americans implanted within Fitzgerald's classic text has opened up vistas of discourse, usually ignored by readers, and thereby limiting a holistic understanding of the brilliant layered text. Singh and Courage refer to the publication of *The Rising Tide of Color Against White World-Supremacy* by Lothrop Stoddard, published in 1920 by Scribner's, Fitzgerald's own publisher, that exposes racial prejudice and much more as Stoddard later joined the Ku Klux Klan. In 2025, this re-reading expands our understanding of Fitzgerald's novel beyond the clichéd parameters of telling and showing.

H. Kalpana's Marxist reading of Fitzgerald's novel, which is about the burgeoning capitalist entrepreneurs whose source of phenomenal income is shrouded in enigma, is compared with the award-winning Indian diasporic novel *The White Tiger* by Aravind Adiga. Both novels foreground economic class structures and class divide, and the dichotomous relationships of the urban rich and the urban poor. While Fitzgerald's novel was published in 1925, Adiga's novel was published more than eighty years later, in 2008. In the era of rapid globalisation and the economic neoliberal policies, Kalpana argues that the divide between the rich and poor and perceptions of false consciousness have further escalated deepening tensions, angst and physical violence. In all cultures, it seems, capitalism has effectively driven a wedge between citizens due to economic disparities. Often the economic disparities have led to the eruption of wrath and violence. Kalpana tracks the slippery passages and tightrope-walking that connect the lives of the rich and the poor, where no one seems to have achieved happiness and the dreams of material success and personal power remain as elusive and illusory as dreams usually are.

Amit Shankar Saha's perceptive essay asserts that *The Great Gatsby* will remain an enigmatic novel, as the author, the narrator and the characters create the impression of being drifters on a futile search, which remains unresolved. So love is delusional, the American Dream, like all dreams remains illusory. Disenchantment destabilises the key characters, who are either fractured or destroyed in the pursuit of material power and the impassioned unreason of obsessive love.

Neeraj Pizar's essay focusses on imagery and symbolism in the novel, the valley of ashes, green light, the owl eyes and Gatsby as a suffering Christ figure, tormented and triumphant in accosting the vagaries of fortune. Gatsby can well symbolise the successful American Dream, if acquiring enormous material wealth can be the sole interpretation of the American Dream. Pizer argues that the self-made, self-reliant business entrepreneur learns as he lives that enterprise and monetary success can be a part of a capitalist dream, but in terms of social and personal relationships, intangible factors as etiquette, education, sophistication, heredity and social behaviourism all contribute to securing the Dream, which is often tipped towards transforming into a nightmare.

By referring to the English poets Shelley and Keats and their evocative poems, Suchandana Bhattacharyya's essay delves deep into the aura of the American Dream that lured Jay Gatsby only to surrender to the delusions that dreams underpin. Gatsby became a victim of an uncontrolled existential crisis as he was neither sagacious nor corrupt, but a simple, average man, of average general intelligence in pursuit of his lady love, whose love and fidelity he could win only if he was richer than her affluent husband Buchanan, who was extremely arrogant about his class elitism. Bhattacharyya also carefully analyses Fitzgerald's use of colour symbolism in his novel, that contributes to deepening the play of emotional desires and tensions in the novel.

Bennet Schaber's in-depth and detailed essay zooms beyond the literary text and explores the interconnections between the original printed literary text and the evolving qualifications of its visual texts. The politics and problematics of inter-semiotic translations and screenplays have been explored carefully in this essay. Schaber foregrounds film adaptations of Fitzgerald's early-twentieth century novel *The Great Gatsby*, referring to the emergence of the film noir or dark film in Hollywood since the 1940s, influenced by German filmmakers who fled to Hollywood during the Second World War. Film noir was characteristically cynical; money had primacy over love, and depressive, violent and tragic conclusions were normative. By discussing the neo-impressionist aesthetics of the modern novel, Schaber carefully traces how a fictional narrative is coaxed into malleability by fusing the experimentations of content and style of the modern novel with the burgeoning cinematic language and technique of the early American films. Schaber refers to the need for a cinematographic correlative and refers in some detail to the affinity between the early American films like *Citizen Kane, Scarface* and, specifically, *Sunset Boulevard* and Fitzgerald's novel *The Great Gatsby* that appeared in 1925. Schaber suggests that the American Dream of self-enterprise and success, in reality, has the potential to corrupt and ruin what idealistically remains incorruptible, caught between the duality of inferno and paradise, Eros and Thanatos, and the psychological torture of unrequited love.

III

One has to agree with Fitzgerald's biographer Jeffrey Meyers's qualitative assessment of *The Great Gatsby* in which he states that the semi-autobiographical novel transcends Fitzgerald's life and expresses the important themes of American literature: 'the idealism and morality of the American West (where most of the characters originate and where Nick returns at the end of the novel) in contrast to the complexity and corruption of the East (where the novel takes place); the frontier myth of the independent self-made man; the attempt to escape the materialistic present and recapture the innocent past; the predatory power of rich and beautiful women; the limited possibilities of love in the modern world; the heightened sensitivity to the promises of life; the doomed attempt to sustain illusions and recapture the American dream' (1994, 145).

Similarly in the essay 'Color and Cosmos in *The Great Gatsby*' A. E. Elmore states that 'Although, in an age of unbelief and vast carelessness, the romantic idealist like Gatsby is almost certain to be defeated before he reaches his particular goal, there remains the enduring consolation, superseding tragedy and perhaps making it impossible, that the visionary pilgrim who is faithful to the end will find the journey sufficient victory. *The Great Gatsby* endures as a monument only to that notion but also to Fitzgerald's underrated power build a universal theme from a brilliantly effective technical structure' (1970, 443).

As the novel concludes, Fitzgerald leaves it to Nick Carraway, the narrator-participant who steers the novel's unfolding, to say the last words about Jay Gatsby, who was not just a tragic hero but an incorrigible romantic—'Gatsby believed in the green light, the orgiastic future that year by year recedes before us. It eluded us then, but that's no matter—tomorrow we will run faster, stretch out our arms farther.... And one fine morning— So we beat on, boats against the current, borne back ceaselessly into the past' (Fitzgerald, 196).

Among the other novels published in 1925, Virginia Woolf's *Mrs Dalloway*, Franz Kafka's *The Trial* and Theodore Dreiser's *An American Tragedy* have stood the test of time and new interpretations have opened up opportunities for further research on these classics.

Fitzgerald's novel *The Great Gatsby*, first published in 1925 and re-read in 2025, proves that a timeless literary text, despite its rootedness in space and time, remains relevant and relatable even a century later, echoing T. S. Eliot's proclamation in 'Burnt Norton', the first poem in the *Four Quartets* (1943)—

> Time present and time past
> Are both perhaps present in time future
> And time future contained in time past.
> If all time is eternally present
> All time is unredeemable.

Works Cited

Donaldson, Scott. 1983. *Fool for Love: F. Scott Fitzgerald*. New York: St Martin's Press. edition

Elmore, A. E. 1970. 'Color and Cosmos in *The Great Gatsby*. *The Sewanee Review* 78(3): 427–443.

Fitzgerald, F. Scott. 1933. *Tender Is the Night: A Romance*. New York: Charles Scribner's Sons.

Fitzgerald, F. Scott. 1936. 'The Crack-Up'. *Esquire*, February 1936.

_______. 1950. *The Great Gatsby: The Tale of a Man Who Built Himself an Illusion to Live By*. New York: Penguin Books.

_______. 2010. *Flappers and Philosophers*. With an introduction by Sarah Churchwell. London: Penguin Classics.

_________. 2018. 'Echoes of the Jazz Age'. In *The Crack-Up: Essays* by F. Scott Fitzgerald. Surrey: Alma Books.

Gray, Richard. 2011. *A Brief History of American Literature*, Oxford: Wiley-Blackwell.

Guha, Sourin. 2012. *Critical Approaches to Scott Fitzgerald and Ernest Hemingway*. Kolkata: Avantgarde Press.

Hanzo, Thomas A. 1956. 'The Theme And the Narrator of *The Great Gatsby*'. *Modern Fiction Studies* 2(4): 183–190.

Magistrale, Tony, and Mary Dickerson. 1989. 'The Language of Time in *The Great Gatsby*'. *College Literature* 16(2): 117–128.

Mandal, Somdatta. 1997. *F. Scott Fitzgerald: A Centennial Tribute.* New Delhi: Prestige Books.

Meehan, Adam. 2014. 'Repetition, Race, and Desire in *The Great Gatsby.*' *Journal of Modern Literature* 37(2): 76–91.

Meyers, Jeffery. 1994. *Scott Fitzgerald: A Biography.* New York: Harper Collins.

Mizener, Arthur. 1951. *The Far Side of Paradise: A Biography of F. Scott Fitzgerald.* London: Heinemann.

Parr, Susan Resneck. 1981. 'Individual Responsibility in *The Great Gatsby*'. The Virginia Quarterly Review 57(4): 662–680.

1

The Great Gatsby and the Lost Narratives

Sachidananda Mohanty

Described as a 'great American novel', F. Scott Fitzgerald's *The Great Gatsby* (1924), has been variously hailed as 'a historical document of the lost generation', and a 'text that captures a fractured collective psychic terrain of a nation and the citizens of privilege'.

I shall argue in this essay that while we may legitimately celebrate the many achievements of the novel, in terms of substance and style and see the way it appealed to a certain generation of readers in America, becoming, in due course, part of the American literary canon, the work, in cultural and ideological terms, does not go far enough in dealing with many of the underlying issues of its times. These include the question of immigration and race relations, the experience of black people and hyphenated Americans, the participation of women in the public sphere, the question of women's suffragette and campaigns for contraception, the place of labour, labour rights and immigration laws in a capitalistic order (we may note here in passing that the October 1917 Russian Revolution had greatly influenced the intellectual class, especially the American socialists, in the Ivy League universities in America) (Meier 2008), the role of the American State during World War I and in its aftermath, and finally the question of pacifism and conscientious objection to war.

These issues are not generic; they had taken centre stage in the aftermath of the Great War (1914–18) in America. It may therefore be useful to have a contextual reading of the novel while making a renewed assessment of the work in its centenary year. I shall examine the novel primarily through the prism of contemporary history and historicism.

Contextual Reading

To argue that Fitzgerald's main aim in writing *The Great Gatsby* was not to offer a political study of the Roaring Twenties, and that he had consciously chosen to present a slice of the social reality of the Jazz Age may not be entirely convincing. For any novel of substance, say of Conrad, Lawrence, Hemingway, Tolstoy, Dostoevsky or the great Victorians like Dickens, Hardy and George Eliot, or, for that matter, the fiction of celebrated Indian authors like Fakir Mohan Senapati, Premchand or Bibhuti Bhushan Bandyopadhyay, must grapple with the pivotal issues of its times. And since *The Great Gatsby* aspires to be a candidate for the 'great American novel' (according to many it has reached this status), we must judge the work against the larger ideological and historical backdrop of its times.

The Novel

Written during the 1920s in the context of an upwardly mobile America, the novel centres around the affluent and profligate, party-hopping elites of Long Island's North Shore, near New York City, in America. While early critics faulted the novel's non-adherence to a realistic mode, the author declared that he had intended the work to parallel the main contours of his life experience.

Indeed, Fitzgerald's life as a young Midwesterner from Minnesota who received education at Princeton and met his sweetheart Ginevra King, the sixteen-year-old socialite, follows, in some measure, the life narrative of the millionaire Jay Gatsby and his former lover Daisy Buchanan. There are major differences though. While the lifestyle of the nouveau riche and the dubious sources of wealth acquired through illicit bootlegging, are apparently based on the close observations of Fitzgerald, the author was no millionaire. Despite the relative success of his early novels, *This Side of Paradise* (1920) and *The Beautiful and the Damned* (1922), Fitzgerald found himself as a struggling author. The success he so desired, eluded him during his lifetime.

The Great Gatsby's narrator Nick Carraway, a Yale alumnus, travels to New York to work as a bond-salesman like Fitzgerald who went to Princeton; he resides in the Long Island village of West Egg, next to the estate of the wealthy Jay Gatsby. We learn that Gatsby's one time lady-love Daisy Jordan is married to Tom Buchanan. Nick meets Jordan Baker, a 'flapper', the liberated woman of her times, a member of the newly emancipated group known for their defiance of dress codes and sexual mores. Then there is Myrtle Wilson, introduced to us as the mistress of Buchanan, a domineering male given to machismo and periodical outbursts of violence against women. Gatsby pursues Daisy relentlessly and tragically with the hope that his current wealth and social status will help him bring Daisy back to his life.

There are other memorable characters—George Wilson, a mechanic and owner of a garage, Myrtle Wilson, George's wife, and Tom Buchanan's mistress. Gatsby and Daisy's car tragically hits Myrtle who dies. The Plaza Hotel suite, a familiar landmark of its times, witnesses a showdown between Jay Gatsby and Tom Buchanan over Daisy and Gatsby is fatally shot. Critics have pointed out that the murder at the Plaza Hotel, as an *affair de Coeur*, may have been based on the infamous Hall-Mills murder case reported in the contemporary media and known to Fitzgerald.

The publication and circulation history of *The Great Gatsby* is worth recalling on the novel's centenary. Equally important is it to review the book's reception, then and later. The bohemian lifestyle of the Jazz Age was witnessed not only in Long Island but in other parts of East Coast America as well, such as Newport in Rhode Island. The majestic white-painted mansions that line the seafront of Newport (that I visited during 2004–05), are reminders to the visitor of the flamboyance of an earlier era.

While Fitzgerald was happy to get critical endorsements by his respected peers, he was disheartened by the commercial failure of the novel. The manuscript had been submitted to the editor Maxwell Perkins who had settled on the final title, while Fitzgerald preferred different variants he had used prior to the publication of the novel. The author died somewhat heartbroken over the commercial failure of the work.

Winds of Change: Text History

After the passing of the author in 1940, winds of change in America, prompted by the Great Depression of the 1930s and World War II during the forties, brought about a revival of interest in the novel's fortune. The Council on Books in Wartime, we learn, distributed free copies of novels dealing with the American Dream to American soldiers overseas. *The Great Gatsby* was one such volume that appealed greatly to the men in uniform. Its leitmotif, the novel's search for affluence and the tragedy of unrequited love, struck a chord with the contemporary mind. The alleged snubbing by Ginevra's father, namely: 'Poor boys shouldn't think of marrying rich girls', became a refrain that questioned the power of the American Dream: the ability to rise in the social and economic ladder and marry the woman of one's desire. (This is also the staple of Bollywood cinematic love till today.)

In the post-war period, the novel was promoted by influential critics like Edmund Wilson. By 1970, it entered the canon of the 'great American novels', and continues to make an appeal to readers till today.

Significant Absences

While the celebration of *The Great Gatsby* in its centenary year is welcome, it may be rewarding to uncover some of the significant absences in the novel. In other words, if the text is portrayed as a realistic account of its times and captures the dominant mood of the glitterati in the Jazz Age, then it also glosses over much of the underlying malaise of American society from 1915 till 1924. We find such resonances in the avant-garde critical writings of the period including those by the anarchist Emma Goldman who spearheaded, in contemporary America, campaigns and movements related to women's contraception, suffragette and the rights of the working class and immigrants in the labour market. Fitzgerald's novel skips much of the socio-political reality of its times, as captured by Emma Goldman, Alexander Berkman and others.

White Supremacist Ideology

The spectre of white supremacist ideology including the Ku Klux Klan had become a menacing reality again by the time *The Great Gatsby* was published. Similarly, while President Woodrow Wilson led America to victory in World War I (1914–18) and helped establish the League of Nations, he also denied the rights of coloured people to self-determination among the subjugated nations the world over, especially among Asiatic nations like Japan, China and India. As the one-time president of Princeton University, he spoke approvingly of the fanatical Ku Klux Klan and allowed the exhibition of D. W. Griffith's racist film 'The Birth of a Nation' in The White House. Thanks to campaigns in recent times, following the Black Lives Matter Movement, the name of the Woodrow Wilson Centre of Public Affairs, has been changed to Princeton School of Public Affairs (Mohanty 2021b).

Tulsa Race Riots (1921)

Nor were such occurrences rare in America during the 1920s, the period in which *The Great Gatsby* was written. In 2021, America observed the centenary of the Tulsa Race Riots/Massacre which had taken place in Tulsa, Oklahoma, in 1921 (Mohanty 2021b). The race riot, more accurately described as the Tulsa Massacre (since the state was directly implicated in the act), was based on an alleged rape (it turned out to be a false charge) involving a black youth Dick Rowland and a seventeen-year-old white elevator operator Sarah Page. The local press falsely reported that Sarah 'screamed' and Rowland 'fled' from the scene, with the clear innuendoes of a sexual assault, which took place on 30 May 1921 (Du Bose 2021).[1] Thanks to what the American critic Leslie Fiedler aptly calls the 'threat of interracial rape', the event hit the headlines in the local media.

Vigilante justice was soon meted out to the prosperous black community of Tulsa during the next twelve hours spanning 31 May and 1 June 1921. According to a conservative estimate, roughly three hundred black people had been killed in Greenwood's business district and more than a thousand black residences were reduced to ashes (Smithsonian 2021). Using material memory, there have been attempts, in recent times, to curate, preserve and display remnants of the carnage and destruction.

---

[1] The accusation was later recanted by *Tulsa Tribune*, the city's main paper. But the damage was already done.

Lynching as an 'enduring spectacle of power'; Photographs as Trophies

During this entire period, in many parts of the United States lynching was used as an 'enduring spectacle of power'. As David A. Davis tells us in his insightful study 'Not only War is Hell: World War II and Lynching Narratives', returning black soldiers from World War I, far from being treated as war heroes, became victims of racial bigotry. It revealed the 'hypocrisy of American intervention in World War I and the arbitrary nature of American racism', which in brief meant, 'fight for liberty abroad, but condone brutality at home' (Davis 2008). Similarly, photographs of black victims were circulated as trophies widely by white supremacists. Such racial attacks took place in Chicago (1919), Arkansas (1919), Florida (1923), among others. Photographs became powerful emblems of white triumphalism.

The silence of Fitzgerald on the underlying racial oppression and injustice, so ubiquitous during this period, questions the celebratory mood of the Jazz Age depicted in *The Great Gatsby*. While the novel does allude to crimes of passion and social evils like bootlegging and the illicit smuggling of liquor in an era of prohibition, it concentrates primarily on the destiny of the white elites, as was common during the period.

Radical Climate: 1914–24

Already in 1917, the Bolshevist Revolution had taken place and American capitalism had become wary of the way the radical youth and pro-labour sections among students were being influenced increasingly. The Mexican Communist Party was founded by the Indian revolutionary M. N. Roy who was made to flee from America thanks to the pressure exerted by the British foreign office (Roy 1964). Roy had other accomplices in America during this period, like Sailen Ghosh and the American dissident Agnes Smedley (Mohanty 2021a), later companion of Viren (Chatto]) Chattopadhyay (the elder brother of Sarojini Naidu) in Germany during the two wars.

During World War I, campuses such as those of Columbia University became 'a part of the apparatus of the Government of the United States for the preparation and training of men. At Columbia, there was considerable opposition to war, Charles Beard "the young star" of the History Department resigned' (Meier 2008, 35). He was soon to support American intervention in the war after the German submarine torpedoed an American merchant ship. Several radical professors participated in anti-war pacifist rallies in Boston and New York. Several of them faced dismissals as well (ibid).

Many sensitive and idealistic young men and women in American university campuses felt deeply troubled by the display of wealth and affluence amidst growing poverty and inequity among the immigrant labour during this period. Some anarchists participated actively in the socialist and labour movements and earned the wrath of a brutal police and prison system.

John Reeds and V. I. Lenin: 1917–19

Several of the radical youth turned to the newly formed Soviet Union for inspiration and guidance. John Reeds, the young and idealistic socialist reporter, travelled to Russia in 1917, and witnessed the birth of the Bolshevist Republic. His despatches from ground zero caught the imagination of the socialist press in America. His book, *Ten Days That Shook the World*, became a classic (Doherty 2017). Reeds died tragically due to typhus in Russia in 1920. It is worth noting that the introduction to the volume was authored by the main architect of the Bolshevist Revolution in Russia, Lenin, who wrote:

> With the greatest interest and with never slackening attention I read John Reed's book, *Ten Days that Shook the World*. Unreservedly do I recommend it to the workers of the world. Here is a book which I should like to see published in millions of copies and translated into all languages. It gives a truthful and most vivid exposition of the events so significant to the comprehension of what really is the Proletarian Revolution and the Dictatorship of the Proletariat. These problems are widely discussed, but before one can accept or reject these ideas, he must understand the full significance of his decision. John Reed's book will undoubtedly help to clear this question, which is the fundamental problem of the international labour movement.
>
> Nikolai Lenin (Vladimir Ilyitch Ulianov), End of 1919

Some other Americans, in their misguided zeal, joined the Bolshevist espionage network NKVD in Europe, Asia and America. While Emma Goldman and Alexander Berkman retained their integrity throughout and paid the price for opposing the authoritarian state both in the United States and the Soviet Union, others, more naïve idealists like Isaiah (Cy) Oggins became unwitting collaborators and later disappeared behind the Iron Curtain during the Cold War. Both Berkman and Emma Goldman, on the other hand, were forcibly deported from America to the Soviet Union through a transport ship 'Buford' (Berkman 1925). Andrew Meier's well researched *The Lost Spy: An American in Stalin's Secret Service* (2010) in its opening chapters, offers a powerful and vivid throwback to the contemporary intellectual and ideological climate, much of which is relevant to the times of F. Scott Fitzgerald.

As an alumnus of Princeton University, Fitzgerald must have been aware of the climate experienced by Isaiah Oggins. And yet, *The Great Gatsby* is almost silent about such resonances.

Emma Goldman in America, 1924

My purpose here is not to underline the importance of the philosophical or political anarchism of Emma Goldman, but the fact that her critique of capitalist America and Bolshevik Russia had appeared in a mainstream publishing house, Doubleday Page and Company, in 1924 (Bubbins 2020),[2] the year of the publication of *The Great Gatsby.*

---

[2] As Bubbins states: 'Goldman's arrest in Union Square on February 11, 1916, was a result of her outspoken campaign for legalized birth control, believing that contraception was essential to women's social, sexual, and economic freedom… Goldman and a comrade were arrested in New York again on conspiracy charges… She was found guilty and given the maximum sentence—two years in prison and $10,000 fine. Judge Julius Mayer recommended her deportation as an "undesirable alien". Goldman was still in prison when she was served with her last arrest warrant, which included a deportation order, on September 12, 1919.'

Conclusion

I have argued in this essay that *The Great Gatsby* (1924) remains a memorable study of the American Dream during the Jazz Age. The triumph and tragedy of Jay Gatsby signals the strength and limitation of this 'dream'. However, in celebrating Fitzgerald's *The Great Gatsby*, one needs to reflect upon the lost narratives. It is not my claim that a novelist must write to order, according to a preordained ideology or critical dictates; the argument here is simply that any work that aspires to be 'great' must deal with the major issues of the age. By juxtaposing *The Great Gatsby* with the seminal texts and events of its time, I have advocated a more just and measured/nuanced appreciation of the text on the centenary year of its publication.

Indeed, I have argued, all along, that the significant absences of the issues of gender, class, race, ethnicity and ideology, unravelled by me, have rendered the 'absences' more visible. These, in turn, question an unilinear and straightforward interpretation of the novel's truth claims. In other words, the surface reading of the text that has gained currency over time as a story of tragedy and unrequited love, and an unalloyed celebration of the Jazz Age, misses out on the narrative's inability to do full justice to the dominant cultural and ideological issues of its time. Such a facile reading is disrupted by our knowledge of the contemporary society and its politics and draws fresh attention to the significance of the novel one hundred years after its publication.

Works Cited

Berkman, Alexander. 1925. *The Bolshevik Myth*. New York: Boni and Liveright.

Bubbins, Harry. 2020. Emma Goldman, 'The Most Dangerous Woman in America'. *Village Preservation*. www.villagepreservation.org/2020/06/27/emma-goldman-the-most-dangerous-woman-in-america/.

Davis, David A. 2008. 'Not Only War Is Hell: World War I and African American Lynching Narratives'. *African American Review* 42(3–4): 477–91.

Doherty, Barney. 2017. Review of *Ten Days That Shook the World* by John Reed. *Irish Marxist Review* 6(17). www.marxists.org/history/etol/newspape/irishmr/vol06/no17/doherty.pdf.

DuBose Erika. 2021. 'The Real Sarah Page'. *The Black Wall Street Times*. www.theblackwallsttimes.com/2021/08/13/the-real-sarah-page-center-for-public-secrets-reveals-full-identity-of-woman-whose-false-allegation-launched-tulsa-race-massacre/.

Fitzgerald, F. Scott. 1924. *The Great Gatsby*. New Delhi: Fingerprint Classics.

Goldman, Emma. 1921. *Living My Life*. www.theanarchistlibrary.org/library/emma-goldman-living-my-life.pdf.

Lenin, V. I. 1919. 'Introduction'. In *Ten Days That Shook the World*, by John Reed. New York: Boni and Liveright.

Meier, Andrew. 2008. *The Lost Spy: An American in Stalin's Secret Service*. New York: W. W. Norton.

Mohanty, Sachidananda. 2021a. 'Agnes Smedley, Daughter of Earth, Daughter of Earth'. *Frontline Magazine*, 10 September, 2021.

———. 2021b. 'Globalization and Cultural Memory'. *Frontline Magazine*, 19 November, 2021.

Reed, John. 1919. *Ten Days That Shook the World*. New York: Boni and Liveright.

Roy, M. N. 1984. *Memoirs*. Reprint of 1964 ed. New Delhi: Ajanta Publications.

Smithsonian Magazine. 2021. 'Remembering Tulsa: Special Report'. www.smithsonianmag.com/history/remembering-tulsa-180977764/.

2

Around the World in a Century: Internationalising *Gatsby* and the American Dream

Somdatta Mandal

Put simply, the American Dream is the ideal of opportunity for all—of advancement in a career or in society—without regard for one's origin. This ideal was embodied in Thomas Jefferson's 'Declaration of Independence' as 'Life, Liberty and the Pursuit of Happiness'. Jefferson was specifically reacting against the 'closed' European societies, where power and wealth were seen to be in the hands of an aristocratic governing elite. Thus, the dream idealises those who are 'self-made' as opposed to those who gain wealth and status through inheritance. One of the most common critical approaches to F. Scott Fitzgerald's *The Great Gatsby* (1925) has been to see it as a new myth of America, a myth partaking in the flavour of the 1920s. We are well aware that the term 'Gatsby' has become a generic term used in the American context to allude to a lot of concepts—the Jazz Age, its fabulous parties, the idea and pursuit of the American Dream, democratic idealism wherein the mythic Gatsby is said to be 'a son of God' having 'risen from a Platonic conception of himself' and waiting eternally for the 'green light' to emanate from the end of Daisy's dock. Gatsby is also implicitly linked to some of the other mythic figures of American literature who have similar statuses, in particular to James Fennimore Cooper's Natty Bumppo and to Mark Twain's Huck Finn. These characters are supposedly mythical in that they manifest the abstract ideals attractive to Americans—personal freedom, a self-reliant individuality and a belief in personal integrity rather than conformity. On the other hand, Fitzgerald's myth seems to be about the decadence of American values. Gatsby's dream, although it finally tragically destroys him, raises him above the other characters, giving him a dignity that the other characters had never possessed.

In a letter written on 31 December 1925 to F. Scott Fitzgerald, T. S. Eliot wrote:

> Dear Mr Scott Fitzgerald,
> *The Great Gatsby* with your charming and overpowering inscription arrived the very morning that I was leaving in some haste for a sea voyage advised by my doctor. I therefore left it behind and only read it on my return a few days ago. I have, however, now read it three times. I am not in the least influenced by your remark about myself when I say that it has interested and excited me more than any new novel I have seen, either English or American, for a number of years.
>
> When I have time I should like to write to you more fully and tell you exactly why it seems to me such a remarkable book. In fact it seems to me to be the first step that American fiction has taken since Henry James....
>
> With many thanks,
> Yours very truly, T. S. Eliot

This praise was particularly meaningful because Eliot was a notoriously rigorous critic who rarely complimented contemporary writers. The letter was sent to Fitzgerald after the poet read the inscribed copy, which Fitzgerald had effusively dedicated to him as 'the Greatest of Living Poets'. In his reply, Eliot assured Fitzgerald that the inscription did not influence his judgment. The praise from Eliot was especially significant given that *The Great Gatsby* received mixed or poor reviews upon its initial publication and was not a commercial success during Fitzgerald's lifetime.

Standing on the verge of exactly a hundred years after its publication, the objective of this essay is to explore how the 1925 canonical American text *The Great Gatsby* can be read and interpreted many decades later through different multi-ethnic texts. Since intertextuality refers to far more than the 'influences' of writers on each other, it is also interesting because it shows how the iconic figure of Jay Gatsby, the protagonist, has long ago transcended American shores to rest in various forms in the psyche of men and women from diverse cultures across the world. Apart from analysing this beautifully written rags-to-riches narrative, this essay deals with the use of the novel, the myth behind the American Dream of success as well as the representation of the protagonist Gatsby in different avatars, in cross-cultural settings, showing how the text's canonical status can never be overestimated.

As mentioned earlier, the influence of Fitzgerald's immortal text has led to occasional references in different contexts around the literary world. The noted British writer of Pakistani descent Hanif Kureishi, in his memoir *My Ear At His Heart: Reading My Father* (2004), tells us in detail about the books and writers that influenced him in his creative process and states:

> As a young man, if I discovered a writer, I'd look out for anything written about him. He or she, as well as the work then became the subject, the source of the words. If he liked hats, I would think about getting a hat; reading about Scott Fitzgerald always inspired me to go to the pub. The fact is, the place writers and artists hold in the public imagination exists beyond their work. (65)

Though Kureishi does not specifically mention this particular novel, *The Great Gatsby* makes its appearance in a unique postmodern story by the British writer Ali Smith. Titled 'The Universal Story', it concerns a man buying used copies of *The Great Gatsby* for his sister, who has an arts grant to make boats. Inspired by the line 'so we beat on, boats against the current', she makes a 'seven-foot boat made of copies of *The Great Gatsby* stuck together with waterproof sealant [which] was launched in the spring, in the port of Felixstowe ... [It] stayed afloat for three hundred yards before it finally took in water and sank.'

At first, the story talks about a woman working in a second-hand bookshop in a town no one visits anymore, capturing the decline of little England through the shelves gathering dust. But then the narrator's attention is drawn to a fly in the shop, and suddenly the story begins again—'there was a fly'. Smith's interest in forensic detail takes over here, with the fly's story, its timeline, its need to breed, its excreting and vomiting on the pages of a book, all being captured and the fly's story defining the parameters of the world. But then, the story becomes the story of the book—*The Great Gatsby*—that the fly landed on, and here the story relaxes more into comedy, as Smith describes the book's bibliographic details and then its litany of owners, all of whom have inscribed their names. There are several amusing details here: the young woman who finds the book immensely boring, who then passes it on to her young male friend who thinks it's the most important thing ever and quotes it under his breath, only to then go to university and hold forth about how it's overrated compared to *Tender Is the Night*.

One can go on recounting many other instances where there are cursory references to the text, or where the Gatsby-like rags-to-riches story becomes significant. In a recent novel *How Opal Mehta Got Kissed, Got Wild and Got a Life* by Kaavya Viswanathan, the young protagonist Opal 'felt [her] breath coming more and more quickly' when she saw her heartthrob Sean carrying a copy of *The Great Gatsby* under his arms. This text, which was a 'required senior-lit reading' was probably prescribed in this Ivy-League institution as a canonical guide to the American Dream of success. The Gatsby myth of success was once again referred to in a memoir published in 2005 where the narrator states:

> From the beginning, there was a touch of unreality about my life in the fast lane.... The balcony of my home in Bel Air, California, faced the Pacific and from it I could see Catalania Island, miles off shore. Its golden hills were haloed by the setting sun, its mythically named port of Avalon teased me—a self-made millionaire—just as the green light on Daisy Buchanan's pier had taunted Jay Gatsby, reminding him that in spite of his accomplishments, he would never truly belong to her world. (13)

These lines, taken from Mani Bhowmik's *Code Name God: The Spiritual Odyssey of A Man of Science* (2005), the memoir of an Indian scientist whose hard work and brilliance led him to co-invent the excimer laser used in corrective eye surgery, speak a lot about the myth of Gatsby and the American Dream that Fitzgerald had created more than eighty years ago. Coming from a man whose success won him a spot on *Lifestyles of the Rich and Famous*, this comparison becomes more interesting when the author states:

> My journey from mud to marble was complete, and like Fitzgerald's Jay Gatsby, I sought to wipe clean all traces of the poor non-immigrant boy I had been. Within just a few years, I owned six hilltop houses with million-dollar postcard views, Beverley Hills, Bel Air, Palos Verdes, Malibu—each one was a bulwark against the fate of my ancestors. I drove a Rolls-Royce. (96–97)

The two other memoirs that we discuss in this essay in detail are Wu Ningkun's *A Single Tear: A Family's Persecution, Love, and Endurance in Communist China* (1993) and Azar Nafisi's *Reading Lolita in Tehran: A Memoir in Books* (2003). Trying to teach the Fitzgerald text in environments hostile to Western ideas and according to 'prior codes', bring forth unprecedented problems both in communist China and under the Khomeini regime in Tehran during the height of its religious fundamentalism; studying these memoirs, therefore, becomes a new means of assessing the canonical text intertextually and interculturally.

***

Wu Ningkun's *A Single Tear* is a gripping narrative that tells the story of a young, conscientious and sensitive Chinese professor of English, who was educated in America, and whose decision to return to China from America after the 1949 Mao Zedong Revolution had lasting and potentially tragic implications for both him and his family. Like the many Chinese who had emigrated to other parts of the world after World War II, Wu answered to the call of his homeland as he believed that China will be able to enter a better, prosperous and independent phase with the new Mao regime. Leaving his doctoral dissertation at the University of Chicago incomplete, he was pressed to join the Department of Western Languages and Literature at Yenching University in Peking. Though not particularly political and ignorant of Marxism, he agreed, abandoning his prospects in literary America. Although quickly disillusioned, Wu and his family remained in China and were subject to persecution, imprisonment, deprivation, poverty, betrayal and humiliation. By the time of Mao's death in the 1970s, the Wu family had been moved—separately and together—from city to country and back again, persecuted for their religious beliefs as Christians, and became distrustful of neighbours and friends because of their constant denunciations that had become standard practice. After enduring this pogrom for forty years, the family ultimately survived and when Wu wrote this memoir, he believed that the truthful account of his experiences over three tragic decades, though intensely personal, would 'contribute to a compassionate understanding of history and men' (viii).

One may ask, how does Gatsby come in here? Well, in the very first chapter of the memoir, aptly titled 'The Return of a Native, 1951–52' Wu Ningkun narrates how he left America without any doubt in his mind put his expertise to some good use for a new China, thinking that he would eventually go back home. Full of optimism, he thought that he 'would be welcomed as a patriotic intellectual who had given up an attractive profession in the most affluent capitalist society to come home and serve the socialist motherland' (4). Soon after Wu joined the new university, all the professors, including Wu, were ordered to examine their past for pro-American bourgeois ideology and subjected to criticism by students at public meetings. It was in this 'self-criticism' session that Wu was first denounced politically for exposing his students to capitalistic propaganda like *The Great Gatsby*.

> My righteous accuser pointed to the cover, which pictured a hand with painted fingernails holding a glass of wine, and demanded with indignant eloquence, 'Is this the kind of crap you've brought back from the US imperialists to corrupt the young minds of New China with?' The novel was *The Great Gatsby*. (20)

The tragedy, of course, did not end but actually began from then. Summing up at the end of the session, the chairman pointed out that Wu's 'thinking had been polluted by [his]

American education and by his reluctance to cast off 'bourgeois individualism' and accept 'ideological remolding' (30). Since Marxists believed in facing the facts and relieving the load on one's own mind by telling the party everything, Wu was looked upon as a suspect and the next stage in his 'thought reform' was to make him take a pledge. This was just his first taste of the all-powerful state's arbitrary treatment of the individual this would become the inflexible law of life for Wu in the decades to follow. That he was a bourgeois rightist seemed a foregone conclusion. In an interview given to CNN in 1997, Wu states how this examination and confession was most frustrating. He felt he was being conscientious in coming home to China, so he got more and more frustrated by the treatment meted to him. As he got angrier and angrier, the more he kept talking and talking and talking. In doing so, he got himself into more and more trouble, because he did not know that at the time everything he said was actually being monitored and whatever he said among his colleagues or to other people was recorded in detail. By 1956, once again, he found himself 'the number-one political villain' (57) and finally, at a general faculty meeting on the day before the festive National Day, he was 'formally denounced as a "poisonous weed" of the worst kind—an "ultrarightist, a backbone element of the reactionary right wing of the bourgeoisie"' (59). In Wu's own words, this was how things went:

> My heinous crimes were characterized as anti-party, anti-people, and antisocialism, which made me a 'Three-Anti' counterrevolutionary and an enemy of the people. The charges were numerous.... Placed in a chair by myself facing my tribunal, I burst into tears and pleaded guilty. My compulsory confession, in which I thought I had gone far in besmirching myself, was denounced as insincere and treacherous. (59–60)

Wu then found himself being torn from his young family and packed off for thought reform to a forced labour camp in the Great Northern Wilderness, on the Soviet border facing Siberia, where the starving prisoners and their frightened visitors' condition was beyond shedding a single tear. With nothing much to keep him company but a copy of *Hamlet* in an old laundry bag, Wu's habit of quoting Shakespeare to himself at particularly bad moments is profoundly touching. Nearly starved and frozen, he survived some of the Maoist experiments and was released, only to be denounced again as a 'cow demon' in the infamous Cultural Revolution of the 1960s. Wu was finally rehabilitated in 1979–80. Jay Gatsby, who is said to have risen 'from a Platonic idea of himself', thus became the catalyst of this sincere professor's ruin.

***

Fitzgerald's text plays a greater role in the next memoir Azar Nafisi's *Reading Lolita in Tehran* published in 2003. Like Wu Ningkun, literature professor Azar Nafisi returned to her native Islamic Republic of Iran in 1979 after a long education abroad. After winning a fellowship from Oxford, she taught English literature at the University of Tehran, the Free Islamic University and the University of Allameh Tabatabai which had been 'singled out as the most liberal university in Tehran' (Nafisi 2003, 9). In the fall of 1995, she was expelled from the University of Tehran for refusing to wear the veil and left Iran permanently for America in 1997. Her total stay in her motherland was about eighteen years. Every Thursday morning for those last two years that she was in Iran, Nafisi indulged herself and decided to fulfil a dream. She secretly gathered seven of her most committed female students to read forbidden Western classics in the privacy of her own home and the theme of these classes would be the relation between fiction and reality. As Islamic morality squads staged arbitrary raids in Tehran, fundamentalists seized hold of the universities and a blind censor stifled artistic expression, the girls in Nafisi's living room risked removing their veils and immersed themselves in the worlds of Jane Austen, F. Scott Fitzgerald, Henry James and Vladimir Nabokov. In her book, Nafisi recollects how each student took off more than their scarves and robes in her room, gained outlines and shapes and gradually becoming their own inimitable selves. Living in a culture that denied any merit to literary works, Nafisi records in details the bleak reality of the times:

> Our world under the mullah's rule was shaped by the colorless lenses of the blind censor. Not just our reality but also our fiction had taken on this curious coloration in a world where the censor was the poet's rival in rearranging and reshaping reality, where we simultaneously invented ourselves and were figments of someone else's imagination. (25)

In this extraordinary memoir, the students' stories thus become intertwined with the ones they were reading. As Michiko Kakutani states in *The New York Times*, 'the refuge from ideology that art can offer to those living under tyranny, and art's affirmative and subversive faith in the voice of the individual' become the hallmark of this memoir.

But first we must understand how Fitzgerald travels back to the 1979 Revolution. At the very beginning of the second part of her memoir entitled 'Gatsby', Nafisi narrates how, like Wu Ningkun, she had returned to her homeland with a lot of optimism and hope. From the airplane she saw, suddenly, a blanket of lights that signalled that she had arrived in Tehran and recounts that she felt that on arrival there was always a particular moment of epiphany. Like Jay Gatsby waiting for the green light at the end of Daisy's dock, 'For seventeen years', Nafisi says, 'I dreamed of those lights, so beckoning and seductive. I dreamed of being submerged in them and of never having to leave again' (81). Along with her other personal items, the customs officer picked up her books *Ada, Jews Without Money* and *The Great Gatsby*, 'as if handling someone else's dirty laundry. But he did not confiscate them—not then. That came sometime later' (82).

On joining the English Department at the University of Tehran, she offered to teach a course where she would do a comparative study of the literature of the Twenties and Thirties, the proletarian and the non-proletarian texts. The best author to read for the Twenties for her was, of course, Fitzgerald, though she was curious to know why in the Thirties, people like him were pushed out by a new breed of writers. In trying to be politically balanced, alongside *The Great Gatsby* and *A Farewell to Arms*, she planned to teach works by Maxim Gorky and Mike Gold. Before the new term began in September 1979,

Nafisi had to spend most of her time hunting for the books on her syllabus. In one bookstore, as she was rummaging through a few copies of *The Great Gatsby* and *A Farewell to Arms*, the bookseller advised her to pick up and store whatever books were available; soon enough the government blocked the distribution of foreign books in Iran.

On the first day, she went to the university armed with the trusty *Gatsby*: 'It was showing signs of wear: the dearer a book was to my heart, the more battered and bruised it became' (92). Anxious about how her class would receive her because of the worrisome political upheavals in the country, she entered the class, hands full of all the books and xeroxes she had brought for the class, and found the students unusually quiet. She asked her students what they thought fiction would accomplish, why one should bother to read fiction at all. One thing the authors she would be teaching all had in common was their subversiveness and she told the students how the best fiction always forced one to question what they took for granted. One day, when her leftist students had cancelled classes protesting the fresh murder of three revolutionaries, Nafisi was stopped by a few students. They had already read *Gatsby* and wanted to know whether Fitzgerald's other books were similar to it. Nafisi remembered this incident for a long time and wrote how they went on talking as they walked through the campus where a rather large crowd had assembled in front of a wall plastered with newspapers.

> We walked onto the hot asphalt and sat on one of the benches by the stream running through the campus, and talked like children sharing coveted stolen cherries. I felt very young, and we laughed and we talked. Then we went our separate ways. We never became more intimate than that. (96)

We are then told about one of her colleagues who always worried about losing his job. Having just divorced his wife, he had to maintain her, plus his home and swimming pool and somehow inappropriately kept comparing himself to Gatsby, calling himself Little Great Gatsby. But Nafisi's first culture shock came when one day she had a stimulating discussion on the implications of the words—*literature*, *radical*, *bourgeois* and *revolutionary* with one of the best students in her class, Mr Bahri. At the end of the talk, she was so excited that she reached out to him in a gesture of goodwill and friendship. He silently, deliberately, withdrew both his hands behind his back, as if to remove them from even the possibility of a handshake. She was later informed by a colleague that the gesture meant that no Muslim man would or should touch a *namaharam* woman—a woman other than his wife, mother or sister. Still, that aborted handshake did not prepare her to dislike Mr Bahri fully, though she developed a habit of blaming him and holding him responsible for everything that went wrong.

Initially, Nafisi had felt the imminent problems of teaching a text like *Gatsby*. Amid shouts of 'Death to America' and every now and then the burning of the American flag, the text seemed a strange choice for students burning with revolutionary zeal. Later, in retrospect, Nafisi felt that it was the right choice as the values that shaped the novel were the exact opposite of those of the revolution. Because of the constant interruptions, Nafisi begun to teach the *Gatsby* text in November 1979 but could not finish it until January 1980. Nafisi's choice of the text was not based on the political climate of the time but on the fact that it was a great novel. Though she read and re-read *Gatsby* 'with greedy wonder', she was held back by a strange feeling that she did not want to share it with anyone. Her students were 'slightly baffled' by the text. The story of an idealistic guy so much in love with this beautiful rich girl who betrays him, could not be satisfying to those for whom sacrifice was defined by words such as *masses*, *revolution* and *Islam*. Passion and betrayal were, for them, political emotions, and the meaning of love far removed from the stirrings of Jay Gatsby for Mrs Tom Buchanan. Adultery in Tehran was one of so many other crimes, and the law dealt with it accordingly: it was punished by public stoning.

As the teacher tried to explain to her students, *Gatsby* was an American classic, in many ways the quintessential American novel; it was also different from the ideologies of her own country. 'We in ancient countries have our past—we obsess over the past. They, the Americans, have a dream: they feel nostalgia about the promise of the future' (109).

She then tried to explain the concept of the American Dream. When the students come to the point in the text where Gatsby is visiting Daisy and Tom Buchanan's house for the first time and Tom has a sudden awareness of their relationship, the students expressed mixed reactions about the idea of love. Mr Nyazi said that the Iranian youth didn't have time for love right now as they were committed to a higher, more sacred love. The teacher diffused the tension in the classroom by adding that a novel was not an allegory and to read a novel was to 'inhale the experience' (111).

The next day Mr Nyazi met Professor Nafisi in earnest and with all goodwill, and made his complaint about Gatsby. He was not against Mr Gatsby himself but against the novel which was immoral. It taught the youth the wrong stuff; it poisoned their minds—surely she could see that? Nafisi reminded him that *Gatsby* was a work of fiction and not a how-to manual. But the gentleman was adamant, and he thought that maybe Mr Gatsby was all right for the Americans, but not for their revolutionary youth of Iran. Since America was poison for them, all Iranian students should be taught to fight against American immorality.

In those days of public prosecutions in Iran, Nafisi suddenly had a mischievous notion and suggested that they put *Gatsby* on mock trial in class. Mr Nyazi would be the prosecutor, and he should also write a paper offering his evidence. There would also be a judge, a lawyer for the defence and a defendant; the rest of the class would be the jury. Since no one volunteered to be the defendant, the teacher had to take it up. Zarrin volunteered to be Nafisi's lawyer and wanted to know if she was Fitzgerald or the book itself. They decided that the teacher would be the book: Fitzgerald may have possessed or lacked qualities that they could detect in the book. It was agreed that in this trial the rest of the class could at any point interrupt the defence or the prosecution with their own comments and questions. But no one wanted to speak for *Gatsby.*

The Great Gatsby thus became the set-piece of a courtroom drama in the classroom. 'And so began the case of the Islamic Republic of Iran versus *The Great Gatsby*' (124), writes Nafisi. After a long invocation 'In the Name of God', Mr Nyazi, the Islamist prosecutor, ranted against the novel for its moral ambiguity about the characters' decadence. He said that Imam Khomeini wanted to purge the country of decadent Western culture and so as a Muslim he could not accept *Gatsby* as it preached illicit relations between a man and woman. Americans were decadent and in decline because of their immoral Dream, and the book was therefore the 'last hiccup of a dead culture!' (127).

When Zarrin was summoned to defend her case, she accused the prosecutor of committing a mistake as he could no longer distinguish fiction from reality. Stating that *Gatsby* is being put on trial because it disturbed the students, she cited the famous trials of *Madame Bovary*, *Ulysses*, *Lady Chatterley's Lover* and *Lolita* and explained how in each case the novel won. While both the sides elaborated on their own points of view, Nafisi became rather excited. She wanted to tell them that the book was not about adultery but about the loss of dreams. Going back to Fitzgerald's own explanation of his novel, she advised her students in more concrete and practical terms:

> You don't read Gatsby to learn whether adultery is good or bad but to learn about how complicated issues such as adultery and fidelity and marriage are. A great novel heightens your senses and sensitivity to the complexities of life and of individuals, and prevents you from the self-righteousness that sees morality in fixed formulas about good and evil. (133)

Mr Nyazi was, of course, unable to understand the logic. He thought it would be easier for Gatsby to get his own wife than to win Daisy back. When it was time to hear from the jury, a few of the leftist activists defended the novel. Nafisi felt that they did so partly because the Islamist activists were so dead set against it. In essence, their defence was not so different from Nyazi's condemnation. They said that they needed to read fiction like *The Great Gatsby* because they needed to know about the immorality of American culture. They also felt they should read more revolutionary material, but that they should read books like Gatsby as well to understand the enemy. It was much later that Nafisi discovered that though most of the other students personally liked the book, they lacked enough self-confidence to express their views eloquently. Nafisi's colleagues who were surprised that the debate in class was Fitzgerald versus Islam instead of Lenin versus the Imam, praised Mr Bahri for quieting down the voices of outrage and somehow convincing the Islamic association of the university that she had 'put America on trial' (137), Personally, the *Gatsby* 'trial' had opened a window into Nafisi's own feelings and desires. A totalitarian regime would have to dislike uncertainty or doubt, for its existence would rely heavily on absolutes: good, evil, God, etc. Nafisi shows us that the absence of doubt contributes to the disappearance of empathy, the very heart of any novel. The 'blind censor' does not empathise; he only wants to wipe out imagination. The text, thus, becomes an allegory of the struggle between Iran's Islamists and Leftists to control the legacy of the revolution. At the end of the trial, while trying to explain to Mr Nyazi that dreams are perfect ideals, complete in themselves and cannot be imposed on a constantly changing imperfect, incomplete reality, Nafisi undergoes a kind of self-discovery and realises how their own fate was becoming similar to Gatsby's.

Years later as she read faxes and emails from some of her former students in Iran while in her office in Washington DC, Nafisi tried to decipher something beyond the hysteria of their words. She wonders where Mr Bahri was right now, what happened to his dream of the revolution, and what they should do with all those corpses on their hands.

***

Jay Gatsby's journey back to New York at the end of the twentieth century occurs through an interesting debut novel by an American writer of Puerto Rican origin. Set in the Spanish Harlem section of New York City, Ernesto Quinonez's *Bodega Dreams* (2000) is a direct take on the Fitzgerald novel and speaks a lot about the multicultural context of contemporary American society, especially with the influx of innumerable illegal immigrants from Latin American countries. It talks about the survival of these people through drug peddling, fights, real estate brokerage and also the benefaction of a self-made leader of the group, a man called Willie Bodega who taught the Hispanics to shed their past and create themselves from nothing.

Divided into three sections, the novel begins with a section called 'Because Men Who Built This Country Were Men from the Streets'; the second section is called 'Because a Single Lawyer Can Steal More Money Than a Hundred Men with Guns'; and the last section is titled, 'A New Language Being Born'. Any reader can clearly notice that the novel has several thematic and linguistic similarities with *The Great Gatsby.* Willie hankers for a Daisy-like deserter, Vera, who is now someone else's wife; he is nervous to meet her and by showing off his newly acquired wealth (like Gatsby's boot-legging, here it is drug peddling that brings in money), wants to bring back and recreate the past. In the end, he is shot down and unlike the dreary setting of Gatsby's funeral where hardly anyone was present, the whole of Spanish Harlem joins in Willie's funeral procession. On a positive note, the narrator realises that Spanglish, the language of the future, was a new language of a new race and being born out of the ashes of two cultures clashing with each other. The novel ends *Gatsby*-like with the hope of fresh life in the new world:

> The way a picture that's been hanging on a wall for years leaves a shadow of light behind, Bodega had kicked the door down and left a green light of hope for everyone. He had represented the limitless possibilities in us all by living his life, striving for those dreams that seemed to elude the neighborhood year after year. But in that transitory moment when at last the pearl was about to be handed to him, like Orpheus or Lot's wife, he had to look back to find Vera.
>
> No matter.
>
> Tomorrow Spanish Harlem would run faster, fly higher, stretch out its arms farther, and one day those dreams would carry its people to new beginnings.... The neighbourhood might have been down, but it was far from out. The people far from defeat. They had been bounced all over the place but they were still jamming.
>
> It seemed like a good place to start (213).

To conclude, I reiterate the idea of intertextuality with which I began this essay. According to some critics, the term is not a mere cross-referencing or interdependence of texts, it also includes the attitude that one text exhibits towards another. Taking the term in its widest sense, the memoirs discussed here also exhibit boundary-crossings between texts. With multiculturalism changing the face of the American literary scenario, the Barthesian idea—that writing is always an iteration which is also a re-iteration, a re-writing which foregrounds the trace of the various texts it both knowingly and unknowingly places and displaces—takes on an added meaning in this analysis. In *The Great Gatsby*, F. Scott Fitzgerald had written a myth specifically about America and American society but it seems that the themes of the novel have transcended such particulars of time and place and attained a wider relevance. In the meantime, as the canonical novel completes its hundredth year of publication in 2025, we will continue to witness more of Jay Gatsby's cross-cultural travels around the globe.

Works Cited

Bhowmik, Mani. 2005. *Code Name God: The Spiritual Odyssey of a Man of Science*. India: Penguin.

Culler, Jonathan. 1981. *The Pursuit of Signs: Semiotics, Literature, Deconstruction*. London:

Routledge and Kegan Paul.

Fitzgerald, F. Scott. 1925. *The Great Gatsby*. New York: Scribner's.

Eliot, T.S. 1925. Biblioklept. https://biblioklept.org/2013/02/12/t-s-eliot-writes-to-f-scott-fitzgerald/#:~:text=The%20Great%20Gatsby%20with%20your,your%20book%20for%

Kakutani, Michiko. Book of the Times: https://www.nytimes.com>2003/04/15>books -

Kureishi, Hanif. 2004. *My Ear At His Heart: Reading My Father*. London: Faber & Faber.

Nafisi, Azar. 2003. *Reading Lolita in Tehran: A Memoir in Books*. New York: Random House.

Ningkun, Wu. 1993. *A Single Tear: A Family's Persecution, Love, and Endurance in Communist China*. London: Hodder & Stoughton.

———. 1997. 'Cold War-China'. CNN, 8 February.

Quinonez, Ernesto. 2000. *Bodega Dreams*. New York: Vintage.

Smith, Ali. 2003. 'The Universal Story'. In *The Whole Story and Other Stories*. London: Hamish Viswanathan, Kaavya. 2006. *How Opal Mehta Got Kissed, Got Wild, and Got a Life*. Boston: Little Brown and Company.

3

Roots and Wings: The 'Space' of *The Great Gatsby*

Manju Jaidka

> All great storytellers have in common the freedom with which they move up and down the rungs of their experience as on a ladder. A ladder extending downward to the interior of the earth and disappearing into the clouds is the image for a collective experience to which even the deepest shock of every individual experience, death, constitutes no impediment or barrier.
>
> Walter Benjamin, 'The Storyteller'

According to Walter Benjamin, a story is like 'a ladder extending downward to the interior of the earth and disappearing into the clouds'. It may take its origin in a particular spot, located firmly in a specific time and place, and then reach out to a world beyond. *The Great Gatsby* skilfully recreates the America of the Roaring Twenties and the Jazz Age, capturing the essence of an era defined by opulence and excess. Through the unfathomable character of Jay Gatsby, the novel delves into the American Dream and the relentless pursuit of success, even at the cost of ethical values. It is a powerful reflection of the age in which it was written. At the same time, it has elements that carry it across spatio-temporal borders, making it relevant to cultures and sensibilities distanced from it in time and space, captivating readers across different eras and geographical locations. As Goethe once said, 'The great creations of world literature, while rooted in the soil of a single people, reach upwards into the sphere common to all men'.

This essay focuses on the temporal and timeless aspects of the novel, keeping in mind that a great piece of literature contains within it traces of all that has preceded it in literary history; simultaneously, it influences traditions that follow. This is a commonality that characterises literary masterpieces and makes them relevant for all times to come. By maintaining a dialogue with the past and simultaneously anticipating the demands of readers in an unknown future, F. Scott Fitzgerald's novel remains a classic for all times.

The Classical and the Canonical

A literary classic is widely recognised for its enduring quality and significance. It is a text that has withstood the test of time and continues to be read and appreciated across generations. Literary classics often have high intellectual merit and possess elements that cut across boundaries of time and space, offering profound insights into human nature. They may also significantly impact literature and culture, influencing other works and shaping literary traditions. Although the designation of a literary work as a classic is subjective and can vary based on cultural, historical and individual perspectives, certain characteristics are associated with classic literature, the most important being their enduring relevance. They address universal themes and explore fundamental aspects of the human condition that remain meaningful across different time periods and societies, transcending cultural and geographical boundaries. They reach out to readers from diverse backgrounds and continue to be relevant across generations. The characters that people their worlds often exhibit richness and depth in their exploration of values and ideas, providing an insight into human nature, society, morality or other fundamental aspects of life. They may inspire other works, shape literary traditions, or contribute to social and intellectual movements. They may showcase innovative writing styles, narrative techniques or linguistic mastery. They tend to maintain popularity and continue to be widely read long after their initial publication, finding new audiences, reaching out to readers across different generations, offering a window into the values, beliefs and societal norms of the particular era that they represent. Approved by connoisseurs, literary critics and scholars, they may receive awards or be the subject of academic study contributing to their lasting influence, thus finding a place in the literary canon.

A literary canon comprises representatives of the best or most important works in a particular literary tradition, period or genre. The formation of a literary canon is a complex and dynamic process influenced by various factors. Works that receive critical acclaim from scholars, critics and literary experts are often considered for inclusion in a canon. Academic analyses, reviews and scholarly discussions play a role in shaping perceptions of a work's literary merit. Some works gain canonical status due to their reflection of or response to important historical events or movements. The inclusion of a work in educational curricula can significantly contribute to its canonical status. Texts taught in schools and universities become part of the shared literary knowledge of a given society and may continue to be valued over time. It is, however, important to note that the formation of a literary canon is an ongoing and dynamic process. Over time, canons can evolve and adapt to changing cultural and societal perspectives, leading to the inclusion of new voices and the re-evaluation of existing ones.

The status of a novel as a classic is not determined by a single factor but emerges through a combination of critical appreciation, cultural impact, enduring relevance and the recognition of its literary merit. The process of becoming a classic is not immediate, and recognition often develops over time. The perception of a novel as a classic can also vary among different cultures and literary communities. While some novels achieve classic status relatively soon after publication, others may take years or even decades to be widely recognised as such.

A novel intricately weaves its narrative within a tapestry of social, cultural and historical contexts—its milieu. The milieu encapsulates the environment shaping the novel, from cultural nuances influencing customs, beliefs and values, to historical events profoundly impacting themes and narratives. Social structures, relationships and interactions within the narrative are influenced by societal norms and power dynamics, while the physical environment and geography contribute to a palpable sense of place. The social milieu engages with the landscape, ideologies and power structures of the time, often serving as a commentary on political and social issues. Economic factors, including wealth disparities and challenges, drive character motivations and plot developments, contributing to the overall social fabric of the novel. The linguistic milieu, encompassing the author's command of language and literary traditions, leaves an imprint on the novel's style, echoing the linguistic nuances of the society in which it is written. Together, these diverse milieus converge to shape the novel, providing insights into the author's perspective on the world and reflecting the multifaceted dynamics of the human experience. Thus, when we refer to the milieu of a novel, we are taking into consideration the complex interplay of cultural, historical, social, geographical, political and economic factors that shape the narrative and themes of the work. Understanding the milieu of a novel is crucial for interpreting the meaning of a text as it provides insights into the author's perspective and the broader context in which the literary work is situated.

The transition of a text from its original milieu to a timeless zone is a testament to its enduring qualities and universal appeal. This process occurs when a text transcends the specific cultural, historical and social context in which it was created and continues to appeal to readers with the passage of time. Literature that delves into fundamental and universal themes, capturing the essential aspects of the human experience—like love, loss, morality and the human condition—tends to endure longer than works focused on topical issues. These themes connect with readers on a deep, emotional level, making the text relevant to diverse audiences regardless of their cultural or historical background. As for the characters that populate these texts, they embody relatable qualities and emotions, contributing to the timeless quality of the world they live in, a world that may be fictional but is deeply rooted in reality. The artistic merit of a text, including its writing style, narrative technique and overall craftsmanship, also elevates it to a timeless status. For these reasons, despite being rooted in a specific historical and cultural context, some novels remain relevant through their ability to address enduring human concerns. Whether exploring the consequences of power, the search for identity or the quest for meaning, such literary creations remain compelling. At the same time, the process of achieving timelessness is organic and often unfolds over an extended period until ultimately a work stands outside the limitations of time and cultural specificity.

When dealing with the timeless aspects of a novel, one may use the concept of 'roots and wings' which refers to the dual nature of a text and its enduring qualities—it is deeply rooted in a specific cultural, historical or social context (roots) while possessing the capacity to transcend these specificities and soar into a realm of universality and timelessness (wings). This duality allows a classic to maintain relevance and retain its appeal across different times and cultures although it may be firmly grounded in the cultural milieu from which it emerges, connected to the historical events and circumstances of its time. Despite its cultural and historical roots, a classic novel often explores themes related to human experience that do not perish with time, portraying fundamental aspects of a shared human experience, emotions, relationships, challenges and triumphs. This is what gives the text its wings. The issues explored remain pertinent, allowing readers to find contemporary relevance in the novel's themes and messages.

The interplay between roots and wings is essential for a classic to achieve timelessness. The roots provide authenticity, grounding the novel in a specific context and making it a product of its time, and its wings—represented by universal themes, relatable characters, and enduring insights—allow the text to transcend its origins and appeal to a broader, timeless audience. In essence, the 'roots and wings' of a classic create a dynamic tension that allows the novel to be firmly rooted in its cultural and historical context while simultaneously soaring to heights of universality, ensuring its continued significance across spatio-temporal boundaries.

Space and Time

While discussing the idea of roots and wings, we are dealing with space—a space which is limited in terms of area and geography, as against that which is far beyond these limitations.

In literature, space is of utmost importance, connecting the past with the future, tradition with contemporaneity, then with now and beyond. Spatial theory in literature explores how physical and metaphorical spaces shape the narrative and its characters. It examines the relationship between the setting, the characters' identities, and the events of the story. Space can represent power dynamics, social structures and psychological states. Several critics have differing viewpoints on its use while interpreting a literary text. Critics like Henri Lefebvre and Edward Soja highlight the role of space in literary analysis. Their theories may be cited in the present context.

Edward W. Soja, a geographer and urban planner, is known for his contribution to spatial theory which challenges traditional dualistic perspectives and offers a more nuanced understanding of space. His concept of firstspace refers to physical, objective and measurable space. It encompasses the traditional, empirical understanding of space as a geometric, Cartesian entity. Firstspace is associated with the tangible aspects of spatial relationships, such as distances, coordinates and physical boundaries. The secondspace, in Soja's framework, refers to lived or experienced space. It incorporates the subjective and qualitative aspects of space, including personal perceptions, emotions and cultural interpretations. Secondspace recognises that individuals experience and interpret space in diverse and often subjective ways. Soja's most significant contribution is the concept of thirdspace. This represents an effort to overcome the limitations of dualistic thinking (firstspace vs. secondspace) by introducing a more inclusive and integrative perspective. Thirdspace is a hybrid and transformative space that emerges from the dialectical interplay of physical space and lived experiences. It encompasses the complexities of social, cultural and individual interpretations of space. In its triad—firstspace, secondspace and thirdspace—Soja's spatial theory reflects the layered and dynamic nature of spatial experiences, acknowledging the interplay between physical space, lived experiences and transformative possibilities. By encouraging scholars and researchers to move beyond binary thinking about space and consider the intricate relationships between the physical and the experiential dimensions of space, this theory has been influential in fields such as geography, urban studies and cultural studies.

Comparable, yet distinct, is the spatial theory of Henri Lefebvre, the French Marxist philosopher and sociologist whose influential works, particularly the trilogy *The Production of Space*, presents a comprehensive examination of space as a social product. Lefebvre, too, introduces a triad of spatial categories—perceived space (of perceptions and experiences), conceived space (of conceptualisations and plans imposed by authorities) and lived space (of daily practices and social interactions)—which forms the basis for understanding the complexity of spatial relationships and how different spatial dimensions interact. He identifies three components of spatial practice: physical activities, perceptions and symbolic representations, arguing that space is produced through the intersection of these practices. Representations of space, including maps, images and language, contribute to shaping the way people perceive and understand their environment. Lefebvre emphasises the existence of contradictions within spatial relations that arise from the tensions between different modes of production and the struggle for control over space. Lefebvre critiques the alienating aspects of modern urban life, where abstract space dominates at the expense of lived space. He argues for the reappropriation of everyday life and the creation of spaces that enhance social interactions, creativity and the fulfilment of human needs. His spatial theory has been influential in critiquing traditional urban planning and challenging dominant power structures; his ideas have inspired scholars to explore the social, cultural and political dimensions of space, contributing to a richer understanding of the dynamic relationship between society and its spatial environment.

Against these theories, it is possible to assess a text like *The Great Gatsby* and investigate the reasons for its continued appeal through the ages, its timelessness and its enduring impact. The first space in *The Great Gatsby* is the physical space in which Jay Gatsby lives and dreams; the second is the one he hopes to attain, the fulfilment of his dreams and desires. His story moves from the first and second space to an outer world across time, surviving even a hundred years later. *The Great Gatsby* has an enduring appeal across generations. Through the lenses of the spatial theories of Soja and Lefebvre, we can appreciate how Fitzgerald's work critiques the American Dream and illustrates the persistent tensions between physical reality and personal ambition. The novel serves as a poignant exploration of the interplay between space and identity, demonstrating that our understanding of spaces—both physical and lived—remain relevant and impactful even a century later. In this way, *The Great Gatsby* transcends its time, inviting readers to reflect on the complexities of aspiration, identity and the social structures that shape our lives.

Other critical viewpoints may also be cited in this context. For example, Harold Bloom emphasised the concept of the 'anxiety of influence' and argued that great works of literature possess a timeless quality by engaging in a creative dialogue with the works that came before them (1997). He believed that literature transcends its historical context and continues to resonate with readers across generations. Or we may refer to Northrop Frye who proposed the concept of 'archetypal criticism' and suggested that literature taps into universal patterns and symbols that are ingrained in the human psyche (1951). According to Frye, these archetypes give literature its enduring relevance and make it accessible to readers from different time periods. T. S. Eliot, in his essay 'Tradition and the Individual Talent', argued that great literature is characterised by its ability to maintain a dialogue with the past while also remaining relevant to the present. He believed that literary works, through their timelessness, contribute to the continuous development of cultural and artistic traditions. Virginia Woolf explored the concept of time in literature and emphasised the capacity of novels to transcend the limitations of temporal boundaries. In her novel *Orlando*, she depicted a character who lives for centuries, highlighting how literature can challenge conventional notions of time and connect readers to different historical periods. Roland Barthes examined the concept of the 'death of the author' and argued that once a literary work is created, it takes on a life of its own, independent of its author's intentions or historical context (1977). This perspective emphasises the ageless and autonomous nature of literature. These critics, among others, have contributed to the discussion surrounding the timelessness of literature, recognising its enduring power and its ability to transcend temporal boundaries.

The exploration of time and space in literature is, thus, a rich and multifaceted topic that has been the subject of various theories and approaches. The idea of the chronotope, for instance, coined by Mikhail Bakhtin refers to the intrinsic connection between time and space in literary works (1982). Bakhtin argued that every literary text creates a unique chronotope that shapes the narrative and the characters' experiences. The chronotope establishes a relationship between the fictional world and the social and historical context in which it is situated. Postmodern literature frequently plays with notions of time and space. It disrupts linear narratives, incorporates intertextuality and fragmentation and challenges traditional notions of history and reality. Postmodern writers like Italo Calvino and Jorge Luis Borges have experimented with non-linear storytelling and created intricate narratives that traverse different temporal and spatial dimensions.

These theories and approaches provide frameworks for analysing the intricate interplay of time and space in literature, illuminating how authors manipulate these dimensions to convey meaning, challenge conventions and shape the reader's experience.

Jay Gatsby's Story

F. Scott Fitzgerald is widely regarded as one of the prominent figures in American literature, particularly for his portrayal of the Jazz Age and the Roaring Twenties. His works, notably *The Great Gatsby*, have earned a lasting place in the literary canon by vividly capturing the spirit and excesses of the Jazz Age; his portrayal of the American social landscape during the 1920s remains unparalleled. Fitzgerald critically examined the American Dream, particularly its materialistic and often elusive nature. A powerful commentary on the pursuit of wealth and success in the American context, *The Great Gatsby* stands out not just for its portrayal of an era lost in time but also for Fitzgerald's prose style, celebrated for its elegance and lyricism. His ability to craft sentences with poetic beauty and precision has left a lasting impact on American literary aesthetics. Moreover, the characters created by Fitzgerald, complex and nuanced, often grappling with identity, societal expectations and the consequences of their choices, remain deeply etched in literary history. Through his novels, Fitzgerald offers his observations on class, privilege and morality, focusing on the cultural and social dynamics of his time. His cultural commentary, while rooted in the American experience, has a global relevance and his examination of the human condition, the impact of societal changes and the consequence of excess, applies to a broad range of cultural and historical contexts. Fitzgerald's works continue to be studied and appreciated in literature courses worldwide. The enduring legacy of *The Great Gatsby* and his other novels ensures his place in the global literary canon.

Gatsby is set during the Roaring Twenties, narrated by Nick Carraway, who moves to Long Island and becomes entangled in the lives of his mysterious neighbour Jay Gatsby and his cousin Daisy Buchanan. Gatsby is a wealthy and enigmatic figure known for hosting extravagant parties in the hopes of attracting Daisy, with whom he has had a romantic history. As the narrative unfolds, it becomes clear that Gatsby's opulent lifestyle is driven by his desire to win back Daisy, who is married to the wealthy but unfaithful Tom Buchanan. The novel explores themes of the American Dream, love, wealth and the moral decay of society. Tragedy ensues as Gatsby's dreams collide with reality, and the characters grapple with the consequences of their choices. Fitzgerald's elegant prose and multi-layered characterisation paint a vivid picture of the Jazz Age, offering a critique of the superficiality and moral ambiguity of the era. *The Great Gatsby* remains a literary signpost celebrated for its exploration of the illusions of success and the elusive nature of the American Dream, making it a timeless and thought-provoking work in the canon of American literature.

'The Roaring Twenties' is a term often used to describe the cultural, social and economic dynamism of the 1920s in the United States. This era is vividly portrayed in *The Great Gatsby*, represented by the flamboyant parties hosted by Gatsby:

> There was music from my neighbor's house through the summer nights. In his blue gardens men and girls came and went like moths among the whisperings and the champagne and the stars. At high tide in the afternoon I watched his guests diving from the tower of his raft, or taking the sun on the hot sand of his beach while his two motor-boats slit the waters of the Sound, drawing aquaplanes over cataracts of foam. On week-ends his Rolls-Royce became an omnibus, bearing parties to and from the city between nine in the morning and long past midnight, while his station wagon scampered like a brisk yellow bug to meet all trains. And on Mondays eight servants, including an extra gardener, toiled all day with mops and scrubbing-brushes and hammers and garden-shears, repairing the ravages of the night before. (Fitzgerald 1925, 32)

The opulence of the age is epitomised by these extravagant parties. The gatherings at Gatsby's mansion are lavish, with abundant food, flowing alcohol and a lively atmosphere. The excesses reflect the indulgent and carefree spirit of the time. It may be noted that the novel is set against the backdrop of prohibition, a constitutional ban on the production and sale of alcoholic beverages. However, Gatsby's parties, rife with illegal alcohol, highlight the widespread flouting of prohibition laws. This reflects the rebellious and law-defying attitude prevalent during the Roaring Twenties.

Fitzgerald coined the term 'Jazz Age' to capture the cultural atmosphere of the 1920s in the United States. This label originated from the popular music of the time—an improvised, earthy style characterised by syncopated rhythms and quick tempos. Jazz not only embodied the spirit of liberation but also represented a society deeply engaged in the pursuit of pleasure and excess. The genre reflects the era's hedonism and cultural shifts, which play a prominent role in Jay Gatsby's extravagant parties. These grand celebrations epitomise the opulence and carefree lifestyle of the time, marked by an abundance of alcohol, lively dancing and an overall atmosphere of indulgence. The Roaring Twenties fostered a consumer culture driven by a desire for luxury, with jazz music serving as both a soundtrack and a symbol of the social changes and rebellious spirit of the era. Earlier, T. S. Eliot had mentioned jazz music in *The Waste Land* (1922) with something close to disdain: 'But / O O O O that Shakespeherian Rag—/ It's so elegant / So intelligent…'. Eliot's line has echoes of rag-time music that was much in vogue in the early decades of the twentieth century with its 'ragged' rhythm. In the scintillating world of Jay Gatsby, Daisy Buchanan embodies the spirit of the flapper—an independent, young woman who defied traditional gender norms. The Roaring Twenties saw a shift in women's roles, and Daisy's actions and choices reflect the changing social dynamics of the era. According to Daisy, 'a fool—that's the best thing a girl can be in this world, a beautiful little fool' (Fitzgerald 1925, 15).

Gatsby's immense wealth, acquired through mysterious means, symbolises the American Dream—the belief that anyone can achieve success and happiness through hard work and determination. However, despite the superficial glamour and vitality, the Roaring Twenties also saw moral ambiguity and decay. The characters in *The Great Gatsby* engage in reckless behaviour, and their pursuit of pleasure often masks a deeper sense of disillusionment and emptiness. The highs and lows of the age, the excesses and emptiness and the collision of dreams with the harsh realities of life are thus effectively captured in the story that unfolds, making it a quintessential portrayal of the Jazz Age. But amid this gathering gloom of hedonism and decay comes the symbolism of the 'green light'. Gatsby's famous green light across the bay serves as a symbolic beacon representing hope, dreams and the relentless pursuit of success. It encapsulates the optimism and aspirations of the Roaring Twenties while also foreshadowing the inevitable disillusionment with it. Symbolising ambition, greed and the urge to get rich quick, the green light is deceptive; it lures the dreamer (of the American Dream) who, like many others of his time, expends all of his energy in pursuit of a goal that keeps moving farther away. The metaphor of the green light, representing both hope and disillusionment, characterises both Gatsby's struggle and the elusive American Dream. Despite his desires, what Gatsby does not know is that the green light which has enticed him so, is already behind him, somewhere in the dark obscurity of the past which has propelled him to this place. Jay Gatsby will never know this and yet he is destined to stretch out his arms towards a goal that will forever be out of reach, and ultimately he will pay for it with his life.

Even as the novel portrays the shining, ephemeral world of the 1920s with its glitter and glamour, its hopes and aspirations, it also explores the darker side of this dream at the same time, highlighting the moral compromises and disillusionment that can accompany the pursuit of wealth. Beneath the shining veneer, the Jazz Age was marked by moral ambiguity and a sense of disillusionment. The characters in the novel engage in morally questionable behaviour, and the pursuit of pleasure often masks deeper existential emptiness and dissatisfaction. Fitzgerald weaves together themes of music, social change, materialism and the elusive nature of the American Dream together with human greed and ambition. So, the novel stands as both a celebration and a critique of the era, offering multiple perspectives of the cultural climate that defined the 1920s. As Jay Gatsby embodies the spirit of the Jazz Age, his mysterious background, rapid rise to wealth and lavish parties reflect the social mobility and the pursuit of success that defined the era. His unrequited love for Daisy is also a poignant symbol of the fleeting and sometimes elusive nature of happiness during this period, characterised by materialistic opulence and flamboyance. Other characters, like Tom Buchanan and Jordan Baker, also reflect the societal values and contradictions of the era. Their roles further illustrate the complexities of the social landscape Fitzgerald critiques.

Across Chronotopic Borders

The Great Gatsby by F. Scott Fitzgerald remains relevant today for several reasons. It explores the theme of wealth and social class, portraying the stark contrast between the opulence of the upper class and the struggles of the working class. In contemporary society, issues of wealth inequality and class divisions continue to be pertinent, making Gatsby's narrative relevant to current discussions on socio-economic disparities. The American Dream is a central theme in the novel, and Fitzgerald's critique of its materialistic interpretation remains relevant. In today's context, where discussions about the attainability of the American Dream persist, Gatsby's story prompts reflection on the pursuit of success, its consequences and the illusions as well as disillusionments associated with it. The materialistic excesses and the emptiness of consumer culture of a century ago is echoed in the contemporary era, where consumerism and the pursuit of status symbols are prevalent. Gatsby's lavish parties and the desires of his characters offer a critique of the pursuit of happiness through material possessions.

Gatsby's idealised vision of Daisy and the stark contrast between appearance and reality are themes we are familiar with today in the age of social media and curated identities. The novel's exploration of the consequences of living in a world of illusions and the harsh realities of life continues to be relevant. Complex interpersonal relationships in the novel, characterised by unrequited love, betrayal and societal expectations, mirror contemporary challenges in personal relationships. Gatsby's attempt to climb the social ladder and reinvent himself underscores the ongoing theme of identity and self-presentation in society. In a world where individuals often strive to project a fabricated image through social media, the novel prompts us to contemplate the authenticity of personal identity.

Environmental issues are not neglected. Fitzgerald's descriptions of the valley of ashes, a desolate industrial area, touch upon environmental degradation. In today's context, discussions around climate change and environmental concerns draw parallels with the novel's depiction of a deteriorating landscape.

> This is a valley of ashes—a fantastic farm where ashes grow like wheat into ridges and hills and grotesque gardens; where ashes take the forms of houses and

> chimneys and rising smoke and, finally, with a transcendent effort, of men who move dimly and already crumbling through the powdery air.
>
> The valley of ashes is bounded on one side by a small foul river, and, when the drawbridge is up to let barges through, the passengers on waiting trains can stare at the dismal scene for as long as half an hour. (Fitzgerald 1925, 19)

A century after its publication, what keeps *The Great Gatsby* alive in the popular imagination is the silver screen where several adaptations of the novel have been showcased ever since the novel first appeared. It has been adapted into several film versions, each offering a unique interpretation of the novel. In some adaptations, there are narrative elements that differ from the source material. *The Great Gatsby* (1926) directed by Herbert Brenon is a silent film, the first adaptation of Fitzgerald's novel. Due to the limitations of the silent film era, the adaptation simplifies the narrative and lacks the depth of characterisation found in the novel. A later adaptation in 1949 directed by Elliott Nugent stars Alan Ladd as Jay Gatsby and Betty Field as Daisy Buchanan. The film takes liberties with the plot and characters, altering details to fit the constraints of a feature-length movie. Some critics argue that the film does not capture the essence of the novel as effectively as later adaptations. The 1974 version directed by Jack Clayton is perhaps the most well-known adaptation, featuring Robert Redford as Jay Gatsby and Mia Farrow as Daisy Buchanan. While faithful to the novel in many respects, this adaptation has been criticised for its glamorous portrayal of the characters and its tendency to romanticise the story. Additionally, some subtleties and complexities from the novel are lost in the translation from print to film. In 2000, the novel was adapted for a TV film directed by Robert Markowitz, starring Toby Stephens as Jay Gatsby and Mira Sorvino as Daisy Buchanan. This adaptation takes creative liberties with the plot, updating the setting to contemporary times. While the core narrative remains intact, the modernisation of certain elements changes the contextual nuances of the story. *The Great Gatsby* (2013), directed by Baz Luhrmann, is a visually striking adaptation that stars Leonardo DiCaprio as Jay Gatsby and Carey Mulligan as Daisy Buchanan. Luhrmann's adaptation is known for its stylised visuals, incorporating contemporary music and a more flamboyant portrayal of the Roaring Twenties. The film also utilises framing devices, including Nick Carraway narrating the story from a sanatorium, which is not present in the novel.

Film adaptations of literary works often necessitate alterations to fit the cinematic medium, and each version of *The Great Gatsby* brings its own interpretation to the narrative. These adaptations vary in their fidelity to the source material, creative choices and the degree to which they capture the essence of Fitzgerald's novel. However, they all serve to keep alive the story of Jay Gatsby, taking it from one generation to another through the years.

Conclusion

To sum up, in *The Great Gatsby*, F. Scott Fitzgerald provides a poignant commentary on the American Dream and its potential for failure. Set in a period of economic prosperity and social upheaval, the novel explores the hollowness that can accompany the pursuit of an elusive dream. Gatsby represents the quintessential American Dreamer, believing in the possibility of self-invention and upward mobility. His relentless pursuit of wealth and social status is driven by the belief that these achievements will secure his place in elite society and win back Daisy's love. However, Fitzgerald suggests that Gatsby's version of the American Dream is illusory—a superficial construct built on material success and social acceptance. The tragic narrative of Jay Gatsby underscores the unattainability of his dream. Despite accumulating immense wealth and hosting extravagant parties, Gatsby is unable to bridge the gap between his idealised vision of the American Dream and the harsh reality of his life. His tragic end serves as a cautionary tale about the limitations and pitfalls of an ideal that promises boundless possibilities. As for Daisy, who is also often seen as a symbol of the American Dream herself, she is symbolic of one whose desires are entangled with the pursuit of wealth and social status. Her inability to choose love over societal expectations reflects the corrupted nature of the American Dream, where personal happiness is sacrificed at the altar of societal conventions. The novel, thus, exposes the darker side of the American Dream, particularly during the Jazz Age, characterised by excess and decadence and the downside of the pursuit of wealth for its own sake, disconnected from genuine human connections. Gatsby's story, boldly tracing the trajectory of the protagonist's insatiable pursuit of pleasure without moral grounding, provides a critique of the excesses of hedonism. These issues remain pertinent in the contemporary era, where discussions about sustainability, overconsumption, and its consequences persist.

Through his novel, Fitzgerald urges readers to reflect on the true essence of fulfilment and meaning beyond the superficial trappings of success. Transcending the boundaries of time and space, *The Great Gatsby* continues to hold a timeless appeal that captivates readers across generations and cultures. Whether in the bustling streets of New York City or a quiet corner on the opposite side of the globe, the novel's examination of the human condition and the search for a better life strikes a chord with readers, ensuring its enduring relevance.

> Gatsby believed in the green light, the orgiastic future that year by year recedes before us. It eluded us then, but that's no matter — tomorrow we will run faster, stretch out our arms farther.... And one fine morning .... So we beat on, boats against the current, borne back ceaselessly into the past. (Fitzgerald 1925, 144–145)

Gatsby's story, thus, has valuable lessons for contemporary readers and could inform their views on ambition, success and fulfilment in a changing world. It jolts us out of our complacency and prompts us to confront the realities of life that are often hidden beneath superficial distractions. The allure of high society might offer temporary comfort, but ultimately, it comes with a cost that may lead us to an outcome we never intended.

Works Cited

Bakhtin, M. M., Holquist, Michael, et al. 1982. *The Dialogic Imagination: Four Essays*. Reprint edition. Austin: University of Texas Press.

Barthes, Roland. 1997. 'The Death of the Author'. 1977. In *Image, Music, Text* translated by Stephen Heath, 142–148. London: Fontana Books.

Benjamin, Walter. 1968. 'The Storyteller: Reflections on the Works of Nikolai Leskov'. In *Illuminations*, edited by Hannah Arendt, 83–107. New York: Harcourt Brace Jovanovich.

Bloom, Harold. 1997. *The Anxiety of Influence: A Theory of Poetry*. Oxford: Oxford University Press.

Eliot, T. S. 1982. 'Tradition and the Individual Talent'. *Perspecta* 19: 36-42.

Fitzgerald, F. Scott. 1925. *The Great Gatsby*. Unabridged Kindle edition.

Frye, Northrop. 1951. 'The Archetypes of Literature'. *The Kenyon Review* 13(1): 92–110.

Lefebvre, Henri. 1991. *The Production of Space*. Translated by Donald Nicholson-Smith. Oxford: Wiley-Blackwell.

———.2008. *Space, Difference, Everyday Life*. New York: Taylor and Francis.

Soja, Edward. 1996. *Thirdspace: Journeys to Los Angeles and Other Real-and-Imagined Places*. Oxford: Blackwell Publishing.

———.2000. 'Postmodern Geographies: The Reassertion of Space in Critical Social Theory'. In *Seeking Spatial Justice, Globalization and Community*, Book 16, edited by Edward W. Soja, 3–22.

4

'Can't buy me love': A Study of Failed Relationships in F. Scott Fitzgerald's *The Great Gatsby*

Tania Chakravertty

F. Scott Fitzgerald's phenomenal novel, *The Great Gatsby*, celebrating its centennial in 2025, is a recollection of events that took place in the summer of 1922. The world portrayed in this novel is a sham and hollow one; one of bitter disappointment, of unsatisfied hopes and unfulfilled dreams, and of failed relationships. When Gertrude Stein referred to the 1920s post-war generation as 'lost' she actually indicted a generation of youth who were disenchanted, disoriented and disillusioned, a generation of youth worshipping a new god—money—and drowning in the drunken excesses of revelry and debauchery. The era has been referred to as the Roaring Twenties, and Fitzgerald referred to this era as the Jazz Age. Something else was also happening in the 1920s, something very significant. From the 1910s, old Victorian patterns of sexual behaviour and morality had begun to be shunned by modern young women and armed with higher education, and having a potential foothold in the job market, women had become far more assertive, sexually and otherwise. Right from the beginning of his career, Fitzgerald was very much associated with the youth culture that developed in the 1920s and expectedly, in the Roaring Twenties, the fiction of Fitzgerald and his friend Hemingway are full of men trying to come to terms with a world in which gender roles were changing.

In this context, one needs to talk about the appearance of the flapper. The social changes that began in the 1890s saw the college-educated Gibson Girl, who was not buxom and matronly but slender and athletic. Then appeared the flapper in 1913 who seemed almost 'mannish' in looks and behaviour to traditionalists. The Gibson Girl was soon replaced by the flapper, who Rena Sanderson says was 'more sexualized', and 'one who aimed at attracting men', adding that 'both female types shared a refusal to play the selfless angel whether of the house or of the nation' (2002, 146). As a chronicler of the 1920s, F. Scott Fitzgerald not only portrayed but also popularised the flapper. Fitzgerald's writings document the evolution of the modern American woman, and this is particularly commendable because the documentation, perception and analysis of female psychology came from a male author. In this era, the independence of the career woman remained a threat to men and male authors, and in contrast, the flapper became a far more positive ideal for modern women in male-authored texts. Assisted by his wife Zelda, Fitzgerald offered his readers 'an image of a modern young woman who was spoiled, sexually liberated, self-centered, fun-loving, and magnetic' (Sanderson 2002, 143). Critics and sociologists now often pin the flapper down as a trend limited to the Jazz Age but it needs to be kept in mind that, as an authentic personage in American history in the Modernist age, she was cherished, envied, emulated and imitated for almost four more decades. In fact, caught in the flux of awe and fear, Fitzgerald himself, like the young men of his times, was ambivalent towards this 'creation' of his. As Sanderson says, increasingly he used the somewhat rebellious flapper 'as a symbol not only of a new order, but also of a social disorder and conflict'. In a letter to Edmund Wilson in May 1925 Fitzgerald wrote, 'If I had anything to do with creating the manners of the contemporary American girl I certainly made a botch of the job' (Bruccoli 1994, 110). Whether or not he had botched up his creation, in an interview taken by Margaret Reid, Fitzgerald himself praised his early flappers, stating that:

> [t]he girls I wrote about were not a type—they were a generation. Free spirits—evolved thru the war chaos and a final inevitable escape from restraint and inhibitions. If there is a difference, it is that the flappers today are perhaps less defiant, since their freedom is

> taken for granted and they are sure of it. In my day, ...they had just made their escape from dull and blind conventionality (Bruccoli and Bryer 1971, 279).

He also traced the American flapper to several influences; among them were the rise of a new moneyed class in the American Midwest, and the popularisation and influence of Sigmund Freud on wealthy young girls, instigating them not to remain victims of repressed desires. Though Fitzgerald did not create the flapper, he did popularise her, much with the help of his wife Zelda. In a popular essay, published under Fitzgerald's name, Zelda wrote, 'I believe in the flapper as an artist in her objective field, the art of being—being young, being lovely, being an object' (quoted in Prigozy 2002a, 8). In another one, Zelda argued that if women were allowed freedom, and full freedom of expression, they would become content to marry and settle down, and the number of divorces would also be lessened. Eminent historian Christina Simmons describes the flapper thus:

> This figure both embodied the popular notion of the free woman and retained a softness that did not threaten men. The flapper participated in the male world, probably working at a job as well as leading an independent, sexually integrated social life. She found men exciting, interesting comrades and did not take a condescending or disapproving attitude toward their ways. Her combination of daring spirit and youthful innocence was precisely what made her attractive to men. (1993, 31)

This description could very well describe Daisy Fay Buchanan except for the fact that she does not work at a job. In fact, Simmons specifies that 'the flapper cared more about men and babies than about paid work or her development as an individual through work' (31) and this is one the reasons that leads to complications in the relationships portrayed in *The Great Gatsby*. The flappers in Fitzgerald's fiction are usually young women belonging to families with wealth and legacy, used to material comforts and economically dependent on men.

'The Diamond as Big as the Ritz' (1922), 'Winter Dreams' (1922), 'Dice, Brass Knuckles and Guitar' (1923) and 'The Sensible Thing' (1924), have plots and themes very similar to *The Great Gatsby*. 'Winter Dreams' revolves around a poor boy from the Midwest, Dexter Green, who falls in love with a rich young woman, Judy Jones. Judy Jones turns out to be cruel and manipulative who first encourages him and then treats him with indifference and contempt. The tale turns out to be one of misplaced revenge; Dexter turns cruel too as he gets engaged to and then abandons a young woman. In 'The Sensible Thing', a young engineer, George O'Kelly, struggles to acquire money and success in New York in the insurance business so that he can marry the girl he loves, Jonquil Cary. Apprehensive about George's prospects, she breaks off their engagement, 'the sensible thing' to do, as she feels in such a situation. There is another story titled 'Absolution' (1924) which 'was to have been the prologue of the novel' as Fitzgerald informed Perkins, 'but it interfered with the neatness of the plan' (quoted in Pelzer 2000, 79). Young men must have money because the women they fall in love with are otherwise beyond reach—this became a recurrent pattern in his fiction. Fitzgerald's own experiences with Ginevra King and with Zelda Sayre may have had something to do with this. In the Christmas of 1914, Fitzgerald met and fell in love with the beautiful sixteen year-old Ginevra King who came from a wealthy Illinois family. He kept corresponding with her and meeting her occasionally until Ginevra ended the relationship in August 1916. He met Zelda Sayre, the daughter of the Associate Justice of the Supreme Court of Alabama, at a Montgomery Country Club dance in July 1918. Charles Scribner's Sons rejected a draft of his novel which he had called *The Romantic Egoist* in August. He revised and resubmitted it but that too got rejected in October the same year. As second lieutenant he was sent to Long Island, New York; and as he awaited overseas duty the war ended. In 1919, after his discharge from the army, by February, Scott and Zelda got engaged, and Scott Fitzgerald began working in an advertising agency. Unsure of their future together, Zelda broke off the engagement in June.

Fitzgerald resigned from the job, went to live with his parents in St Paul and began rewriting the novel, this time calling it *This Side of Paradise*. Scribner's accepted the novel finally in September and his short stories that had been rejected earlier also finally found place in magazines. In January 1920, F. Scott Fitzgerald and Zelda Sayre got engaged again and in April 1920, he got married to her. Like the author himself, Fitzgerald's heroes are often jinxed because of their social inferiority and are rejected. Scott Donaldson, Fitzgerald's biographer calls him a man 'who feared, expected, and even dreamed of rejection' and mentions 'the Princeton plutocrats who detected the intruder in their midst to Judge Anthony Dickinson Sayre who at death's door declined to tell his son-in-law that he believed in him' (2001, 42); he adds that, for consolation and for validation of his worth as a human being, Fitzgerald turned to women. One woman friend, for example, whom Fitzgerald found immensely appealing was Nora Flynn, 'an attractive, vivacious woman, part of whose appeal for Fitzgerald came from her background and her unconventional life' (Donaldson 2001, 129). As Donaldson mentions, she was the youngest of the famous Langhorne sisters of Virginia. The oldest amongst the sisters was Lady Nancy Astor; and interestingly, another had married Charles Dana Gibson, the American illustrator who created the fashionable and independent Gibson Girl. Donaldson documents that Nora Flynn 'had fled from her first marriage in order to run off with Lefty Flynn, a former football player at Yale and—like Nora herself—a gifted musician. Fitzgerald enjoyed her wit, envied her happiness, and admired her fearlessness'. Yet, disdain and indifference by rich girls he took to be the norm and thus, what his biographer says about him could very well befit the men in his fiction, and that includes Jay Gatsby; as Donaldson says, 'If he could win the heart of the girl—especially the golden girl over whom hung an aura of money, beauty, and social position—surely that meant that he had arrived, that he belonged' (43). And we may add that Zelda very well befits the heroines of most of his stories. In January 1921 Fitzgerald said in an interview for a magazine called *Shadowland*, 'Indeed, I married the heroine of my stories. I would not be interested in any other sort of woman' (Milford 1960, 77).

Of course, biographical details account only partially for the way the Gatsby story shaped up. Critics have always referred to the Gatsby story as a typical American story, rather as the story of an individual and Gatsby's dream has been referred to as the American Dream. The Gatsby story could very well be a story of the 'self-made man'. Why then does Gatsby's dream not come to fruition? And why is it that relationships fail in the novel? Hieke Paul begins his chapter 'Expressive Individualism and the Myth of the Self-Made Man' by quoting, Irving G. Wyllie who stated that 'The legendary hero of America is the self-made man' (2014, 367) in *The Self-Made Man in America*. The myth of the self-made man therefore, in the hegemonic context is related to individualism and individual success, traits which are typically American. In order to achieve this the self-made man ideally, therefore, must be part of a utopian classless society, one that allows vertical social mobility. Benjamin Franklin, among others, epitomised the self-made man in American culture. In addition to this, before Fitzgerald there was the oeuvre of Horatio Alger (1832–99) with his rags-to-riches stories, very popular amongst middle-class readers. Indeed, Donaldson too mentions, 'Scott Fitzgerald grew up at the turn of the century reading the Alger books and believing in the gospel of success' (5). Fitzgerald's protagonist differs slightly from the stereotypical self-made man. Gatsby amasses property and thinks of achieving not just success but also happiness; his pursuit of happiness and success epitomised in his golden girl, Daisy.

Such is the plotting that when the novel begins, the reader finds a number of people whose lives become entangled—Gatsby pursuing Daisy Fay Buchanan married to Tom Buchanan who is having an affair with Myrtle Wilson; and Nick Carraway, the narrator, whom Daisy wishes to 'fling … together' (Fitzgerald 2021, 15) with her friend Jordan Baker. Unfortunately, all the relationships fail. Bryer claims that, '[t]he secret of the problem of F. Scott Fitzgerald is that the author and his wife actually believed that money could buy happiness' (quoted in Prigozy 2002, 17), their belief manifested in the lifestyle they had, a lifestyle with much of glamour and a lust for popular acclaim. In *The Great Gatsby* however, money fails to buy happiness, and most importantly money fails to buy, and buy back, love. Ronald Berman reminds us that *The Great Gatsby* 'inhabits a different world, with barriers between men and women, Protestants, Catholics, and Jews, rich and poor, capital and labor, educated and half literate' (2002, 79). These are the barriers that lead to the failures in relationships in the novel—whether based on love or sexual attraction. In this context, Berman mentions the protagonist of Balzac, Stendhal, and Dickens, who 'tries to conquer the social world of London or Paris. He is able to do so because under the new industrialism, money has taken the place of class' (80). Indeed, what had been for centuries the stuff fairy tales are made of, poor boys turning into princes, had become possible, owing to historical and social changes. This possibility had become all the more palpable in America, a land which had not carried over from the 'old world' the feudal class structure and the typical European upper-class contempt for those in trade or physical labour. Yet, in reality, Gatsby and Myrtle become made painfully aware that equality exists on pen and paper only as a socio-political ideal. In the novel, Jay Gatsby not only wishes to attain success, he wants to be a gentleman and Myrtle Wilson, because of her affair with a rich gentleman, begins to think of herself as a lady. More than money, what goes against them and their dreams is, ironically, class-hierarchy.

A few days before the novel was published, Fitzgerald wrote to John Peale Bishop, '[one of the] cheerfulest things in my life [is] … the hope that my book has something extraordinary about it' (quoted in Miller 1968, 19). Love, marriage, affairs, both pre-marital and extra-marital—these themes have been ubiquitous in novels. But the plot of *The Great Gatsby* is rather unusual. The plot revolves around what Judith P. Saunders calls an 'unusual and elaborate mate-poaching scheme devised by the title character' (2018, 138). Jay Gatsby who fell in love with Daisy Fay about five years back, continues to pursue her even after she has become a wife and mother, married to Tom Buchanan for three years before the story opens; and this serves as the raison d'être for him.

The novel describes Gatsby's romance with Daisy Fay, in two phases. The first phase, the reader comes to know, was in the summer of 1917 when the twenty-five-year-old Gatsby was, 'a penniless young man without a past' (Fitzgerald 2021, 119) enchanted by the eighteen-year-old Daisy with beauty, high social status and wealth. Nick Carraway speaks of Gatsby's experience with women, 'he knew women early, and since they spoiled him he became contemptuous of them' (79). Amidst such women, he had happened to come across Daisy, 'the first "nice" girl he had ever known', an acquaintance made possible by the 'invisible cloak of his uniform' (119) with which he transcends social class; the uniform camouflaging his lower-middle-class background. He continues wooing this 'nice' girl who is upper class and unattainable. Though Gatsby's initial objective is frivolous, and his mind bent on seduction, 'to take what he could and go' (120), he soon turns serious as Daisy declares that she is in love with him, after yielding to him sexually. This emotional involvement happens when he is wooing her with the deception, letting 'her believe that he was a person from much the same strata as herself—that he was fully able to take care of her' (119–20). In fact, he continues to deceive both Daisy and himself as he keeps on writing to Daisy, encouraging her to believe that they will eventually marry.

With Jay Gatsby gone, the task of choosing whom to marry becomes a little difficult for Daisy Fay because of her emotional involvement with him. After her debut the following year, sponsored by her parents, she is coerced by 'the pressure of the world outside' to be wooed by eligible bachelors, and to keep 'half a dozen dates a day with half a dozen men' (Fitzgerald 2021, 121). Evolutionary psychology may help the reader understanding why Daisy chooses to marry Tom Buchanan in Gatsby's absence. Quoting from *The Evolution of Desire: Strategies of Human Mating* by David Buss, Saunders analyses how Daisy's marriage with Tom, represents the choice of a mate following predictable patterns. Buss says, similarities in 'values and interests' along with shared 'race, ethnicity, and religion' reflect 'the tendency for like people to mate' (quoted in Saunders 2018, 139). Along with race, ethnicity and religion, Daisy and Tom have similar backgrounds, elite socio-economic statuses and wealth—in fact, Tom's family turns out to be far more affluent as compared to hers. At nineteen, in the most desirable bracket of the marriageable age, Daisy chooses not to wait for Jay Gatsby: 'something within her was crying for a decision. She wanted her life shaped now, immediately' (Fitzgerald 2021, 121). Instead of wasting her prime years waiting for a man that too in the military service, she lets herself be swayed by the 'wholesome bulkiness [of Tom Buchanan's] person and his position' (121–22) and eventually marry him in spite of her drunken insistence at the eleventh hour that she will not marry Tom Buchanan and wait for Jay Gatsby. It would be interesting to speculate what might have happened had Gatsby not been called abroad on military duty. The relationship would definitely have snapped had Daisy's family known about his financial situation. And, scrutinising Daisy's subsequent actions, it seems that Daisy herself would have backed out from any real commitment had she known that the young Gatsby was penniless. The modernist author would not have sentimentalised this issue, had she backed out; Nancy Milford mentions that F. Scott Fitzgerald boldly stated in the January 1921 interview for *Shadowland* that instead of, 'the sex-less animals writers have been giving us', he was in favour of the 'the young woman of 1920 flirting, kissing, viewing life lightly, saying damn without a blush, playing along the danger line in an immature way—a sort of mental baby vamp.... Personally, I prefer this sort of girl' (77). Daisy, like many of Fitzgerald's flappers, is a spoiled daughter from a wealthy family, economically dependent on male providers who would continue to provide her with the material comforts that she is used to in her parental household. Fitzgerald found nothing wrong with it; evident in this advice he gave to his sister Annabel, that a girl must 'learn to be worldly. Remember in all society nine girls out of ten marry for money and nine men out of ten are fools' (quoted in Sanderson 2002, 150).

The relationship between the Buchanans fails owing to multiple reasons and both of them are to blame. Tom Buchanan, the womaniser, marries Daisy not for love but because of her beauty and social position; but he keeps on hunting for sex partners, most of them short-term, and the stupendous amount of wealth he possesses allows this social privilege. Jordan Baker reveals how Tom's affair with a hotel chambermaid three months after his marriage to Daisy got flashed in the newspapers. She reports how he had run into a wagon with his rough and aggressive driving which ripped one of the front wheels off his car and '[t]he girl who was with him, got into the papers, too, because her arm was broken' (Fitzgerald 2021, 61). And, at one of Jay Gatsby's parties, Tom begins flirting, in the presence of Daisy, with a woman whom she finds 'common but pretty' (85). All this womanising continues when Tom is married to the beautiful Daisy and also has Myrtle Wilson, the wife of a garage owner, as a steady mistress. According to Buss, 'men's standards for sexual affairs reveal a precise strategy to gain sexual access to a variety of partners' (quoted in Saunders 2018, 141) adding that in contrast to their preference in wives who are expected to demonstrate sexual reserve and fidelity, men seek temporary affairs with women having sexual experience and high sex drive. The married and sexually experienced Myrtle Wilson fits in perfectly with what Buss says about short-term partners; Myrtle being a woman 'in the middle thirties ... [who] carried her flesh sensuously as some women can' with 'an immediately perceptible vitality about her as if the nerves of her body were continually smouldering' (Fitzgerald 2021, 20). She had responded with physical passion to Tom Buchanan right at their first meeting, as strangers on a train.

The serious liaison between the wealthy Tom Buchanan and the lower-class Myrtle Wilson also reveals much about social protocol. Myrtle's act of sitting in Tom's lap in front of Nick not only violates etiquette, it clearly reveals her working-class background. This class difference works to Tom's advantage. Tom Buchanan makes a modest financial investment, given his immense wealth, but an investment amount that is more than enough to keep Myrtle supremely happy, a woman without the tastes and expectations of the upper-middle class. Ronald Berman says that '[w]hen we see Myrtle's arrangements we see the inside of her mind' (2002, 89) adding that the blue-collar Myrtle surrounds herself with the artefacts of the middle class without even understanding them. Unfortunately, for her, this could also mean that her perception of the very wealthy Tom could be deficient too. She feels happy using what she thinks are expensive face creams, perfumes and items of clothing. She installs fancy furniture and keeps on buying books and magazines and pictures for the apartment he has rented for her. She remains supremely happy because she feels that Tom Buchanan is generous with his resources. Berman rightly says, 'Myrtle has tried to *accumulate* her social character' adding that she keeps on buying things, 'because of the urgings of advertisements which promise status through acquisition'. The affair lets her indulge in unplanned purchases—new dresses, and a puppy for example, and in impulsive whims—taking a massage, riding in a garish lavender-coloured taxicab—and offers her temporary respite from the unattractive life with Wilson in the garage. Not only does Myrtle feel 'regal' (Fitzgerald 2021, 22) when she enters the love nest in New York City, she also begins to feel that she has risen in terms of social class. She begins to think of her husband as someone hierarchically inferior, not really 'a gentleman' and not 'fit to lick [her] shoe' (27). Her lower-middle class background coupled with her sparse knowledge and experience regarding the affluent upper-middle class make her vulnerable to Tom Buchanan's duplicity. He keeps on implying that he would probably marry her sometime in the future, and lies to her that it is his wife's religion, which forbids divorce, that is hampering their union. In spite of some emotional attachment, the lack of commitment towards Myrtle becomes clear during their violent row in the New York City apartment. Myrtle's words and actions manifest jealousy inciting Tom to first forbid Myrtle to mention his wife's name, and then strike her, making her bleed through the nose, as she refuses to comply. This clearly shows that he has no plans to marry Myrtle and that he considers her much inferior to the wife he cherishes. In spite of such treatment, Myrtle continues to stay in this loveless relationship, because of the material benefits the affair brings.

'Tom's got some woman in New York' (Fitzgerald 2021, 12), Nick understands, is an open secret, a secret that Daisy would also obviously come to know about. To Tom Buchanan, keeping a mistress is not really an embarrassment; rather to him it becomes a show of power and wealth. It also gives him the crude pleasure of humiliating and cuckolding the poor and innocent Wilson '[who's] so dumb he doesn't know he's alive' (21). Wilson is disgraced also by his wife's sexual disloyalty. Tom keeps Myrtle's name and the rented apartment a secret from his wife but his mistress telephones his home and that triggers Daisy's suspicions; Nick witnesses 'that turbulent emotions possessed her' (13). Also, in one of Gatsby's parties that the Buchanans attend, Tom leaves Daisy, saying that 'a fellow's getting off some funny stuff' (85), which, in this case, is a euphemism for a short-term seduction; and Daisy with mock-geniality replies 'Go ahead, … and if you want to take down any addresses here's my little gold pencil' (85). This little incident like many others shows that though Daisy has desensitised herself against his womanising, she torments him with her sarcastic comments. She asserts herself with her sarcastic wit and innuendos, thus demeaning Tom Buchanan. If Tom has a crude flaunting of money and sexual prowess, Daisy pays him back with words and innuendos that lead to embarrassment and humiliation in public. Marriages like that of the Buchanans involving a wealthy husband and a trophy wife were not uncommon in that era. A wonderful example would be the marriage of Grant and Jane Mason who served as prototypes for Hemingway's short story 'The Short Happy Life of Francis Macomber' (1936). The relationship between the Buchanans is similar to that of the Macombers. Hemingway writes: '… They had a sound basis of union. Margot was too beautiful for Macomber to divorce her and Macomber had too much money for Margot ever to leave him' (21). The odd relationship between the Buchanans, and the Macombers, can be referred to as a 'symbiotic' one. Harold Searles says that in symbiotic processes, 'just as self and object are not clearly demarcated, neither are hate and love clearly differentiated' (quoted in Chakravertty 2022, 112). The spouses hold on to a relationship in which love and hate intermingle.

What makes the Buchanan marriage doubly adulterous is Daisy's renewed interest in Jay Gatsby. Jay Gatsby surprises everybody by renewing his pursuit of the woman he loved five years back. Saunders states that the tactic he uses is a clever one. He first disappears from Daisy's life only to rè-enter with elan.

'Unlike many other men in similar circumstances, in life or in literature (for example, Goethe's *Werther*), he does not seek meetings or correspondence with her. … He avoids presenting himself in the guise of cringing hanger-on or emasculated loser—male types women reject as mates.' (Saunders 153)

By the time he re-enters with flair, he has acquired material resources more than enough to compete with her immensely rich husband who has given her an extraordinarily expensive lifestyle. He holds fancy parties 'always full of interesting people, night and day. People who do interesting things. Celebrated people' (73) in his enormous European-style mansion, and in his first meeting with Daisy, he shows her around, the 'Marie Antoinette music rooms and restoration salons', taking her through the 'period bedrooms swathed in rose and lavender silk … through dressing rooms and poolrooms, and bathrooms with sunken baths' finally leading her to his bedroom, showing her his 'toilet set of pure dull gold' and throwing the high-priced British shirts he possesses before her which land in a 'many-colored disarray' (Fitzgerald 2021, 74). His tactics work—the attracted Daisy begins to smooth her hair with his brush, and Gatsby's shirts 'of sheer linen and thick silk and fine flannel' make her weep profusely. Gatsby then shows her his collection of newspaper clippings featuring her, 'a lot of clippings—about you' (75), he says, and hopes to impress her with his devotion which, as he wishes to manifest, has not waned over the years.

Jay Gatsby fails in his attempts to win back Daisy however. As the nouveau riche, he fails to understand that wealth alone does not bring status. Even Nick is aware of the differences between the raw splendour of West Egg, where Gatsby has taken up residence, and the suave, sophisticated and fashionable East Egg where the Buchanans have purchased property. By East Egg standards, Gatsby's display of wealth is gaudy and tasteless. His home, which is an imitation of a European hotel, is ostentatious and the parties are nothing but 'many-coloured, many-keyed commotion' (Fitzgerald 2021, 83–4). Unlike the blue coupé, of Tom Buchanan, who possesses old money,

Gatsby's car is garish, of 'a rich cream colour, bright with nickel, swollen here and there in its monstrous length with triumphant hatboxes and supper-boxes and toolboxes, and terraced with a labyrinth of windshields that mirrored a dozen suns' (50). Such are the ornate embellishments that the upper-class Tom Buchanan labels it a 'circus wagon' (96). To bring Daisy back to himself, Daisy's husband simply reminds her of the class difference, he reminds her of the risks involved in a life shared with 'Mr Nobody from Nowhere' (104). Not only does Tom expose Gatsby's lack of elite upper-class status and connections, he offers information about Gatsby's shady, and possibly criminal, business dealings so far. He informs her that Gatsby belongs to the lower class, with folks who deliver 'the groceries to the back door' (105) and that Gatsby himself is 'a common swindler' (107)' and 'a bootlegger' (107). With a show of pseudo affection, Tom shrewdly offers his analysis of Daisy's adulterous affair as foolishness rather than disloyalty, adding that his affection, in spite of the occasional straying, is genuine: 'The trouble is that sometimes she gets foolish ideas in her head and doesn't know what she's doing ... And what's more, I love Daisy too. Once in a while I go off on a spree and make a fool of myself, but I always come back, and in my heart I love her all the time.' (105). Gatsby who 'felt married to her' (120) fails to obliterate Daisy and Tom's past and begin afresh by turning back the clock to 1917. Tom Buchanan in fact dismisses Gatsby's five-year devotion to Daisy as a 'presumptuous little flirtation' (108) and he achieves the desired effect. The moment Daisy recognises that marriage to Gatsby would make her lose her own socio-economic and cultural milieu, she holds herself back. Tom talks intently to his wife after all this, covering her hand with his own. As Nick says, 'They weren't happy ... and yet, they weren't unhappy either. There was an unmistakable air of natural intimacy' (117) that they manifest. It is no wonder that Daisy, who Gatsby says, possesses a voice 'full of money' (96), chooses to cling on to her husband who offers her money and security, things more substantial as compared to ephemeral love.

The Horatio Alger rags-to-riches stories were far from innocent. Ideally, one would expect that in (classless?) America, a self-made man would be proud of his achievements. But Jay Gatsby keeps on hiding his past. Berman rightly says that one of the principal messages in the Alger stories where working class heroes fight for their success, in books like *Sink or Swim* (1870) or *Strong and Steady* (1871), is that getting rich is easier than being accepted. It is not money but the 'social order [which] is against them, usually personified by a rich man's son who understands that when poor boys rise, rich boys have less space to breathe in' (2002, 80). Men like Braddock Washington in 'The Diamond as Big as the Ritz' (1922), Anson Hunter in 'The Rich Boy' (1926), and of course Tom Buchanan of *The Great Gatsby* control, threaten and exclude intruders who dare to emulate or imitate the elites like themselves. Interestingly, in the stories mentioned, these individuals cause at least one death. In *The Great Gatsby*, like her husband, Daisy also excludes, though inadvertently, an upstart who wished to be a lady and who was also a sexual rival. The hit-and-run case, where she was at the wheels, shows cowardice as well as carelessness, traits associated with the very affluent. Jordan Baker, in spite of her adulation of Daisy, decides to hone her talents as a self-reliant woman, but as Nick says, she turns out to be 'incurably dishonest' (Fitzgerald 2021, 46) as she is revealed to cheat at golf. In spite of her talents, her relationship with Nick Carraway doesn't even commence because of her basic dishonesty though Nick admits at the end that he is 'half in love with her' (143) when they part ways. Jordan mentions, how in Chicago, the Buchanans moved 'with a fast crowd, all of them young and rich and wild' (61) and at the end of the novel, Nick proclaims that the Buchanans are careless people, self-centred to the core, oblivious to individuals of other social strata with interests other than their own, ones who 'smashed up things and creatures and then retreated back into their money or their vast carelessness, or whatever it was that kept them together' (144). It is no wonder, that those shared privileges ironically keep the Buchanan marriage from falling apart, love or no love.

Works Cited

Berman, Ronald. 2002. '*The Great Gatsby* and the Twenties'. In *The Cambridge Companion to F. Scott Fitzgerald*, edited by Ruth Prigozy, 79–94. Cambridge: Cambridge University Press.

Bruccoli, Matthew J. 1994. *F. Scott Fitzgerald: A Life in Letters*. New York: Charles Scribner's Sons.

Bruccoli, Matthew J., and Jackson R. Bryer. 1971. *F. Scott Fitzgerald In His Own Time: A Miscellany*. Kent: Kent State University Press.

Chakravertty, Tania. 2022. *Ernest Hemingway and the Fluidity of Gender: A Socio-Cultural Analysis of Selected Works*. London: Routledge.

Donaldson, Scott. 2001. *Fool for Love: F. Scott Fitzgerald*. New York: Authors Guild Backinprint.com. 2001.

Fitzgerald, F. Scott. 2021. *The Great Gatsby*. New Delhi: Penguin Random House, India.

Hemingway, Ernest. 1938. *The First Forty-Nine Stories*. London: Arrow Books-Random House.

Milford, Nancy. 1970. *Zelda: A Biography*. New York: Harper and Row.

Miller, James E. 1968. 'Boats Against the Current'. In *Twentieth Century Interpretations of The Great Gatsby*, edited by Ernest H. Lockridge, 19–36. Englewood Cliffs: Prentice-Hall, Inc.

Paul, Heike. 2014. 'Expressive Individualism and the Myth of the Self-Made Man'. In *The Myths That Made America: An Introduction to American Studies* by Paul Heike, 367–420. Bielefeld: Transcript Verlag. http://www.jstor.org/stable/j.ctv1wxsdq.11.

Pelzer, Linda C. 2000. *Student Companion to F. Scott Fitzgerald*. Westport: Greenwood Press.

———. 2002. 'Introduction: Scott, Zelda, and the Culture of Celebrity'. In *The Cambridge Companion to F. Scott Fitzgerald*, edited by Ruth Prigozy, 1–27. Cambridge: Cambridge University Press.

Sanderson, Rena. 2002. 'Women in Fitzgerald's Fiction'. In *The Cambridge Companion to F. Scott Fitzgerald*, edited by Ruth Prigozy, 143–163. Cambridge: Cambridge University Press.

Saunders, Judith P. 2018. '*The Great Gatsby*: An Unusual Case of Mate Poaching'. In American Classics: *Evolutionary Perspectives*, 138–74. Brighton: Academic Studies Press, 2018.

Simmons, Christina. 1993. 'Modern Sexuality and the Myth of Victorian Repression'. In *Gender and American History Since 1890*, edited by Barbara Melosh, 17–42. London: Routledge.

5

The Great Gatsby in the Twenty-First Century: Memory, Masculinity and the 'Fictitious Capitalist'

Avishek Parui

This essay aims to examine F. Scott Fitzgerald's *The Great Gatsby* (1925) as a novel about memory and masculinity, emerging from an anxiously euphoric age and how these themes correspond to the construct of the 'fictitious capitalist' as described by Karl Marx, a concept further problematised in this reading. The essay will particularly study the interplay of nostalgia and future-projection which gets manifested through the use of unreliability and mystery in the narrative technique espoused in the novel as well as in its characterisations. Drawing on established scholarship on *The Great Gatsby* as well as by locating the relevance of the story in the twenty-first century, the essay will highlight how Fitzgerald's literary representation of the character of Gatsby bears interesting parallels with the cultural acceptance of and the anxiety around the mysteriously wealthy male subject in the contemporary age, particularly in post-liberalisation India. Of special interest in the essay is the theme of the unknown past of the newly-emergent capitalist who was once a weak former lover, a symbol of masculinity appearing also in Emily Bronte's *Wuthering Heights*. This connects complexly with the merger of memory and erasure and how that shapes the mystery of the fictitious capitalist whose sources of income are not materially defined or calibrated but rather exist in a state of fluidity and proleptic projection, ironically undercut by the sudden and unnatural death of the eponymous character in Fitzgerald's novel. Finally, the essay will revisit the theme of 'anxious euphoria' manifested in the many balls and parties of *The Great Gatsby* and study those as signs of cannibalistic consumerism which almost becomes a mandatory part of middle-class behaviour, a theme eerily resonant with the credit-based capitalism of the twenty-first century where the use of money is defined more through investments in a spectral future rather than being grounded in a real, tangible present.

In volume three chapter twenty-nine of his *Capital*, Karl Marx described the fictitious nature of the contemporary credit system as a machinery where everything turns into 'duplicate and triplicate, and it transformed into a mere phantom of the mind' (1981, 603). In the same volume, Marx defines the dual qualities that shape the spokesperson for credit, who becomes, in this reading, a 'mixed character of swindler and prophet' (572–73). The fictitious capital and the fictitious capitalist exemplify and inhabit an anticipatory system that 'circulates without production yet having been realised, representing a claim on a future real valorisation process' (Durand and Broder 2017, 57). Literary historians such as Mary Poovey and Marieke de Goede have argued that the culture of credit economy which emerged in Europe in the eighteenth and nineteenth centuries were shaped by and in turn shaped the institutional differences between fact and fiction, involving 'the development of the discrete separation between factitious texts, including modern journalism and economic ledgers, and fictitious ones, including, notably, the novel' (Haiven 2014, 31–32). Combining elements of a cheater as well as a seer, the fictitious capital's 'anticipation of future accumulation implies a radical form of fetishism liable to mutate into unsustainable phantasmagoria' (58). The fictitious capitalist is, thus, both a figure of anticipation and destruction standing on a fragile present where all that is solid melts into air, while celebrating the unreal signifiers of success which also embodies decadence and a slow death, in an economy of 'fictions that animate society' (6). This culture of fictitious animation and amplification, dramatically accelerated today, receives one of its earliest and finest literary representations in F. Scott Fitzgerald's complex fictional depiction of what he classified as the Jazz Age, a culture where poor American boys from the hills could become wealthy businessmen–gentlemen by bootlegging, gambling, loansharking and selling stolen bonds.

The futuristic and ultimately unachievable quality of capital which is associated with growth and greatness in Fitzgerald's novel is reflected in Gatsby's belief 'in the green light, the orgiastic future that year by year recedes before us' causing such believing subjects to 'beat on, boats against the current, borne back ceaselessly into the past' (Fitzgerald 1993, 141). If the promise of the fictitious capital is illusory and slippery, *The Great Gatsby* gives us a world where such illusions are embodied and enacted by the aspiring male subjects through imaginative projections which are also already nostalgic in quality, thereby dramatising a complex interplay of memory, anticipation and masculinity. The anxiety and ambiguity associated with financial prosperity and sustainability in *The Great Gatsby* are interestingly comparable to the post-liberalisation Indian economy that saw ontological changes in the notions of the billionaire and the financial conman, whereby the sudden rise and fall of risk-based capital publicly and, sometimes, spectacularly displayed the blurring borderlines between promise and precarity in a culture characterised by a great appetite for aspirations. As Kanchan Chandra argues in a study of the relocation of patronage in post-liberalisation India, patronage transactions that determined the rise and fall of private businessmen necessitated that aspirant subjects 'cultivate relationships with state officials as a necessary evil to get work done in an ambiguous environment' (2015, 47). This relationship of symbiotic patronage and privilege is often contingent upon a futuristic investment and the necessary renegotiation of permission and privilege, especially in the form of loans and waivers, creating a culture which sees the sudden growth (and destruction) of massive capitalists and mysterious billionaires in a post-liberalisation economy which operates with 'a new system of licenses, leases, concessions, permits, and contracts that regulate the entry of the private sector to the newly de-reserved areas (48). This is often accompanied with unprecedented patronage on the part of the government to selected private businesses in the form of 'land, raw materials, and credit'. This creates a cultural and economic ecosystem that facilitates the fictitious capital to be invested in the quick rise of businessmen and businesses, and is also characterised by enigmatic self-made wealthy subjects with new cultural self-fashioning, themes which are dramatised and cautioned against in Fitzgerald's novel.

This essay will explore how the memory and masculinity dramatised by the eponymous character of *The Great Gatsby* are interestingly connected to the extended economy of fictitious capital in an age where the borderlines between the gentleman and the crook are blurred and mutable, creating a social situation where, as Tom Buchanan says to Nick Carraway, 'A lot of these newly rich people are just big bootleggers' (Fitzgerald 1993, 114). Published in 1925 and depicting the economic and moral changes of post-First World War America, Fitzgerald's novel is set in the summer of 1922 and presents the story of Jimmy Gatz who eventually becomes Jay Gatsby by working variously as a farm boy, fisherman and steward, and ending as a decorated major who made money as a bootlegger and a swindler, exemplifying the mutating moral codes and compasses in *The Great Gatsby*. The memory–masculinity complex in *The Great Gatsby* is a product of an age in which, as the philosopher John Dewey wrote soon after the publication of Fitzgerald's novel, 'the loyalties which once held individuals, which gave them support, direction, and unity of outlook on life, have well-nigh disappeared' (Prigozy 2001, 83) and where Gatsby becomes a great man through his bootlegging despite being 'Mr Nobody from Nowhere' (Fitzgerald 1993, 137). The gentleman–criminal that Gatsby ultimately becomes is marked both by his garish and excessively phallic car which is of 'rich cream color, bright with nickel, swollen here and there in its monstrous length with triumphant hatboxes and supper-boxes and tool-boxes, and terraced with a labyrinth of wind-shields that mirrored a dozen suns' (51) as well as a photo of himself 'cricket bat in hand' (53) from his Oxford days, metonymic markers of a memory and a masculinity Gatsby aspires to produce and preserve. The memory–masculinity associated with Gatsby's Oxford education is not without its sinister subcurrents, as Nick observes: '[Gatsby] hurried the phrase "educated at Oxford", or swallowed it, or choked on it, as though it had bothered him before. And with this doubt, his whole statement fell to pieces, and I wondered if there wasn't something a little sinister about him, after all' (42). Along with the subliminal sinisterness, memory and masculinity in Fitzgerald's eponymous character are also marked by a sense of spectrality, as the social rise of Gatsby is always haunted by the ghosts of his dead family, and the narrative almost implies that they had to die to ensure Gatsby 'came into a good deal of money' (42). This somber spectral tone is highlighted in Nick's description thus: 'His voice was solemn, as if the memory of that sudden extinction of a clan still haunted him' (42). Through its narrative and symbolic economy, Fitzgerald's novel illustrates how growth and death are organically connected with each other in an age where the moral as well as capitalist currency are dangerously mutable as well as uncertain. The precarity of capital and the problematic proximity of prosperity and catastrophe as depicted in *The Great Gatsby* are also historically borne out by the fact that the US stock market crash in 1929 and the subsequent Great Depression emerged from the deceptively opulent Jazz Age depicted in the novel. The mystery and uncertainty about wealthy self-made subjects such as Gatsby compare complexly with the precarity and unknowability associated with a post-liberalisation economy. As Amitava Krishna Dutt argues in a study of the post-1990 liberalisation India, such an economy of credit and capital-building often operates with imperfect information, uncertainty and instability; the information asymmetry causing the need to 'put up collateral to overcome moral hazard problems' (2006, 1851). In close correspondence to this, the stolen bonds and bootlegged alcohol which shape the greatness of Gatsby in turn create an economy of financial and moral hazards, where information is asymmetrically available and at best translucent and where self-fashioning male subjects operate in close proximity to criminality, moral deviancy and death.

In *Image Patterns in the Novels of F. Scott Fitzgerald*, Dan Seiters examines how the colour imagery in *The Great Gatsby*, particularly in relation to the garish cream yellow automobile owned by Gatsby, is a 'combination of the white of the dream and the yellow of money, of reality in a narrow sense' (1986, 58). Interestingly, the shift in the colour imagery associated with Gatsby's car is also an indication of the increasing moral degeneration of Gatsby in the novel, which may be examined as a fictional depiction of economic and moral volatility in an age of artificial appearances. Thus, after causing Myrtle Wilson's death, the car is described simply as 'a yellow car' (Fitzgerald 1993, 148), with yellow indicating 'purely and simply corruption. White, the color of the dream, has been removed from the mixture' (Seiters 1986, 58). The fragile construct of Gatsby's masculinity is, thus an interplay of things possessed as well as emotions lost and remembered only through symbolic objects, of wealth exhibited as well as values cherished but abandoned in an age of advertisements and superficial self-fashioning through a fictitious and cannibalistic capital. The visual vocabulary of consumerist violence characterising the hyper-capitalist gaze in the novel is accentuated by a strange satisfaction 'that the constant flicker of men and women and machines gives to the restless eye' (Fitzgerald 1993, 37). The flicker—a classic Modernist literary trope used by writers such as T. S. Eliot and Joseph Conrad to convey the changing wavelengths of cognition and consciousness—is used here by Fitzgerald to describe a restless metropolitan modernity which is scopophilc as well as neurotic in quality, reflective of how commodity fetishism in the American Jazz Age ironically also generates existential exhaustion and a nostalgia for a pastoral past. As Leo Marx argues in *The Machine in the Garden: Technology and the Pastoral Ideal in America*, 'In the *Great Gatsby*, as in *Walden, Moby Dick*, and *Huckleberry Finn*, the machine represents the forces working against the dream of pastoral fulfilment' (1964, 358). In its rags-to-riches story, complexly corresponding to as well as exposing the dark underbelly of the American Dream, Fitzgerald's novel is interestingly resonant with the anxieties and aspirations of post-liberalisation India where memory and masculinity are similarly tied to a mutable and fictitious capital of credit and investment apropos of social growth, where the boundaries between the gentleman and the criminal may be mutated and blurred, and where 'lifestyles and buying habits, valorised in TV and print ads, give rise to processes of status emulation that guide the conduct and channel the ambitions of others' (Krishna and Bajpai 2015, 70).

In examining race and identity in *The Great Gatsby* and connecting it to the Obama era of American culture, Joseph Vogel reads Baz Luhrmann's film adaptation of Fitzgerald's novel and highlights how both texts, resonating with the social structures and economic conditions of two different ages, rely on the 'currency' (both cultural and financial) invested in an 'intersectional exploration of identity' (Vogel 2015, 31), which in turn is illustrated in the complex 'consequences of white supremacy' (32) that unfolds into a panic in the novel's plot. The currency in both the original Fitzgerald text and the Luhrmann film operate as intersectional instruments of race, masculinity, and money through which the cycle of cultural aspirations and exhaustions take place. In line with the argument espoused in this essay, Vogel states that *The Great Gatsby* as a novel, despite being so organically and culturally associated with the Jazz Age, carries profound 'cultural relevance as a multi-media text in the twenty-first century' (32) in its assertion of aspiration, fantasy and fear of failure. What emerges in Fitzgerald's novel is how gentlemanly prosperity and criminality, success fetish and failure phobia are inextricably linked, generating an economy of emotions significantly resonant with the cultural landscape of opportunities, overreaching excesses, insecurities and alienation in post-liberalisation India. Consequently, the death of the eponymous character in Fitzgerald's novel is, as Vogel argues, 'not merely the death of an overreacher, but the death of an infiltrator who gets swallowed by the brute force of a system operating as intended' (50), flagging up again the manipulations, mendacity and menace always existing in close proximity to death in an anxiously aspirational age. In this reading, *The Great Gatsby* achieves more cultural currency in contemporary times than in its original setting, by dramatising 'a value system, a convenient tool of exclusion, misdirected rage, and oppression' (51) beneath its superficial structures of social stardom and celebration.

In his reading of Gatsby as a Prohibition gangster and businessman, Stephen Brauer studies the analogy Gatsby's father Henry Gatz makes between his deceased son and James J. Hill towards the end of Fitzgerald's novel, declaring with paternal pride and bereavement, if Gatsby had lived he would have become as great a man as Hill. An interplay of nostalgia and the imagined future, this projection connects Gatsby to a historical figure, a railroad industrialist who was a significant player and contributor to the American economy four decades before the time in which *The Great Gatsby* is set. This also situates the character of Gatsby as a self-made subject, in line and comparable to historical American industrialists such as John D. Rockefeller and Andrew Carnegie, also highlighting how the boundaries between business tycoons and gangsters were problematic in that age, exemplified by 'the 1920s culture that linked business and crime' (Brauer 2003, 51). This had a significant impact on literary imagination as well in terms of characterisation and figurative representation, as post-First World War fiction such as Fitzgerald's *The Great Gatsby* repositioned the criminal–businessman, not necessarily 'as figures operating on the margins of the culture, but also as individuals looking to move into the mainstream and into the seats of power'. The Gatsby-masculinity which receives a literary projection in Fitzgerald's novel is thus an amalgam of moral hybridity and reorientation, and a complex of nostalgia and nihilism, exemplified by the romantic remembrance of a lost time and the sudden and violent death of the eponymous character. The memory and masculinity of the self-made, self-serving subject in a morally ambivalent age are also invested with 'a Machiavellian rhetoric that suggests that the means to success do not matter so much as the results' (52). This theme is articulated by John Cawelti in Apostles of the Self-Made Man (1965) thus: 'The main trend in the development of ideas of self-help was away from the earlier balance of political, moral, religious, and economic values and in the direction of an overriding emphasis on the pursuit and use of wealth' (169). These tenets of self-help for the enterprising man were problematically similar to the success stories of contemporary gangsters such as Al Capone.

Indeed, Fred D. Pasley in *Al Capone: Biography of a Self-Made Man* (1930) highlighted how Capone 'had quit school in the fourth grade to help his parents in the struggle for existence in the slums' and, after a life of tricks and techniques on the streets and alleys, 'had soon commanded respect by reason of his fighting ability and fast thinking' (17). The cannibalistic violence associated with aspirational imagination and drive for success in Fitzgerald's novel is depicted in the characterisation of the young Gatsby, then named James Gatz, whose 'heart was in a constant, turbulent riot. The most grotesque and fantastic conceits haunted him in his bed at night' (Fitzgerald 1993, 105). Unsurprisingly, Gatsby, amidst all his new business enterprises, looks like he had 'killed a man' (142), foregrounding Fitzgerald's complex craft and 'ability to render Gatsby as both sympathetic and also despicable' (Brauer 2003, 67).

The character of Dan Cody serves as a symbolic precursor to the Gatsby-figure in Fitzgerald's novel. A self-made man who makes his fortune in Montana copper, Cody is also described as 'the pioneer debauchee who during one phase of American life brought back to the eastern seaboard the savage violence of the frontier brothel and saloon' (Fitzgerald 1993, 106). The constructed categories of social identities in *The Great Gatsby*—a novel where opposites often meet in cannibalistic ways to consume each other—are also exemplified by the tensions in sound patterns. The event at Plaza Hotel is marked by marriage music which is drowned when the 'compressed heat exploded into sound' with a 'burst of jazz' eating up the 'portentous chords of Mendelssohn's Wedding March' (99–100). The novel itself begins with a deceptive harmony of 'the sunshine and the great bursts of leaves growing on the trees' (7) only for words to be perceived later as 'babbled slander' as Gatsby departs to 'clamor' and 'tumult' (106). Fitzgerald's novel dramatises scenes where machines drown minds in cacophonous conditions created by the aspirant subjects chasing an elusive capital, where moral valences are forgotten and remembered strategically, sometimes through metafictional moments. This is corroborated in Barbara Will's study of obscenity in *The Great Gatsby*, which examines how Fitzgerald's novel 'also self-consciously inscribes the process of forgetting into its own narrative' (2005, 126) whereby Gatsby's greatness emerges only after the readers are made to forget that he is a criminal bootlegger. Will shows how this interplay of foregrounding and forgetting also shapes the politics of presentation and visibility in the text. The obscene word 'scrawled by some boy with a piece of brick' on the white steps of Gatsby's mansion, which to Nick appears at the end as a 'huge incoherent failure of a house' (Fitzgerald 1993, 140), thus becomes a marker that must be forgotten in order to remember Gatsby's greatness. However, even as Nick tries to rub the word out by scratching the stone with his shoe, in order to restore the fact that Gatsby 'turned out all right in the end', Fitzgerald foregrounds 'the process of erasure', dramatising the attempt to unremember, thereby 'problematizing the inevitability of the text's ending' and thus reminding the reader that Gatsby's greatness can be created and consolidated 'only if we forget, or repress, his obscenity' (Will 2005, 127). Loaded with symbolic significance, this scene corresponds to the broader cultural condition described in *The Great Gatsby*, illustrating how greatness in the unreal Jazz Age economy is a strategic construct of memory, masculinity and fictitious capital, which may be generated and superficially celebrated, but is never without its dark, sinister and obscene objects. More broadly, Fitzgerald's novel exemplifies how 'forgetting emerges as an act of production in fiction, whereby spectrality is produced as an articulation of absence' (Parui 2022, 8) that is also invested in identity production and preservation. The focus on the obscene word scrawled on Gatsby's house at the end of the novel generates further significance, as Will argues, when one examines the Latin root word *obscenaeus* which means both against representation and unrepresentable. *The Great Gatsby*, thus, eventually emerges as a novel which literally as well as metaphorically exemplifies Karl Marx's description of all that is solid melting into air and also 'points to a signifying void' (Will 2005, 127) at the heart of the human condition, dramatically embodied by Fitzgerald's eponymous character who is described by the narrator as 'an elusive rhythm, a fragment of lost words' (Fitzgerald 1993, 87).

Suzanne Del Gizzo's reading of the unhinged American Dream compares Fitzgerald's *The Great Gatsby* with Chuck Palahniuk's *Fight Club* (1996) and highlights how both texts foreground orders of memory and masculinity shaped and reshaped by reification and alienation, with both texts inhabiting periods of time characterised by major cusps of change in contemporary social behaviour, and argues that 'the world of Fight Club is a logical extension of the culture of commodification at the center of *The Great Gatsby*' (71). Both novels show how capital consumes the human subject vampirically, creating a credit system of production and consumption where the boundaries between the rich and the rogue have well-nigh vanished, and where violence is embedded in the enactment of wealth, prosperity and progress, a violence which is 'an unwavering side-effect of the American dream' (Del Gizzo 2007, 81). Both novels exhibit capital gone awry and the rapid swings between 'enchanted objects' (Fitzgerald 1993, 98) and sudden deaths, dramatising what the young Jimmy Gatz describes as the 'unreality of reality' (105). As Jacqueline Lance illustrates in a study of colour and automobile imagery in *The Great Gatsby*, 'Fitzgerald consistently uses the automobile as a vehicle to reveal the carelessness and materialism ofhis characters and he extends the scope of the automobile to that most feared and mysterious human condition of all, death' (2000, 29). The materiality and monstrosity of the automobile in *The Great Gatsby* foreground the entanglement of velocity and violence in the novel, dramatising how the marker of mobility and progress also becomes the vehicle of death, symbolically described as the 'death car' (Fitzgerald 1993, 144) which kills Myrtle Wilson. The phallic quality of Gatsby's garish car becomes monstrous and ultimately self-destructive, anticipating the rise-of-machine narrative associated with postmodern orders of spectrality and masculinity. *The Great Gatsby* and *Fight Club* both present orders of masculinity in their organic as well as socially transformative extensions, which correspond to psychological situations including 'lost time, forgetfulness, alienation, and most importantly, a split sense of self' (Del Gizzo 2007, 73), exemplified in Fitzgerald's novel by the floating cocktails and the yellow music (Fitzgerald 1993, 44). The split self emerges as the ephemeral subject of a cannibalistic cultural materiality fuelled by the greed and velocity of a vanishing capital that is always already elsewhere, comparable to the fictitious condition theorised by Marx, and enacted by the 'schizoid sensibility Fitzgerald began to detect and represent in The Great Gatsby' (Del Gizzo 2007, 80). In this transformative economy of fictitious capital, bootleg alcohol becomes the 'milk of wonder' (Fitzgerald 1993, 117) and Daisy Fay becomes the 'golden girl' (127) of Fitzgerald's novel. Memory and masculinity, as dramatised in *The Great Gatsby*, combines a romantic nostalgia for an idyllic America and an anxious aspiration for an urban utopia marked by velocity and violence symbolically connected, as Joseph Vogel contends in a study of the novel's relevance in the Obama era, to the monstrous spectres of white supremacy. The novel is also significant in its description of how such racial embodiments of prosperity and metropolitan modernity ultimately turns to trash, instantiated by the visceral violence perpetrated as well as suffered by the white male subjects increasingly exhausted by the fictitious capital they seek to acquire by outrunning each other, a theme that connects *The Great Gatsby* again to *Fight Club*. The racial otherness of Gatsby, what Barbara Will describes as his 'off-white' status, is associated 'with creole or Jewish difference' from the pure-white American fantasy (2005, 132). The vanishing subject of Gatsby, wherein 'his character can only be revealed through the moments in which he vanishes from the narrative, through oxymorons, through dashes—all of which point to an unrepresentability at the center of this textual reality', corresponds to the vanishing quality of capital in Fitzgerald's novel, reflective of a culture where ontological density is replaced by ephemerality, where the greatness of the fictitious capitalist is also associated with criminality, spectrality and obscenity.

In 'Echoes of the Jazz Age' published in 1931, Fitzgerald had described the era as 'the most expensive orgy in history' which was 'borrowed time anyhow', when even bankrupt subjects did not worry about money 'because it was in such profusion around' (5). Marked by the Janus-faced projections of prosperity and precarity, Fitzgerald's America may retrospectively be examined as a false euphoria which shattered when 'its essential prop received an enormous jolt, and it didn't take long for the flimsy structure to settle earthward' (5), culminating into a catastrophic economic decline with the Great Depression. Like all great works of literature, *The Great Gatsby* is penetrative as well as prophetic as a representation of its epoch, dramatising an interplay of nostalgia and anticipation, memory and masculinity. At the time when it was first published, Fitzgerald's novel sold only 23,870 copies going out of print by the time its author died in 1940, with its second edition's copies wearing away unsold in a warehouse (Scribner 1925, 203). As this essay has attempted to show, its relevance is perhaps more immediate today than at the time in which it first appeared. A novel written by a white American male with anxieties about non-white immigration, exemplified in his 1921 letter to Edmund Wilson where Fitzgerald advocated raising the bar for immigration to allow 'only Scandinavians, Teutons, Anglo Saxons + Celts to enter' (1994, 47), who wrote about an unreal opulent economy that preceded the stock market crash and the Great Depression in the United States, *The Great Gatsby* is in dialogue with the aspirations and anxieties of post-liberalisation India where it is uncertain whether the 'increase in consumption expenditure' is a healthy extension of 'increased incomes that will continue to grow further' or symptomatic of an artificial growth which is essentially 'credit-driven, which is vulnerable to fizzle out in the event of an economic downturn' (Krishnan and Hatekar 2017, 46). In its tale of unsustainable economic growth and unreal prosperity, dramatised through the life, success and death of its eponymous character, the world and human subjects in Fitzgerald's novel which precedes the catastrophic consequences of the Great Depression and the share market collapse in America, carry significant commonalities with the play of privilege and precarity in post-liberalisation India which saw 'rapid urbanisation and fast growth with incoming global investments, the IT boom, and expanding middle class', also accompanied by 'agrarian crises, farmers' suicides, food insecurity, and corruption' (Das Gupta 2019, 1). Lastly,

Fitzgerald's *The Great Gatsby*, like its great nineteenth-century predecessors and qualitative counterparts such as *Heart of Darkness* and *Crime and Punishment*, shows how the affective literary medium 'as a special and stylized system of codes reflects, represents, and defamiliarizes culture and lived reality through an interplay of matter, metaphor, and memory' (Parui 2022, 178). Its political and cultural relevance in the centenary of its publication, in our post-digital economy of production, consumption, circulation and self-fashioning, cannot be overestimated.

Works Cited

Brauer, Stephen. 2003. 'Jay Gatsby and the Prohibition Gangster as Businessman'. *The F. Scott Fitzgerald Review* 2: 51–71.

Cawelti, John G. 1965. *Apostles of the Self-made Man*. Chicago: University of Chicago Press.

Chandra, Kanchan. 2015. 'The New Indian State: The Relocation of Patronage in the Post-Liberalisation Economy.' *Economic and Political Weekly* 50(41): 46–58.

Das Gupta, Sejuti. 2019. *Class Politics and Agrarian Policies in Post-liberalisation India*. Cambridge: Cambridge University Press.

Del Gizzo, Suzanne. 2007. 'The American Dream Unhinged: Romance and Reality in *The Great Gatsby* and *Fight Club*.' *The F. Scott Fitzgerald Review* 6: 69–94.

Durand, Cédric, and David Broder, trans. 2017. *Fictitious Capital: How Finance Is Appropriating Our Future*. London: Verso.

Dutt, Amitava Krishna. 2006. 'Flawed Logic of Capital Account Liberalisation.' *Economic and Political Weekly* 41(19): 1850–1853.

Fitzgerald, F. Scott. '1931. 'Echoes of the Jazz Age'. *Scribner's Magazine*, XC(5): 1–6.

———. 1993. *The Great Gatsby*. Ware, Hertfordshire: Wordsworth Editions Limited.

———. 1994. *A Life in Letters*, edited by Matthew J. Broccoli. New York: Touchstone.

Haiven, Max. 2014. Cultures of Financialization: Fictitious *Capital in Popular Culture and Everyday Life*. London: Palgrave Macmillan.

Krishna, Anirudh, and Devendra Bajpai. 2015. Layers in Globalising Society and the New Middle Class in India: Trends Distribution and Prospects. *Economic and Political Weekly* 50(5): 69–77.

Krishnan, Sandhya, and Neeraj Hatekar. 2017. Rise of the New Middle Class in India and Its Changing Structure. *Economic and Political Weekly* 52, No. 22: 40–48.

Lance, Jacqueline. 2000. '*The Great Gatsby*: Driving to Destruction with the Rich and Careless at the Wheel.' *Studies in Popular Culture* 23(2): 25–35.

Marx, Karl. 1981. *Capital*, Vol III. Harmondsworth: Penguin.

Marx, Leo. 1964. *The Machine in the Garden: Technology and the Pastoral Ideal in America*. London: Oxford University Press.

Parui, Avishek. 2022. *Culture and the Literary: Matter, Metaphor, Memory*. Lanham: Rowman and Littlefield.

Pasley, Fred. 1930. *Al Capone: The Biography of a Self-made Man*. New York: Ives Washburn.

Prigozy, Ruth, ed. 2001. *The Cambridge Companion to F. Scott Fitzgerald*. Cambridge: Cambridge University Press.

Scribner, Charles III. 1925. 'Publisher's Afterword'. In *The Great Gatsby* by F. Scott Fitzgerald, 195–295. New York: Scribner.

Seiters, Dan. 1986. *Image Patterns in the Novels of F. Scott Fitzgerald: Studies in Modern Literature 53*. Ann Arbor: UMI Research Press.

Vogel, Joseph. 2015. '"Civilization's Going to Pieces": *The Great Gatsby*, Identity and Race from the Jazz Age to the Obama Era.' *The F. Scott Fitzgerald Review* 13(1): 29–54.

Will, Barbara. 2005. '*The Great Gatsby* and the Obscene Word.' *College Literature* 32(4): 125–144. Johns Hopkins University Press.

6

Unveiling Spectral Shadows: Studying the Lurking Gothic Elements in *The Great Gatsby*

Madhuchhanda Ray Choudhury

In 1924, a year before the publication of *The Great Gatsby*, F. Scott Fitzgerald made two significant remarks about the novel in his letters. On 11 April 1924, Fitzgerald wrote to writer and editor Moran Tudury that he was 'anxious for people to see [his] new novel which [was] a new thinking out of the idea of illusion'(1924a, 178). Later in August 1924, he wrote to his Princeton classmate Ludlow Fowler that 'the burden of [this] novel' was 'the loss of those illusions that give such color to the world so that you don't care whether things are true or false as long as they partake of the magical glory' (1924b, 179). The illusion that Fitzgerald was referring to was the myth of the American Dream—a myth that had degenerated into the rampant materialism and hedonism of the Roaring Twenties. Indeed Roger L. Pearson asserted that *The Great Gatsby* revealed that the 'American dream, [was], in reality, a nightmare' (1970, 645). In this essay, I demonstrate that Fitzgerald's 'new thinking' about 'the idea of illusion' was encapsulated in his use of Gothic tropes of haunting, eerie landscapes, spectral figures and a Gothic protagonist to explore the dark shadows emanating from a degenerated American Dream. This degeneration was inextricably linked to a cultural decline and concomitant spiritual crisis that plagued America during the 1920s. Beneath the glitter of the Jazz Age lay an insidious shadow of spiritual vacuity and deep existential agony. In this essay, I assert that Fitzgerald not only critiqued this vacuous ethos but masterfully employed Gothic tropes to distil the horror emanating from this milieu.

Scholars have addressed Fitzgerald's critique of a shallow, material culture, moral laxity and hedonism of the Roaring Twenties. Yet there has been no sustained scholarly discussion on Fitzgerald's use of Gothic elements in *The Great Gatsby* to expose the degeneration of the American Dream and the concomitant spiritual vacuity of the time.[1] In his 2018 article titled 'Dark Romantic: F. Scott Fitzgerald and the Spectres of Gothic Modernism', Derek Lee asserted that Fitzgerald's use of the 'Gothic mode' in some of his supernatural short stories and his novel *This Side of Paradise* enabled him to express his 'anxieties about the modernizing world'. However, Lee identified these anxiety-inducing attributes as 'liberalized sexuality, industrialization, immigration and urbanization' (30, 136). He did not connect it to the dread that can emanate from spiritual hollowness lying beneath the glitz and glamour of an economically prosperous America. Lee insightfully noted that there is 'a largely unrecognized spectral superstructure operating within Fitzgerald's mainstream work, including his social realist novels' (136) and identified *The Great Gatsby* as a social realist novel. But he only mentioned the novel in passing without analysing the nuances of the 'spectral superstructure' as it operates in this novel and did not link it to a spiritual emptiness

[1] In the opening chapter of his book *American Gothic Fiction: An Introduction*, Andrew Llyod-Smith notes that though *The Great Gatsby* is not a Gothic novel it uses several Gothic tropes. The tropes he identifies are 'the city as labyrinth; the imprisoned maiden/femme fatale motif; the wasteland wilderness "Valley of Ashes" presided over by the billboard of panoptican optician Dr T. J. Eckleburgh, the mad–scientist god of the wasteland; the sadistic accident in which Myrtle Wilson's left breast is ripped off by Gatsby's speeding yellow Rolls, with Daisy at the wheel; the scene of Gatsby's death when a shadowy, ashen figure comes out of the trees to kill him' (2004, 1). However, he does not provide any sustained analysis of any of these tropes. Instead he states that the Gothic is often about a return of the repressed past and an exploration of a buried secret which a culture does not want to admit. But his study views this Gothic tendency of returning to the repressed past in detecting the repetition of traditional patterns and writings of preceding writers by subsequent ones (1–2).

that plagued Americans during the 1920s. My essay intervenes in this critical gap. I argue that the spectres that insidiously haunt the world of Jay Gatsby can only be understood in the context of the demolition of old-world stabilities and certainties in the blatantly capitalist and materialistic world that emerged after World War I.

The spiritual crisis that plagued America in the 1920s stemmed from a larger disillusionment and ideological despair post World War I as well as the pitfalls inherent in the American Dream. Susan Currell explained that the supposed return to normalcy after 1919 'did not mean a return to pre-war ideals or traditions, but a huge expansion in business freedom and capitalist acquisition that unwove the progressive reforms and ideals of the previous two decades' (2009, 4). Bereft of traditional beliefs and awaiting a new system to replace the old one, Americans were left floundering in an ocean of doubt and unrest. Susan Currell quoted the philosopher George Santayana who, in 1920, detected a 'moral emptiness of a settlement where men and even houses are easily moved about and, no one, almost, lives where he was born, or believes what he has been taught' (36). This sense of being rootless may be connected to the idea of 'drift' that Ronald Berman discussed in his book *Fitzgerald, Hemingway and the Twenties*. Berman defined this 'drift' as 'unanchored distance—to be at the mercy of currents' (2001, 18).

Ironically this 'drift' was linked to the notion of democracy and freedom that underpinned the American Dream. Berman alluded to philosopher Walter Lippmann who exposed the darker side of American democracy where liberty ironically bred despair. In *Drift and Mastery: An Attempt to Diagnose the Current Unrest* (1914) Lippmann noted the quandary of the American in the modern world. He observed that when the 'old absolutisms of caste and church and state' prevailed 'life was organized into ritual and riveted by authority' (Lippmann 1914, 176). But democracy made far greater demands over the modern man. 'The modern world [swung] wide and loose, it [threw] men upon their own responsibility. And for that gigantic task they lack[ed] experience ... No wonder then that those who

[won] freedom [were] often unable to use it, no wonder that liberty [brought] its despair' (ibid).

This sense of hollow liberty can be connected to a gradual perversion of the notion of upward mobility spawned by the American Dream. Though the term entered popular parlance after James Truslow Adams used it in his 1931 work *The Epic of America* the notion of the Dream emerged with the earliest settlers in the New World (Cullen 2003, 4). Jennifer Murtoff defined the American Dream as the 'ideal that the United States is a land of opportunity that allows the possibility of upward mobility, freedom, and equality for people of all classes who work hard and have the will to succeed' (n.d., para 6). Yet by the 1920s this freedom had been reduced to unabashed acquisition of wealth. Unprecedented 'expansion in industry', 'technological innovation' and 'greater availability of consumer goods' (Tredell 2007, 11) aided the process whereby the connotation of Adams's idea of 'a better, richer, and happier life' was distorted into one of hollow luxury. The sense of stability and identity that Americans of this generation sought to create through acquisition of material objects ironically bred a spectral world—paradoxically insubstantial in its vapid materiality.

Jay Gatsby's opulent world of lavish parties and seemingly merry guests encapsulates this paradox, masterfully captured through Nick Carraway's evocative language. Carraway describes a milieu where 'introductions are forgotten on the spot' and 'enthusiastic meetings' take place between 'men and women who never knew each other's names' (Fitzgerald 1925, 76). The men and women who flit through this world are as protean and insubstantial as spectres and Carraway's language aptly captures these attributes. He talks about 'groups [which] change more swiftly', 'dissolve and form in the same breath', girls who, like 'wanderers', 'become for a sharp, joyous moment the centre of a group, and then, excited with triumph, glide on through the sea-change of faces and voices and color under the constantly changing light' (77). Despite their sheer materiality these ever-changing shapes are as vapid as the spectral figures thrown up by the urban junkyard—the valley of ashes. The language of haunting that Carraway uses to describe these guests and the grotesque shapes spawned momentarily by the valley of ashes underscore their similarity. Like restless, lost souls, these guests are as insubstantial as the ashes which 'take the forms ... of men, who move dimly and ... [crumble] through the powdery air' (64). Fitzgerald thus uses the spectral imagery of Gothic literature to portray a lost generation who 'sweep ... insistently through' a modern wasteland (Berman 2001, 18).

Fitzgerald's use of the images of a wasteland connects *The Great Gatsby* to the employment of Gothic images and tropes by Modernist writers in order to capture the pervasive existential crisis in the post-World War I period. William Patrick Day has written about the connection between Gothic and Modernism. In the chapter titled 'The Gothic in the Twentieth Century', Day explains that ' ... the Gothic fantasy introduced a number of themes, ideas and images that the modernists took over' and the Gothic 'provided some of the tools with which the modernists worked' (1985, 167). One such tool was the trope of the barren wasteland. Day asserts that 'the Gothic is full of images of ruins and a blasted landscape ... The chaotic world of the Gothic fantasy is an anticipation of the empty landscape of the grimmest version of the modernist vision' (169). However, he interprets these Gothic wastelands of modernist literature as 'metaphors for the mental state of the protagonists'. And in this context he remarks that in *The Great Gatsby* 'Nick Carraway describes the world to which Gatsby awakens after he finally loses Daisy as "material without being real", and that description fits the chaotic horror of the Gothic world as well'. However, it is Jim Cullen who makes an explicit connection between the barren valley of ashes overlooked by the empty eyes of T. J. Eckelburg and the existential crisis of the modern world. Cullen asserts that the valley of ashes can be interpreted as 'the modernist metaphor for the wasteland of humanity in a godless age' (2003, 181).

This 'godless age' was the price Americans paid for their rebellion. Walter Lippmann's remarks in *A Preface to Morals* (1929) revealed a spiritually barren landscape that confronted young Americans in the early part of the twentieth century. He explained that the Americans had the freedom to engineer their own lives, freed from the shackles of specific conventions, 'gods', 'priests' or 'revelations which they must accept' (Lippmann 1929, 7). Yet this freedom was self-defeating if not terrifying. Though the 'prison door [was] wide open ... [they staggered] out into trackless space under a blinding sun. They [found] it nerve-wracking' (ibid).

Having shattered every shackle and every idol Americans ironically deprived themselves of any comforting assurance in divine or providential power. Thus this rebellion produced a spiritual wasteland, whose denizens were restless, anchorless souls. Lippmann astutely noted in *A Preface to Morals*,

> the modern man who has ceased to believe, without ceasing to be credulous, hangs ... between heaven and earth, and is at rest nowhere.... There is no moral authority to which he must turn now, but there is coercion in opinions, fashions and fads. There is for him no inevitable purpose in the universe, but there are elaborate necessities, physical, political, economic. (1929, 9)

This was a random universe not governed by any divine or providential law and such a universe is bound to breed dread. Lippmann astutely explained the difference between the old and the new order as follows:

> In the old order compulsions were often painful, but there was a sense in the pain that was inflicted by the will of an all-knowing God. In the new order the compulsions are painful and ... accidental, unnecessary, wanton, and full of mockery. The modern man does not make peace with them.... [W]hen he believes that events are determined by votes of a majority, the orders of his bosses, the opinions of his neighbours, the laws of supply and demand, and the decisions of quite selfish men, he yields because he has to yield. He is conquered but unconvinced. (1929, 10)

The darkness that emanates from this milieu pervades Fitzgerald's universe in *The Great Gatsby*. And he transforms two apparently mundane objects into compelling Gothic tropes, namely the valley of ashes and the hollow eyes of T. J. Eckleburg.

While the valley of ashes embodies the spiritual aridity identified by Lippmann, T. J. Eckleburg represents a concocted or false divinity whose empty eyes and sheer inanity capture the horror of a world devoid of any spiritual or religious centre.

It is indeed ironical that these eyes which 'look out of no face' but 'from a pair of enormous, yellow spectacles' are in reality an old, abandoned billboard advertising the practice of an oculist (Fitzgerald 1925, 64). These eyes which are frequently described as brooding over the ashen dumping ground or keeping vigil over its denizens almost like the eyes of God actually embody a hollow, capitalist culture. Those enormous eyes were meant to aid the business of an oculist. Yet, modern Americans, who, according to Lippmann 'without ceasing to be credulous, [hung], ... between heaven and earth' (1929, 9) tried to invest this inane object with some kind of divine, supernatural power. Wilson was such a man. When he found out about his wife, Myrtle's betrayal, he looked at the 'pale and enormous' eyes of T. J. Eckleburg and muttered, 'I told her she might fool me but she couldn't fool God. I took her to the window ... "and I said God knows what you've been doing, everything you've been doing. You may fool me, but you can't fool God!"' (Fitzgerald 1925,160–61). But T. J. Eckleburg neither provided divine retribution nor divine justice. He simply looked on as Wilson persisted in his mistaken belief that Gatsby was responsible for his wife's fatal accident and ultimately killed Gatsby to avenge Myrtle's death. The final scene of meaningless carnage which left two dead bodies in its wake—that of Gatsby and Wilson—represents the horror of a random, godless universe, where one's destiny is as fickle as a mere game of chance.

The horror is underscored by Carraway's description of Wilson as he approaches Gatsby through the garden. He calls Wilson an 'ashen, fantastic figure gliding toward [Gatsby] through the amorphous trees' (Fitzgerald 1925, 162). It seems as though this 'ashen, fantastic figure' is a dark, vindictive spectre spewed by the spiritual wasteland—the valley of ashes. Living over the garage next to the ashen dumping ground, Wilson had literally been covered in ashes. Earlier in the novel Carraway remarked 'A white ashen dust veiled [Wilson's] dark suit and his pale hair as it veiled everything in the vicinity' (66). Yet, it is Fitzgerald's genius that transforms this mundane phenomenon into a compelling Gothic trope. Fitzgerald's employment and reconfiguration of Gothic tropes enables him to capture the contradictions of the modern world—contradictions embodied in Jay Gatsby's trajectory in the novel.

Gatsby represents the bane and boon of both the modern world and the world conceived by the American Dream. In both these worlds the individual was finally free to craft his own destiny. Yet by the early-twentieth century this freedom became self-defeating since it stemmed from a random universe, unanchored to any absolute value system. The First World War opened new opportunities, especially for Americans like Gatsby who served in the war. Yet, it also left the new generation devoid of traditional values and certainties. In the wake of America's prosperity, the only way of shattering class distinctions and achieving the American Dream was through the acquisition of wealth. Berman explains, 'Gatsby is materialistic because Americans do not have any other alternatives. Material life offers one of the few recognized ways in which the American can *express* his idealism' (2001, 57–58). However, Gatsby's idealism itself becomes hollow—as hollow as his label of being an 'Oxford man'. Gatsby's service in the First World War enabled him to create a façade of respectability by opening up the hallowed portals of Oxford University to him. When the snobbish Tom Buchanan expressed his doubt about Gatsby's label of being an 'Oxford man', Gatsby explained, 'It was an opportunity they gave to some of the officers after the armistice, ... We could go to any of the universities in England or France ... It was in nineteen-nineteen, I only stayed five months. That's why I can't really call myself an Oxford man.' (Fitzgerald 1925, 139). Gatsby's academic distinction is thus innately paradoxical. Though technically Gatsby entered the hallowed upper-class circle of Oxford alumni he did not belong to the traditionally wealthy and elite club of Oxford intellectuals. He apparently managed to climb the social ladder yet for the traditionally privileged individuals like Tom Buchanan, he remained 'Mr Nobody from Nowhere' (140).

Gatsby's social status and air of respectability is thus as contradictory as the Gothic décor of the library in his mansion. During his first visit to Gatsby's house Carraway discovered 'an important looking door, and walked into a high Gothic library, panelled with carved English oak, and probably transported complete from some ruin overseas' (Fitzgerald 1925, 80). It is interesting that Fitzgerald uses the word 'Gothic' in this connection. Jerrold E. Hogle opines that right from its use by Horace Walpole the word 'Gothic' came to stand for a counterfeit or a hollowed-out facade. Walpole famously concocted a false claim that *The Castle of Otranto*, the first Gothic novel in English was a translation of a twelfth-century manuscript by a Renaissance priest. He also refurbished his famous property, Strawberry Hill, to give it the appearance of a Gothic castle. Alluding to both these phenomena Hogle asserts that

> The Gothic is founded on a quasi-antiquarian use of symbols that are quite obviously signs only of older signs; ... Indeed, in using symbols from a highly Catholic past in an ultimately anti-Catholic way, as he did in his Gothicized house at Strawberry Hill ... Walpole made his references to the distant past distinctly hollowed out ones, allusions to what was largely empty as well as distant for him, even though Gothic relics could be effective for establishing a useful myth of Gothic ancestry that often proved to be as effective for class-climbing as it was ultimately counterfeit. Such a use of the emptied past in ghosts of counterfeits has consequently allowed the *neo*-Gothic to be filled with antiquated repositories into which modern quandaries can be projected. (2002, 15–16)

Gatsby's Gothic library is such a neo-Gothic element—the embodiment of an 'emptied past in ghosts of counterfeits'. Gatsby's own identity is similarly hollowed-out and therefore Gothic.

In many ways Gatsby both resembles as well as reconfigures the notion of the Gothic protagonist. William Patrick Day traces several characteristics of Gothic protagonists in characters from modernist works and in Jay Gatsby (Day 1985, 167–69). Placing Gatsby in the same league as classic Gothic protagonists like Dracula and Manfred, Day asserts that Jay Gatsby like his predecessors is a 'self-created being' who lives according to his 'own will and desire'. While I agree with Day's interpretation, I disagree with the sense of power that it implicitly endows Gatsby. Unlike classic Gothic protagonists like Dracula or Manfred or even Kurtz in *Heart of Darkness*, Gatsby's power is hollow. While Dracula or Kurtz or Manfred can create darkness, Gatsby can only create ashes—vapid, fleeting yet lethal. Tellingly, Roger L. Pearson interprets Gatsby as a failed prophet. According to him, 'The valley of ashes is the result of Jay Gatsby's testament, the dust of a corrupted and perverted American dream; and like its biblical counterpart, it has its association with the worshiping of a false god, Mammon, incarnate in his son, Gatsby' (1970, 641). However, Gatsby cannot be viewed as any God or prophet. He is as much a product of fortuitous circumstances as his world. Just as the valley of ashes at times blooms into a 'fantastic farm', 'ridges' 'hills' and 'houses and chimneys and rising smoke' and at other times morphs into 'grotesque gardens' and powdery men and women, Gatsby's world momentarily flowers into splendour and then disintegrates into an ashen heap. The very godless universe which enables Gatsby to seemingly become the master of his own destiny also generates the spectral figure of Wilson who ultimately spells his destruction. Wilson is the spectre that emerges from the depths of a modern, American nightmare, the valley of ashes and swallows up Jay Gatsby—the self-made man of the American Dream.

In his horrific and lonely end as a hollowed-out entity, Gatsby most certainly resembles classic Gothic protagonists. Drawing a parallel between Gothic and modern protagonists, William Patrick Day asserts that '[t]he isolation of the Gothic and modernist protagonist is enforced ... by the breakdown of conventional concepts of causality and the idea of wholeness of personality and character' (1985, 168). He further explains that 'The ... characters of Gothic fantasy reflect the breakdown of conventional notions of what constitutes the self. This same disintegration appears, more realistically, in the modernist fascination with states of consciousness and in characters such as ... Jay Gatsby, who appear to be one thing and are another'. While it is true that Gatsby lacks any coherent self, this absence stems from the paradoxical blessings of random material prosperity during the 1920s. As the First World War and its aftermath enable Jimmy Gatz to reincarnate himself as Jay Gatsby and he flits through numerous avatars.

Much like Gothic protagonists Gatsby's identity is shrouded in mystery sparking both splendid and gloomy speculations about the provenance of the man and his wealth. Some of his guests speculate that he had been a bootlegger. Others spin even more sinister stories by claiming that he was the nephew of 'Paul Von Hindenburg (1847–1934), commander-in-chief of the German army during the last half of the First World War, and German president from 1925 to 1934' and that Gatsby killed a man when his background was revealed (Fitzgerald 1925, 91). Mr Wolfshiem, on the other hand, considers Gatsby to be a gentleman because he had been to Oxford. Mr Wolfshiem says, 'I made the pleasure of his acquaintance just after the war. But I knew I had discovered a man of fine breeding after I talked with him an hour' (100). Gatsby himself fuels this illusion by spinning lies about his privileged background. At one point, he claims that after the death of his family he inherited immense wealth and 'lived like a young rajah in all the capitals of Europe—Paris, Venice, Rome—collecting jewels, chiefly rubies, hunting big game, painting a little, things for myself only ...' (94). Through these stories Gatsby creates the myth of being a man of leisure in an effort to disguise his nouveau riche background. Ironically, this false narrative also becomes partly true because Gatsby behaves much more like a gentleman than the privileged Tom Buchanan. Towards the end of the novel Carraway poignantly exclaims: 'They're a rotten crowd', ... 'You're worth the whole damn bunch put together.' I've always been glad I said that. It was the only compliment I ever gave him, because I disapproved of him from beginning to end' (156). So who is Gatsby? Is he a gentleman, a chivalrous war hero or a shady con man? Ironically, Gatsby is all of them and none of them. Like the ashen figures of the urban wasteland, he momentarily assumes one form, then another before crumbling into a heap of powdery dust.

The straggling group of people that assemble at Gatsby's burial ceremony underscore the desolation of this so-called self-made man. A man who was the cynosure of upper class society makes an ignominious exit surrounded only by Carraway, his father and the man with owl eyes who used to be a guest at Gatsby's parties. Jay Gatsby's dogged attempt to inscribe his identity in and through materiality ironically renders him a phantom at best and a spectre at worst. As the splendour of the American Dream and the myth of the self-made man fades into darkness Fitzgerald reveals that the modern world is haunted by new kinds of ghosts. His masterful use of Gothic tropes exposes the horrors of a spiritually barren and glibly self-destructive Jazz Age.

Works Cited

Berman, Ronald. 2001. *Fitzgerald, Hemingway and the Twenties.* Tuscaloosa: University of Alabama Press.

Cullen, Jim. 2003. *The American Dream: A Short History of an Idea that Shaped a Nation.* Oxford: Oxford University Press.

Currell, Susan. 2009. *American Culture in the 1920s.* Edinburgh: Edinburgh UP.

Day, William Patrick. 1985. *In the Circles of Fear and Desire: A Study of Gothic Fantasy.* Chicago: University of Chicago Press.

Fitzgerald, F. Scott. 1925. *The Great Gatsby,* edited by Michael Nowlin, Ontario: Broadview.

———.1924a. 'F. Scott Fitzgerald to Moran Tudury, ca. 11 April,1924'. In *The Great Gatsby,* edited by Michael Nowlin, 178. Ontario: Broadview, 2007. p. 178.

———.1924b. 'From F. Scot Fitzgerald to Ludlow Fowler, August 1924'. In *The Great Gatsby,* edited by Michael Nowlin, 179. Ontario: Broadview.

Hogle, Jerrold E. 2002. 'Introduction: The Gothic in Western Culture'. In *The Cambridge Companion to Gothic Fiction,* edited by Jerrold E. Hogle, 1–20. Cambridge: Cambridge University Press.

Lee, Derek. 2018. 'Dark Romantic: F Scott Fitzgerald and the Spectres of Gothic Modernism'. *Journal of Modern Literature* 41(4): 125–142.

Lippmann, Walter. 1914. *Drift and Mastery: An Attempt to Diagnose the Current Unrest.* Madison: University of Wisconsin Press.

———.1929. *A Preface to Morals.* New York: Routledge.

Llyod-Smith, Andrew. 2004. *American Gothic Fiction: An Introduction.* New York: Conntinuum.

Murtoff, Jennifer. n.d. 'American Dream'. *Encyclopaedia Britannica*, https://www.britannica.com/topic/American-Dream.

Pearson. Roger L. 1970. 'Gatsby: False Prophet of the American Dream'. *The English Journal* 59(5): 638–45.

Riquelme, John Paul. 2014. 'Modernist Gothic'. In *Cambridge Companion to The Modern Gothic,* edited by Jerrold E. Hogle, 20–36. Cambridge: Cambridge UP.

Tredell, Nicholas. 2007. *Fitzgerald's The Great Gatsby: A Reader's Guide.* New York: Continuum.

7

'We're all white here': *The Great Gatsby* in Conversation with the Harlem Renaissance

Richard A. Courage and Amritjit Singh

This jointly authored essay attempts to read F. Scott Fitzgerald's novel *The Great Gatsby* in the wider context of the American 1920s and 1930s, often referred to as the Second American Renaissance. Those years are also associated in literary history with the Harlem Renaissance (henceforth shortened as HR) that signals an emergence of arts among black Americans—including literary expression in all genres, not just in Harlem, New York, but also in many other urban centres around the US.[1] In the late 1980s, our teaching and scholarship began to wrestle with the need to study major Anglo-American Modernists such as Ernest Hemingway, William Faulkner, T. S. Eliot, Robert Frost, Virginia Woolf and F. Scott Fitzgerald

[1] Major scholarly books on HR include Nathan Huggins, *Harlem Renaissance* (New York: Oxford University Press, 1971); Arna Bontemps, *The Harlem Renaissance Remembered* (New York: Dodd, 1972); Amritjit Singh, *The Novels of the Harlem Renaissance: Twelve Black Writers, 1923-1933* (University Park: Penn State University Press, 1976); Jervis Anderson, *This Was Harlem: A Cultural Portrait, 1900-1950* (New York: Farrar, 1983); Houston A. Baker, *Modernism and the Harlem Renaissance* (Chicago: University of Chicago Press, 1987); David Levering Lewis, *When Harlem was in Vogue* (New York: Penguin, 1997). These books have individually and collectively addressed the total absence of black American writers and writing in well-written accounts of modernism, such as Frederick J. Hoffman's *The Twenties* (1962, 1965) and Hugh Kenner, *The Homemade World* (1976).

in conjunction with their black American contemporaries—HR figures like Jean Toomer, Langston Hughes, Rudolph Fisher, Claude McKay, Wallace Thurman, Nella Larsen and Zora Neale Hurston.[2] Like Arnold Rampersad, we too can now imagine a 'Blues Modernism' of HR writers, flourishing next to the 'High Modernism' of Eliot and others or the 'Regional Modernism' associated with Frost and Faulkner (see note 2).

Unlike most white modernists, Faulkner felt compelled to engage with race. In many of his works—for example, his short story 'That Evening Sun' (1931) and his novel *Light in August* (1932)—Faulkner wrestled with the racial legacy of the South through well-developed black characters, both men and women. Most other white American Modernists felt no such need. In fact, even when they created Jewish characters in their novels—

---

[2] Since the 1990s, besides the section introductions in *Heath Anthology of American Literature*, beginning with its fifth edition, many scholars have read HR in the larger context of Modernism: Arnold Rampersad, 'Langston Hughes and Approaches to the Harlem Renaissance', (49–71), in *The Harlem Renaissance: Revaluations* eds., Amritjit Singh, et al, (New York: Garland, 1989); Craig H. Werner and Sandra G. Shannon 'Foundations of African American Modernism, 1910–1950,' in *The Cambridge History of African American Literature*, eds., Maryemma Graham and Jerry Ward, Jr., (Cambridge: Cambridge University Press, 2011), 241–67, 242; James Smethurst, *The African American Roots of Modernism* (Chapel Hill: University of North Carolina Press, 2011); Michael North, *The Dialect of Modernism: Race, Language, and Twentieth-Century Literature* (New York: Oxford University Press, 1994). In his detailed and polemical book, *The Harlem Renaissance in Black and White* (Cambridge: Harvard University Press, 1995), George Hutchinson makes a brave but unpersuasive argument that there had been extensive and harmonious interaction between black writers and white intellectuals. Hutchinson asserts that black critics such as Nathan Huggins, David Levering Lewis and Houston Baker, and black writers such as Langston Hughes (in his autobiography, *The Big Sea*, 1940) were wrong in focusing excessively on the separateness of the HR writers. At the same time, while Hutchinson acknowledges 'race' as a 'powerful social determinant' during the period, his narrative fails to capture the significance of how 'race' engrossed the creative energies of almost all HR writers in all genres in various ways.

such as Robert Cohn in Hemingway's *The Sun Also Rises* (1926) or Simon Rosedale in Edith Wharton's much earlier novel, *The House of Mirth* (1905)—it was not always clear if they were representing antisemitic tendencies in US society or displaying their own conscious or subconscious ethnic prejudices. Major Anglo-American modernist writers, each in their own way, appear caught between a full surrender to the period's norms of whiteness and the impulse to resist them or evade them or engage tangentially with them.

Along with several black American mentors such as Alain Locke, Charles S. Johnson, James Weldon Johnson, and Jessie Fauset, a few white American writers such as H. L. Mencken, Sinclair Lewis and Carl Van Vechten also engaged in collegial conversations with young black writers and sometimes helped them to get published (Singh 1976, chapter 1). But in retrospect, it appears that many more exchanges could have taken place among these artists of diverse backgrounds. It is difficult to estimate how those might-have-been conversations would have transformed the contemporaneous writers of diverse backgrounds or influenced literature or society as a whole. Our essay, focused on reading one novel (*The Great Gatsby*) in relation to HR, may be viewed as an attempt to generate a space, maybe a virtual salon, where black and white writers from the 1920s may work together to enrich and expand conversations that barely took place earlier because of prevalent racial attitudes and barriers. We also hope that this attempt of ours to read *The Great Gatsby* in terms of race and class would make it easier for students of diverse ethnic and racial backgrounds to engage fully with this American classic.[3]

Ways of White Folks

This section's title is borrowed from Langston Hughes's 1934 short story collection to evoke the specific discourses of whiteness

---

[3] In his article, 'A New Way to read *Gatsby*', (*Atlantic*, 1 February 2023), Lorenzo Vereen discusses the challenge of teaching the novel in an impoverished rural community in South Florida to students whose parents were new immigrants from Haiti, Cuba, Mexico and Guatemala.

that dominated US society in the early decades of the twentieth century. In his nuanced short stories of this collection such as 'The Blues I am Playing', Hughes explores the interdependent nature of how black and white Americans experienced their identity. As Amritjit Singh has argued elsewhere, this 'black-white symbiosis' (a term originally used by Nathan Huggins) is not always equally beneficial for both parties. As Singh notes: 'Time and again in American history, the one-sided and unequal relationship between blacks and whites has obliged blacks to serve as eternal footmen holding the identity coats for whites' (1987, 32).

Whiteness has been a powerful presence in US history at all times, changing its attributes every few decades in response to the surrounding conditions.[4] Its negative impact on citizens of African American, Native American, Latino/a, and Jewish ancestry has levelled off considerably through several campaigns for civil rights since the Civil War (1861–65). Immediately after the Civil War, the relatively short-lived Reconstruction (1865–76) surrendered to the notorious Compromise of 1877. The Jim Crow realities of the late-nineteenth century led ultimately to the 1896 *Plessey v. Ferguson* Supreme Court decision that made racial segregation the law of the land—which was successfully challenged in favor of racial integration in high schools in *Brown vs. Board of Education* (1954). The Civil Rights Act (1964) and Voting Rights Act (1965) together opened the doors for African Americans to participate fully in the civic and political life of the US. President Lyndon Johnson who enabled these two transformative acts in response to the Civil Rights Movement led by Rosa Parks and Martin Luther King Jr., also

[4] On the role of whiteness in US history and culture, see Matthew Frye Jacobson, *Whiteness of a Different Color: European Immigrants and Alchemy of Race* (Cambridge: Harvard University Press, 1999); Ian F. Haney-Lopez, *White by Law: The Legal Construction of Race* (New York: New York University Press, 1996); David Roediger, *Wages of Whiteness* (London: Verso, 1991); Michael Omi and Howard Winant, *Racial Formation in the United States* (New York: Routledge, 1986; Rev. ed. 2014).

opened up immigration from all parts of the world through the Immigration Reform Act of 1965.[5]

In the early decades of the twentieth century, in the age of Modernism, anti-black and anti-immigrant sentiments were quite prevalent. Well-known figures such as Henry James, T. S. Eliot, Edith Wharton, and F. Scott Fitzgerald reflected such attitudes in their fiction and non-fiction, even more so in their private correspondence. At the same time, in responding to new developments such as eugenics, Freudian psychology and socialist ideologies, these writers also displayed fascinating tensions and contradictions. One can experience these tensions early on in *The American Scene*, Henry James's travel book based on his US visit in 1904–05. James indicated that black people were not capable of 'alertness' and 'attention', but he also praised W. E. B. Du Bois's *Souls of Black Folk* (1903) as 'most accomplished, ... the only Southern book of any distinction for many a year'. James was also unnerved by the 'horde' of immigrants, their 'strange ways' and their 'babble of tongues', and saw them as a threat to 'American-ness'. Along the Bowery, the most impoverished section of Lower Manhattan, the Jews offended him much more than the Italians. But he acknowledged that for the children of these shabby immigrants, the assimilative forces of the US will work well: 'the younger generation ... will fully profit, rise to the occasion, and enter into the privilege' of full citizenship. In contrast, Ezra Pound—whom T. S. Eliot honoured as 'il miglior fabbro' (the superior craftsman) in the dedication to *The Waste Land*—went off the deep end during World War II by joining the fascists in Italy. After the War ended in 1945, Pound was indicted in 1946 in a Washington DC court on charges of sedition for his anti-US and antisemitic broadcasts from 1941 to 1945 on a short-wave radio broadcast directed at American audiences. Considered unfit for trial based on a psychiatric report, he was released in

[5] On African American history, see John Hope Franklin, *From Slavery to Freedom* (1947; Rev. ed., New York: McGraw Hill, 2021); Mary Frances Berry and John W. Blassingame, *Long Memory: The Black Experience in America* (New York: Oxford University Press, 1982).

1958 and sailed immediately to Italy and died in Venice in 1972. In his 1934 book *After Strange Gods*—based on his 1933 lectures at the University of Virginia—T. S. Eliot expressed racist and antisemitic views that so shocked his friends and readers that he was forced to withdraw and suppress the book. He described the Civil War as a disaster and emphasised the need for 'a homogeneous population' shaped by a 'unity of religious faith', adding, 'reasons of race and religion combine to make any large number of free-thinking Jews undesirable'(20).[6]

In Edith Wharton's fictional writings and correspondence, we can experience the tension we mentioned earlier— the tendency of many modernist writers to identify with the prevailing structures of whiteness, but as imaginative artists also to deconstruct those structures through plot and character. Apparently, as documented by Alfred Bendixen, in editing *Letters of Edith Wharton* (1988), R. W. B. Lewis and Nancy Lewis felt compelled to leave out some letters because Wharton had used 'some racist or antisemitic remarks,' and in one letter, she had made 'some vilely antisemitic comment' (Bendixen 1989, 1,5).[7] But as Dale Bauer has argued persuasively in *Edith Wharton's Brave New Politics*, Wharton the novelist 'became increasingly keen on instructing her audience to remain malleable, since she seemed to imagine the culture rigidifying into dangerous postures' (5). In our reading of *The Great Gatsby*, we suggest that Fitzgerald displays a similar skill as a novelist in exploring the intertwined issues of race and class.

---

[6] See Roz Kaveney, 'T. S. Eliot and the Politics of Culture,' *The Guardian* (28 April 2014); Frances Dickey, 'T. S. Eliot and the Color Line of St Louis', M*m* (*Modernism/Modernity*), 5(4; May 9, 2021); Richard Lehan, *The City in Literature: An Intellectual and Cultural History* (Berkeley: University of California Press, 1998), chapter 13.

[7] According to Lehan (1998, 221), after his bad experiences with the police in Rome, Italy, Fitzgerald complained to Edmund Wilson about such bad blood 'creep[ing] northward to defile the Nordic race'. For Fitzgerald, if northern Europe were to avoid similar degeneration, it must 'raise the bars of immigration and permit only Scandinavians, Teutons, Anglo-Saxons and Celts to enter.'

The Great Gatsby in Black and White

Our analysis of *The Great Gatsby* suggests that, in limning features of American life in his best-known novel, Fitzgerald frequently employed 'race' and 'class' as interchangeable tropes. Understandably class has received much greater attention than race in the teaching and scholarly explorations of this novel. There are several reasons for this, beginning with Fitzgerald's long-standing reputation as an astute commentator on the mores and vagaries of social class, especially the upper classes. For example, his 1925 short story 'The Rich Boy' (from the collection, *All the Sad Young Men*, 1926) includes the oft-quoted observation that: 'the very rich.... are different from you and me, ... They think, deep in their hearts, that they are better than we are because we had to discover the compensations and refuges of life for ourselves.'

More specifically, we note that a structural framing based on social class is evident throughout the text of *The Great Gatsby*. At the centre of the story recounted by narrator Nick Carraway is the love triangle of Jay Gatsby, Daisy Buchanan and Tom Buchanan, which plays out primarily in three locations just outside New York City. These locations are arrayed in a three-tiered hierarchy. On Long Island are the town of East Egg—associated with 'old money' families such as the Buchanans—and the town of West Egg, where Jay Gatsby resides in all the glitter and glamor of the newly—and sometimes mysteriously—wealthy. The third location—a desolate urban patch called 'Valley of Ashes'—lies between West Egg and Manhattan and is inhabited by poor and working-class people like Tom's mistress, Myrtle Wilson, and her husband George. So readily apparent are signifiers of class—from the stabled polo ponies of the old rich to the joyrides and gin-soaked soirees of the nouveau riche to the sad pretensions and thwarted dreams of the working poor—that it is easy to overlook the brief but deeply resonant moments that advance plot and characterisation even as they offer significant insights into race relations in the 1920s.

We highlight and examine several such passages because they are suggestive of Fitzgerald's dexterity in handling intertwined aspects of race and class. We also suspect that these passages would likely have drawn closer attention from HR writers if the conversations imagined in our essay's title had actually taken place.

We envision a scene where Fitzgerald along with a handful of other young white writers are joined by some of their black counterparts from uptown Harlem. Among potential organisers of the Harlem contingent, Alain Locke and Charles S. Johnson seem most likely. Fitzgerald might have been joined by Carl Van Vechten, who supported young black writers but also wrote a bestselling novel, *Nigger Heaven* (1926), that had negatively affected the creative and publication potential of HR writers (Singh 1976, chapter 1). We believe the virtual meeting had to go forward without Van Vechten, who was probably too busy with hosting interracial parties to join.

Alain Locke, a philosophy professor at Howard University in DC, had done his PhD at Harvard. An extensively published art and literary critic, he was a mentor to several young male HR writers. A sociologist and educator, Charles S. Johnson was the founding editor of *Opportunity*, a civil rights journal published by the Urban League that became, along with *The Crisis* and *Messenger*, a leading vehicle for identifying and promoting emerging black writers. Much of the HR's institutional infrastructure and public relations apparatus was the result of Locke and Johnson's extensive collaboration on *Opportunity* in the 1920s (Bone and Courage, 2011).[8]

---

[8] Robert Bone and Richard Courage, *The Muse in Bronzeville: African American Creative Expression in Chicago, 1932–1950* is a study of what is now widely known as the Black Chicago Renaissance (in the 1930s and 1940s), which like HR, was centred on black pride and black consciousness in art and literature. Black Chicago Renaissance, too, was concerned with issues of cross-cultural representations of class and race. For one black novelist's representations of Italian American life, see Fred Gardaphe, 'Dancing with Italians: Chicago's Italians in Fact and in the Fiction of Willard Motley', (47–62) in *Crossing Borders: Essays on Literature, Culture, and Society in Honor of Amritjit Singh,* eds. Tapan Basu and Tasneem Shahnaaz (Hyderabad: Orient Blackswan, 2017).

With *The Great Gatsby* as their focus, a scene in the novel's opening chapter would most certainly have prompted an impassioned discussion. There, narrator Nick Carraway describes a conversation with his cousin Daisy Buchanan, with whom he is becoming reacquainted, and her husband Tom, whom he is meeting for the first time. Nick reports that a chance remark he made to Daisy—'"You make me feel uncivilized",.... was taken up in an unexpected way.' In response, Tom explodes: 'Civilization's going to pieces. I've gotten to be a terrible pessimist about things. Have you read *The Rise of the Colored Empires* by this man Goddard ...? It's a fine book, and everybody ought to read it. The idea is if we don't look out the white race will be—will be utterly submerged. It's all scientific stuff; it's been proved' (Fitzgerald 1925, 12–13).[9]

Everyone present in our virtual salon (and most of Fitzgerald's actual readers) would have recognised Tom's references to *The Rising Tide of Color Against White World-Supremacy* by Lothrop Stoddard, published in 1920 by Scribner's, Fitzgerald's own publisher. Stoddard's book had a lurid black and red cover featuring stereotypical representations of Asians and Africans, who brandish spears, swords and muskets as they scale the ramparts of colonial rule and white supremacy. To defend those ramparts, Stoddard advocated racial segregation, 'Nordic' solidarity, anti-miscegenation laws, eugenic sterilisation and strict limits on immigration by people of colour. However much the Harlem writers might have bristled at Tom's naked assertion of white racial superiority, they would also have recognised that Fitzgerald was accurately portraying the beliefs and fears of millions of white Americans.

The commercial success of Stoddard's book rested on twin pillars. First, the author's PhD from Harvard lent a

[9] Here is a point African American writer Jesmyn Ward makes at the end of her five-page introduction to the 2018 reprint of Scribner's 1925 edition of *The Great Gatsby*: 'This is a book that endures, generation after generation, because [readers continue to] discover new revelations, new insights, new burning bits of language' (Fitzgerald 2018, ix).

veneer of intellectual respectability to his claims about racial differentiation and hierarchy, especially as such claims were echoed and reinforced by professional societies and academic departments across the US. Few writers of any race were as familiar as Charles S. Johnson with the tenets and methods of this ubiquitous racial pseudoscience, and he devoted many pages of *Opportunity* to the fight against its poisonous influence.

The HR writers would be acutely aware that the other pillar of Stoddard's success was his membership in the Ku Klux Klan, then at the very height of its power and influence. The KKK eagerly promoted sales of his book, secure in the knowledge that if 'all [that] scientific stuff' failed to persuade, there were always the lash, the lynching tree, the machine gun, and other instruments of white-supremacist terror. In fact, some HR writers, along with their mentors and promotors, consciously pursued publication and other professional opportunities in the belief that their individual successes might contribute to racial advancement while avoiding the dangers of direct confrontation.[10] James Weldon Johnson, another mentor to young HR writers, had articulated this strategy in his introduction to the 1922 *Book of American Negro Poetry:* 'Nothing will do more to ... raise his status than a demonstration of intellectual parity by the Negro through the production of literature and art.'[11]

Tom Buchanan is a self-deluded and brutish character whose inherited millions only increase his appetite for bootlegged whiskey, violence and philandering. His visceral enthusiasm for Goddard/Stoddard's 'fine book' does not give voice to Fitzgerald's own views but adds an element of complexity to the novel's developing portrait of a society in the midst of crisis and change. The tensions and contradictions of this crisis are

---

[10] In February 1926, DuBois organised a symposium in the pages of *The Crisis* on how to portray black life in art (Singh 1976, chapter 1).

[11] As NAACP's Executive Secretary in the 1920s, James Weldon Johnson had also launched an unsuccessful campaign for the US Congress to pass an anti-lynching legislation. Nearly a century later, in 2022, the Emmett Till Anti-Lynching Act was approved by the Congress and signed into law by President Joe Biden.

embodied in the novel's taut plot and its characters—both major (Tom, Daisy and Jay) and minor (the Wilsons, Nick and his love interest, professional golfer Jordan Baker). While they are relatively fleshed-out, other characters and character types seem to hover suggestively but insubstantially in the book's margins. Some, like the Jewish gambler and fixer Meyer Wolfsheim, are identified by name and/or function and sketched in hazy detail.[12] Some are only glanced, perhaps only imagined, or their presence vaguely sensed as the novel's social commentary becomes more nuanced. As already noted, the significance of such spectral presences is glimpsed during Tom's first meeting with Nick as he 'violently' obsesses over the perceived threat of racial submersion. It becomes even more evident in a protracted scene in chapter seven that begins with a well-lubricated luncheon at the Buchanans' luxurious mansion.

Daisy and Jay have rekindled their old love affair, and Daisy boldly flaunts her affection and physical desire for Jay. The day is swelteringly hot, and Daisy, Tom, Jay, Nick and Jordan decide to drive two cars into Manhattan in search of some diversion. As they enter the vehicles, Daisy suddenly

---

[12] Incidentally, Meyer Wolfsheim was played by Mumbai-based actor Amitabh Bachchan in the 2013 film based on *The Great Gatsby*, directed by Baz Luhrmann, with Leonardo DiCaprio as Gatsby, Toby McGuire as Nick Carraway, Carey Mulligan as Daisy Buchanan. In an email (dated 20 August 2025) to Amritjit Singh, Kurt Hemmer of Harper College, Palatine, Illinois, notes: 'When I teach *The Great Gatsby*, I choose to emphasize Gatsby's relationship with Meyer Wolfsheim, who was based on Arnold Rothstein, mentor to gangsters such as Lucky Luciano, Meyer Lansky, and Bugsy Siegel. The 1949 film adaptation of *The Great Gatsby* starring Alan Ladd portrays Gatsby as this type of murderous gangster. Nick Carraway reports rumors that Gatsby might have killed a man. Wolfsheim feels close to Gatsby and claims that he made him. Is it possible that James Gatz was Jewish, which would help explain why Wolfsheim took him under his wing? Certainly, Gatz is trying to "pass" as someone he is not by becoming Gatsby. Michael Shnayerson, in *Bugsy Siegel: The Dark Side of the American Dream* (2021), argues that Wolfsheim "could just as easily have been Ben Siegel" (18). I would say Gatsby could have just as easily been Bugsy.'

breaks free of her husband's directive grasp on her elbow and leaps into the second car to ride alone with Jay. 'Did you see that?' sputters an astonished Tom to Nick and Jordan (Fitzgerald 1925, 121). Minutes later, he stops at a gas station operated by Myrtle's husband, George Wilson, and learns that the couple are planning to move away. With a hint of schadenfreude, Nick muses on Tom's quandary: 'His wife and his mistress, until an hour ago secure and inviolate, were slipping precipitously from his control' (Fitzgerald 1925, 124). As the five characters reconvene in a suite at the Plaza Hotel, Tom's anger boils over. 'What kind of a row are you trying to cause in my house, anyhow?' he demands of Gatsby, continuing 'I suppose the latest thing is to sit back and let Mr Nobody from Nowhere make love to your wife. ... Nowadays, people begin by sneering at family life and family institutions and next they'll throw everything overboard and have an intermarriage between black and white' (Fitzgerald 1925, 129–30).

Nick's response recalls Tom's earlier outburst about the Goddard/Stoddard screed, 'Flushed with his impassioned gibberish, [Tom] saw himself standing alone on the last barrier of civilization' (Fitzgerald 1925, 130). Here, a furtive presence momentarily steps forward from the fevered mix of racial anxiety, wounded manhood and sheer confusion that roils Tom's sense of himself and his place in the world. The shadow figure of the rapacious black man lusting after white women is conflated with his flesh and blood rival, Jay Gatsby, a rich white man but one of unknown origins and an associate of gamblers, bootleggers and Jews. The interchangeability of class signifiers ('Mr Nobody from Nowhere') and racial signifiers ('intermarriage between black and white') could not be more evident.

Another voice—bored, enervated, detached—rises from the heat in that hotel suite: '"We're all white here", murmured Jordan' (Fitzgerald 2018, 130). Her observation seems intended to aid Daisy in deflecting Tom's ugly attack on Jay. Beyond that, Tom's outburst and Jordan's reaction highlight salient differences in regional and social backgrounds and further demonstrate the role of the racial shadow figure in advancing Fitzgerald's narrative. Tom is from Chicago whereas Jordan and Daisy 'passed' their 'white girlhood' in Louisville, Kentucky (Hopkins 2018; Singh 1976, chapter 1).[13] Tom would have witnessed the profound social and economic changes that overtook Chicago following massive immigration of white labourers from Europe and of black people from the American South. If he were in Chicago in July 1919, Tom might have seen streets running with blood as whites attacked black neighbourhoods, often encountering determined self-defence.[14] Charles S. Johnson was there, barely survived an encounter with a white mob, and subsequently played a leading role in producing a book-length report for the Governor of Illinois on violence—its origins and possible ways to avert future eruptions. Jordan and Daisy, on the other hand, grew up in an 'artificial world [that] was redolent of orchids and pleasant, cheerful snobbery and orchestras which set the rhythm of the year, summing up the sadness and suggestiveness of life in new tunes. All night the saxophones wailed … the Beale Street Blues while a hundred pairs of golden and silver slippers shuffled the shining dust' (Fitzgerald 2018, 151).

The reference to 'Beale Street Blues' evokes not only the towering figure of W. C. Handy, but also a popular song that was part of the minstrelsy tradition, 'Oh, dem golden slippers', which was written in 1879 by a black composer, James A. Bland, as a parody of a spiritual sung by the Fisk Jubilee Singers called 'Golden Slippers'. Harlem writers such as Langston Hughes and James Weldon Johnson were aficionados of jazz and blues, making this passage a potential source of pride during these cross-racial conversations. Yet, in acknowledging the music but not the black musicians who created it, the passage also

---

[13] There is a real possibility that Jordan is a 'high yellow' black woman passing as white and that Daisy and Jordan share that secret. Passing (light-skinned black men and women choosing to lead their lives as whites) has been a well-known phenomenon in US life throughout nineteenth and twentieth centuries and was a common motif in several HR novels by Nella Larsen, Jessie Fauset and others.

[14] Claude McKay wrote a powerful poem ('If We Must Die') in response to the violence directed in twenty-six US cities at black soldiers returning from World War I.

evokes a long history of cultural appropriation and imposed anonymity—a theme explored in Ryan Coogler's 2025 movie, *Sinners*. Significantly, the black presence in *Gatsby* is not figured as a violation as perceived by Tom but rather as an entertaining, benign figure with a fixed place in the 'artificial world' of Louisville's young sophisticates whose fantasies offer a stark contrast to the realities of Charles S. Johnson in Chicago. In both 'Diamond as Big as the Ritz' and *Gatsby*, Fitzgerald demonstrates his skill to offer preceptive readings of race and class. Jordan's apparently unperturbed response to Tom is not just about demographics but reflects her upbringing in a rigidly controlled and predictable social and racial order in the South, one that renders legions of black servants, nannies, labourers, and even entertainers invisible. This passage illustrates, once again, the fluid intertwining of race and class in the novel.

Coda

White American fiction writers who identified with Modernism during the 1920s essentially reinvented their art form. They overturned long-established conventions for plot structure, character development, dialogue, narration and other core elements of the craft, and they created an ever-expanding set of innovations to take their place. Their bold experiments with literary language and form, however, did not necessarily extend to representations of the social text. With the crushing weight of legally enforced 'Jim Crow' segregation, racist pseudoscience was deeply entrenched in the education system, and the Ku Klux Klan remained a powerful and violent presence in all parts of the country. At the same time, depictions of American society in the novels of white Modernists sometimes presented a text of unrelieved whiteness or one dappled by the presence of people of colour whose humanity was not fully recognised. Other novelists wrestled with problems of racial (and social class) representation with varying degrees of success—with an evident commitment to using Modernist innovations to render perceptibly truthful narratives. Our close and contextualised examination of selected passages from *The Great Gatsby* suggests that Fitzgerald's work belongs in this latter category.

To arrive at this conclusion required roiling the surface text of this apparently very white novel, as judged by any listing of characters, settings and major events. When such scenes are closely interrogated, when figures from the margin are forced toward the centre and figures in the shadow are forced toward the light, a subliminal conversation within the psyche of white America begins to surface. The subject of this conversation is the role and status of people of colour, most especially black people, in American society—past, present and future. In today's schools and universities, many teachers and scholars trained in race, gender and ethnic studies, are prepared to conduct such interrogations, for example, to read beneath and against the surface text.

In 1925, when *The Great Gatsby* was first published, this was not the case, but there was one group of potential readers whom we might reasonably assume were up to the task—writers and intellectuals associated with HR. Our imagined gathering of some of these individuals under the leadership of Charles S. Johnson and Alain Locke was informed by their actual gatherings in the offices of *Opportunity*, at its annual awards dinners, and as authors published on the pages of this and other journals and in novels and fiction and poetry collections of their own.

In the same year that *Gatsby* appeared, Locke's anthology *The New Negro: An Interpretation* was published. The black poets, fiction writers and social scientists who filled its pages were quite accustomed to probing the margins and shadows of American society because those were most often the constricted spaces where black life was lived.[15]

We conclude our textual exploration of *The Great Gatsby* by turning to a passage in chapter four that would likely have provoked much animated discussion and perhaps broader speculation about Fitzgerald's artistic and social vision in the context of American literary culture of the 1920s. As it begins, Jay is driving Nick to have lunch together in Midtown Manhattan. En route, Gatsby regales his guest with a lengthy

[15] *The New Negro* was originally published as the March 1925 special issue of the magazine Survey Graphic. The special issue sold forty-two thousand copies in two printings (Singh 1976, 15–21).

and transparently bogus account of his life prior to arriving in West Egg. As their car speeds past the Valley of Ashes onto the climbing lane of the bridge to Manhattan, a thrilling panorama opens and Nick thinks, 'The city seen from the Queensboro Bridge is always the city seen for the first time, in its first wild promise of all the mystery and the beauty in the world.' In a single, beautifully wrought sentence, Fitzgerald compresses the hopes and dreams of all the city's newcomers. We picture Professor Alain Locke heaping praise on Fitzgerald's masterful prose style, then leaning forward with quiet confidence and quoting several of his own pertinent observations from *The New Negro*. He would tell Fitzgerald that New York City was not only a beacon to restless white Midwesterners like Nick and Jay, but that Harlem in Uptown Manhattan had emerged as 'the capital of the Negro world'. He would assert that black migration from farm to factory and from rural South to urban North was not 'a blind flood' but the conscious embrace of 'a new vision of opportunity' (Singh 1976, chapter 1).

We like to imagine that Fitzgerald would have been receptive to the insights of an esteemed African American intellectual, especially as they would serve as a valuable context for the group's examination of the ensuing scene. 'As we crossed Blackwell's Island', Nick continues, 'a limousine passed us, driven by a white chauffeur, in which sat three modish [N] egroes, two bucks and a girl. I laughed aloud as the yolks of their eyeballs rolled toward us in haughty rivalry.' Yes, Nick laughs at that vision, perhaps silently mocking Tom's anxious posturing over white supremacy. Depending on who was participating in this conversation, the racially stereotypical language might have instantly derailed the meeting. A poet like Claude McKay would likely have denounced any white person daring to compare black men to animals ('bucks'), or employing descriptions of their eyes derived directly from the traditions of minstrelsy. Langston Hughes, so skilled in deflecting the uglier ways of white folks with humour, might have created a teaching moment and kept the discussion going.

Nick draws this conclusion from what he and Gatsby briefly glimpsed on that bridge: '"Anything can happen now that we've slid over this bridge" I thought; "anything at all". Even Gatsby could happen, without any particular wonder' (Fitzgerald 1925, 69). The passage resonates with a sense of optimism about the future of American democracy. If a 'rising tide of color' is the stuff of nightmare for Tom and if it is essentially unthinkable to Daisy and Jordan, the sight of 'three modish [N]egroes' in a luxurious vehicle 'driven by a white chauffeur' captures Nick's curious imagination, presenting a vision of new possibilities that would place class and colour lines in flux.

The authors would like to thank Kurt Hemmer, Claudia Jacques, Nita N. Kumar, Peter Schmidt, and Barbara A. Silliman for their valuable feedback on earlier versions of this essay.

Works Cited

Bendixen, Alfred. 1989. 'The Lewises Discuss the Letters'. *Edith Wharton Newsletter* 6(1; Spring 1989): 1, 5.

Bone, Robert and Richard Courage. 2011. *The Muse in Bronzeville: African American Creative Expression in Chicago, 1932–1950.* 33–58. New Brunswick: Rutgers University Press.

Eliot, T. S. 1934. *After Strange Gods: A Primer of Modern Heresy.* London: Faber and Faber.

Fitzgerald, F. Scott. 1925. *The Great Gatsby.* New York: Scribner. 2018.

Hopkins, Lucie. 2018. 'Passing for White in *The Great Gatsby*: A Spectroscopic Analysis of Jordan Baker'. *Explicator* 78(3): 150–154.

Richard Lehan. 1998. *The City in Literature: An Intellectual and Cultural History.* Chapter 13. Berkeley: University of California Press.

Shnayerson, Michael. 2021. *Bugsy Siegel: The Dark Side of the American Dream.* Yale University Press.

Singh, Amritjit. 1987. 'Black-White Symbiosis: Another Look at the Literary History of the 1920s'. In *Harlem Renaissance Re-examined*, edited by Victor Kramer, 32. New York: AMS Press.

Singh, Amritjit. 1976. *The Novels of the Harlem Renaissance: Twelve Black Writers, 1923–1933.* University Park: Penn State University Press.

8

Class Struggle and False Consciousness in Scott Fitzgerald's *The Great Gatsby* and Arvind Adiga's *The White Tiger*

H. Kalpana Rao

The Great Gatsby has solidified its place as a classic through its comprehensive exploration of American values during the turbulent 1920s and 30s. T. S. Eliot famously called it a social novel, highlighting its critical examination of the American Dream and the inevitable disillusionment with it. The narrative exposes how this dream, often romanticised, leads to failure for many—acting as a reflection of society's complexities. Despite facing criticism, the novel remains a quintessential representation of American culture, offering insights into enduring issues like identity, belonging and the relentless pursuit of social status. In this way, it draws parallels to Dickens's *Great Expectations* where similar themes of social aspiration and class struggle emerge. One might argue that Fitzgerald's work embodies nineteenth-century ideals, but it also captures the distinct spirit of a decade marked by rapid change and social upheaval. Reading Aravind Adiga's *The White Tiger* suggests how contemporary narratives continue to address issues rooted in the same values as explored in *The Great Gatsby*. Both novels, despite their different settings, echo themes of ambition and the search for identity.

In the American context, the underlying framework is the American Dream; while in the Indian context, it is neoliberalism and globalisation. The 'American Dream' is often envisioned as a path to material wealth and upward social mobility. However, the term is ambiguous, evolving over time and varying according to historical periods and the individuals who define them. The Oxford English Dictionary defines the American Dream as 'the ideal that every citizen of the United States should have an equal opportunity to achieve success and prosperity through hard work, determination, and initiative.' The Merriam-Webster mentions that it is 'a happy way of living that is thought of by many Americans as something that can be achieved by anyone in the US especially by working hard and becoming successful.' Many scholars trace the origins of the American Dream to the Puritans, yet as the Encyclopedia Britannica notes, 'the phrase itself was coined by American businessman and historian James Truslow Adams in his 1931 book *The Epic of America*'. Adams argues that the Dream is not about material wealth but about a vision of society where each person can reach their fullest potential and be recognised for who they truly are, regardless of race, class or birth. The concept has evolved through various interpretations—religious freedom, political liberty, a comfortable life, equality and dignity. However, the most widely accepted understanding centres on the pursuit of material wealth as the key to success, recognition and identity. Fitzgerald's *The Great Gatsby* critiques the attempt to attain this dream and the tragic consequences that often follow.

Around 1991, India began shifting its economic policy towards liberalisation. This shift favoured finance capital and large businesses, branded selling, liberalising investments and promoting financial growth. As Raju Das notes in his article, by quoting Bhagwati on growth and reform, India's new economic policy represented 'a reversal of the anti-globalization, anti-market, pro-public-enterprise attitudes and policies that produced our dismal growth performance' prior to 1991 (2015, 715–716). Das further elaborates that, as Bhagwati argues, growth generates employment because increased investment provides the government with funds, which can be used to improve the nation's healthcare, infrastructure and other sectors to in turn benefit the poor.

The National Economic Policy (NEP) introduced in 1991 marked a shift towards a capitalist model. As Das observes, it met 'the demands of hegemonic fractions of the domestic and foreign-diasporic capitalist class at a particular stage in the development of Indian and global capitalism' (716).

Under this policy, investments from global organisations facilitated the exploitation of India's natural resources. It served to attract global capital while also gaining access to foreign technology and markets. As Das explains, 'The NEP model pursues the goal of transforming India into a world power by making it an office, a laboratory (for pharmaceutical and biotech companies, for example), and a factory for international capital, based on (relatively) cheap labour, both skilled and unskilled' (716). Many critics and scholars, however, argued that the policy only widened inequality, enriching the wealthy while leaving the poor behind. Neoliberalism has led to significant economic inequality, unemployment and labour exploitation, while slackening many regulations in the name of free trade and growth. In his effort to highlight this gap and raise awareness about the challenges faced by rural and semi-urban Indians in their journey toward social mobility, Adiga utilises the voice of Balram Halwai in *The White Tiger*.

In this essay, I intend to explore several pivotal questions concerning both *The Great Gatsby* and *The White Tiger*: how is class constructed in each narrative? How do the protagonists strive to forge a sense of self amidst societal pressures? In what ways do they attempt to curate their images within their respective societies? How does false consciousness play a role in shaping individual identity? Are the characters able to anticipate social mobility, and can instant material wealth facilitate social acceptance? The chapter, after dealing with the plot narratives, will attempt to analyse both novels through the lens of class dynamics.

The Great Gatsby is set against the backdrop of 1920s America, a period later recognised as the Roaring Twenties or the Jazz Age. This era witnessed a significant migration of Americans from rural areas to burgeoning urban centres, driven by the promise of economic prosperity and a vibrant cultural landscape (Martinez 2024). The booming economy during this time fostered a sense of optimism and possibility, yet it also laid bare the stark divisions within society. In a similar strain the emergence of a liberal economic policy in India, instead of bettering the lives of the poor, only created a bigger divide.

Based on this background, we can gain an insight into how both Fitzgerald and Adiga articulate the complexities of class and identity, thereby reflecting broader societal truths that remain relevant today.

In the United States the economy boomed with a forty percent GDP growth, binding Americans nationwide through advertisements and sales. However Prohibition, though declared, was poorly implemented leading to illegal sales and sudden wealth for many. This surge in consumerism and commercialism set the stage for the Great Depression of the 1930s. Fitzgerald's novel, *The Great Gatsby*, is set during this period. The story is narrated by Nick Carraway, who moves from an affluent Midwestern family to New York to learn about the 'bond business'. Through Nick's perspective, we explore the lives of Gatsby, his neighbour in West Egg, and Nick's cousin, Daisy, and her husband, Tom Buchanan, who live in the wealthy neighbourhood of East Egg. The setting at the beginning of the novel sets the tone of class distinctions and enumerates the distinction between the haves and the have-nots. Nick, moreover, tends to describe Tom as a physically fit person by describing him as a tough, strong male and as an extremely rich man too: 'one of the most powerful ends that ever-played football at New Haven—a national figure in a way…' (5). Nick furthers this revelation by mentioning that Tom had a hard mouth and a supercilious manner; his eyes displayed arrogance and his appearance was aggressive. He sums up this image as a 'body capable of enormous leverage—a cruel body.' (6)

The narrative of *The Great Gatsby* vividly illustrates the stark contrasts of wealth and morality, particularly through the lives of Jay Gatsby, the Buchanans and the society that surrounds them. As the story unfolds, it becomes increasingly clear that the glitz and glamour of the 1920s mask a deeper sense of emptiness and disillusionment. In the aftermath of Gatsby's tragic death, Nick Carraway reflects on the profound loneliness that defined Gatsby's existence. He recognises the sorrow and isolation that surrounded Gatsby despite his immense wealth and lavish lifestyle. The parties that Gatsby threw which attracted the elites and socialites feel hollow and insincere to Nick, making him understand that all this revelry was only a mask for the underlying emptiness. He also understands that Gatsby was an invention of his own imagination: 'So he invented just the sort of Jay Gatsby that a seventeen-year-old boy would be likely to invent ....' (78). Gatsby's funeral, which is attended by only a handful of people, contrasts starkly with the throngs of guests who once flocked to his extravagant soirées. This disparity underscores the superficiality of the relationships that were built around wealth and status.

Meanwhile the Buchanans, particularly Tom and Daisy, embody a privileged class that displays a remarkable indifference to the chaos they create in their lives and the lives of others. They swiftly flee to avoid facing the consequences of their actions, highlighting their moral vacuity. Their decision to escape rather than confront the fallout of Gatsby's tragic demise reveals a troubling truth about their character: they are willing to abandon those who are less fortunate and, in doing so, illustrate the darker side of the American Dream.

Nick's disillusionment deepens as he witnesses this dynamic of privilege and evasion. His experiences force him to confront the unsettling reality that wealth does not equate to integrity, empathy or genuine human connection. This realisation leads him to make the difficult decision to return to the Midwest, seeking solace and a sense of grounding away from the moral decay that permeates both East Egg and West Egg.

Through Nick's journey, the narrative serves as a poignant commentary on the illusion of the American Dream. It exposes the fragility of human aspirations when set against the harsh realities of social stratification and ethical bankruptcy. Nick grapples with the realisation that wealth cannot buy genuine relationships or fulfil deeper emotional yearnings, leaving him profoundly disillusioned and yearning for something more authentic in life. The novel powerfully illustrates that, in a world driven by wealth and status, the true costs of ambition often go unseen and unacknowledged.

Aravind Adiga's *The White Tiger* is set in 2008, a year significantly marked by a financial crisis in India. This period was profoundly influenced by the US mortgage crisis, which triggered an economic recession beginning in 2006. As the crisis unfolded, its repercussions began to extend far beyond American borders, gradually affecting the Indian economy. Several underlying issues contributed to this financial turmoil in India, including the adverse effects of global recession on local markets and financial systems that were poorly regulated and lacked sufficient oversight. The consequences were evident in the nation's GDP, which saw a noticeable decline. A commentary in *The Economic Times* highlights this downturn: 'The global recession started in December 2007. The initial impact on India was muted: GDP growth slowed from 9% in 2007–08 to 7.8% in April-September 2008, still a very high rate. But after Wall Street collapsed in September, India's growth plummeted to 5.8%, 5.8%, and 6.1% in the next three quarters' (Aiyar, 2009).

In this context, Adiga intricately explores a variety of issues through his novel, including low levels of investment in agriculture, an increased emphasis on technological advancement and the widespread migration of individuals from rural areas to urban centres in search of employment opportunities. He delves into the never-ending struggle faced by many to achieve economic stability and improve their living conditions. Once again, India is portrayed as a nation grappling with divisions—not just in terms of religion and caste, but also along economic lines. The stark contrast between the affluent and the impoverished is a central theme of the novel: '...that India is two countries in one: an India of Light and an India of Darkness' (14). Notably, the differences between the US and India regarding wealth distribution are shaped by cultural factors; in the US, class disparities are often oriented toward individuals, while in India, they are more familial in nature and influenced by caste, religion and, at times, gender.

Narrated through a series of letters, *The White Tiger* features Balram Halwai as its central character. Balram's journey begins in the rural landscape of a village in Gaya district in Bihar, from where he finally leaves for Delhi in pursuit of a better life. Faced with harsh realities early in life, he is compelled to abandon his education and take up work in a tea-shop in Dhanbad, contributing to the dowry expenses for his cousin's marriage. In the tea-shop, he absorbs valuable insights about the Indian economy and potential opportunities for advancement through the conversations he overhears among customers. As he learns to drive, he seizes the chance to move to Delhi, where he becomes a chauffeur for Ashok, the son of a wealthy landowner from Laxmangarh. While working in the bustling capital, Balram becomes acutely aware of the pervasive bribery and corruption that characterise the lives of the wealthy elite. His experiences reveal the stark social and economic divisions that exist, prompting him to reflect on the broader implications of these disparities. He poignantly articulates this divide in a striking passage: 'A handful of men in this country have trained the remaining 99.9 percent—just as strong, talented, and intelligent—to exist in perpetual servitude; a servitude so profound that you can hand a man the key to his emancipation, and he will throw it back at you with a curse' (176).

As Balram begins to gain a foothold in this new world, he gradually transitions from driving small cars to larger, more luxurious vehicles. His boss, Ashok, becomes embroiled in a web of dealings with various government officials in order to secure favours for his family's business. A pivotal incident occurs when Ashok's wife, Pinky, in a state of drunkenness, accidentally hits something on the road while driving. It is heavily implied that she has killed a child, leading to a concerted effort to pin the blame on Balram. This moment of crisis compels Balram to reflect on his own entrapment, likening his situation to that of hens confined in a coop. He describes this phenomenon as the 'rooster coop' effect where the hens and roosters in wire meshes know that they may get killed but have no way out: 'They see the bodies of their brethren lying around them. They know they are next, yet they cannot rebel. They do not try to escape. The same is done to humans in this country' (175).

Desperate to break free from this oppressive 'rooster coop' effect, Balram makes a fateful decision: he kills his employer and takes the bribe money Ashok was carrying in the car. He relocates to Bangalore, where he starts a taxi business, viewing this as his opportunity to reshape his destiny. Balram acknowledges the possibility that Ashok's family may seek vengeance by eliminating his relatives back in their village. He grapples with the moral implications of his actions, rationalising that his quest for freedom may come at the expense of others: 'But isn't it likely that everyone in this world ... has killed someone on their way to the top? All I wanted was a chance to be a man—and for that, one murder is enough' (120). In this new narrative, Balram begins to perceive himself not merely as a servant but as an entrepreneur embarking on a journey toward success.

According to the Collins Dictionary, class is defined as 'a collection or division of people or things sharing a common characteristic, attribute, quality, or property' while the Cambridge Dictionary states: 'one of the groups of people in a society with the same social and economic position, or the system of dividing people into these groups'. This definition underscores how class distinctions have structured society into upper, middle and lower tiers. The concept of class became a pivotal issue with the advent of Marxist theory, which introduced the dichotomy between the bourgeoisie and the proletariat. In Marxist ideology, class consciousness serves as a critical framework for understanding economic hierarchies and is instrumental in shaping socio-economic and politico-cultural orders. Class conflict, as a significant aspect of Marxist thought, examines the relationships within society, offering a lens through which to view and challenge the prevailing capitalist structures. It provides a basis for advocating for a new social and economic order founded on the principles of equality and justice.

Class, as evident through the Marxian backdrop, arises due to exploitation and production. As Liam Campling et al. state, 'our class-relational perspective production is not merely a technical relationship between inputs and outputs; rather it is a conflictual process in which work is directed and controlled by the capitalist to ensure that the capacity to labour is realised' (1746). They further point out that class relations occur differently. 'Class relations are related to 'exploitative social relations of production' and additionally 'class is a relational and multidimensional concept ... Class is widespread and understood universally and moreover, class has 'agency which is unevenly constrained and/or facilitated by the social structures with which it is mutually constituted'. (1747)

In *The White Tiger*, Adiga explores the exploitation of Balram's family. Women and men are exploited in different ways. One expects that a marked division of labour, education and societal changes could lead to social transformation. However, the novel repeatedly depicts the failure of the system, of the social division of labour, capitalist competition and, crucially, social mobility. The novel reveals that hierarchy and class is a mark of privilege and power connected to gender and caste.

It is precisely this sense of class that fuels the struggle for significance in the two novels. While Gatsby is a bootlegger, Balram is an entrepreneur. The distinction lies in the moral fibre of these two men. Gatsby, based in the United States, embodies the corrupt nature of capitalism and reflects the 1920s ideals of consumerism and rapid expansion. Balram Halwai, navigating the 2000s, confronts economic crisis and resorts to murder to survive. Both novels expose the intrinsic flaws in societal expectations. The quest for social mobility creates individuals who are morally compromised. Gatsby seeks love from a married woman, Tom engages in an affair and Balram harbours an obsession for his boss's wife, Pinky, and is willing to kill. Much of the narration in *The Great Gatsby* is by Nick, limiting the reader's insight into Gatsby's personal struggles, while Balram, as the narrator in Adiga's novel, provides a vivid account of his life.

One of the aspects of class dynamics that emerges in the novels is the sense of superiority that both Gatsby and Balram gain. Fitzgerald maintains an aura of mystery around Gatsby. Through Nick's narrative we learn that although Jay Gatsby was born as James Gatz in North Dakota and came from a humble home, he desired to gain the American Dream of riches and prosperity and thereby created a new persona and named himself Jay Gatsby. Yet in many ways his life is mysterious and one gets the impression that he is shadowy. Fitzgerald desired Gatsby to be mysterious so that the reader could not judge him morally. Nick Carraway while reporting the facts of Gatsby's life undermines the narrative by making him seem like a superior persona when he mentions, 'The truth was that Jay Gatsby of West Egg, Long Island, sprang from his Platonic conception of himself. He was a son of God ...' (78).

In *The White Tiger*, although Adiga provides a clear picture of Balram Halwai, he also stresses on the nature of his enlightenment and his attempt to glorify himself by moving away from darkness: 'I'm always a man who sees "tomorrow" when others see "today"' (519). At the conclusion of *The White Tiger*, Balram declares himself an entrepreneur in Bangalore. Yet this self-proclaimed transformation narrated in his own epistolatory way is quite dubious. While he appears to convince the reader, the authenticity of his reinvention remains ambiguous. His identity in the contemporary present is as much a product of selective omission and self-fashioning as it is of confession, leaving readers unsure of what is his identity is in the contemporary present.

Fitzgerald once expressed his own experience of class division: 'That was always my experience—a poor boy in a rich town; a poor boy in a rich boy's school; a poor boy in a rich man's club at Princeton .... However, I have never been able to forgive the rich for being rich, and it has coloured my entire life and works' (1994, 352). In the novel, Fitzgerald grapples with creating a class system in which the rich and the poor are continuously interacting and intermingling but it is always the rich who finally gain advantage. The West Egg region, where Tom and Daisy Buchanan live, is the home of the rich while East Egg, where Gatsby and Nick live, is the region that the middle class stay and Dream of becoming millionaires. This is also the region of the lower class, represented by George and Myrtle Wilson, who attempt to uplift themselves but fail. Nick, the narrator who is in many ways an insider due to his relationship to Daisy also recognises that he, too, is an outsider when he mentions, 'in a moment she looked at me with a smirk on her lovely face, as if she had asserted her membership in a distinguished secret society to which she and Tom belonged' (15).

Adiga discusses the stark divide in Indian society regarding the haves and have-nots: 'The dreams of the rich and the dreams of the poor—they never overlap, do they?' (2008). In *The Great*

Gatsby, there exists a secret society among the wealthy while in India, a veil of invisibility prevails. Adiga elaborates as to how he spent time around railway stations and talking to rickshaw pullers and his idea that while the rich struggle with obesity, it is the poor who are intelligent in spite of being thin.

To fit in, Gatsby throws extravagant parties, lives in a castle-like mansion and mimics the behaviour of the wealthy, while Balram strives to present himself as a successful entrepreneur, constructs a false identity and believes he has transformed into a new man. Yet, both men remain excluded from the elite club due to their lack of the socio-cultural context needed to engage in upper-class circles. Simple factors like dress, behaviour, customs of social interactions and mannerisms are cultivated among the elite, and both novels explore how characters outside this sphere fail to embody the upper class's behavioural norms despite their wealth.

In the process of adaptation, the characters in both novels experience a phenomenon known as false consciousness. This term, rooted in Marxist philosophy, describes a situation where the working class is unaware of their true social status and misinterprets the dynamics of production. While the characters do become aware of their oppression and marginalisation, their attempts to liberate themselves ironically lead them to develop a false consciousness, a set of beliefs that perpetuates conditioned thinking and obscures reality. A crucial aspect of this false consciousness is the role of ideology. As Lee Wilson discusses in 'Why They Know Not What They Do: A Social Constructionist Approach to the Explanatory Problem of False Consciousness', ideology shapes perceptions of reality. The belief in wealth and status as desirable ideals is a prominent ideology critiqued by economist Thomas Piketty in his work, *Capital and Ideology*. Piketty argues that wealth arises from systemic inequalities, which he refers to as an 'inequality regime'. This regime comprises discourses and institutional frameworks designed to justify and maintain economic, social and political disparities within society (2020, 2).

Further, Klikauer posits that ideology serves three significant functions: it camouflages contradictions, supports domination and hinders emancipation (2017, 85). This function of ideology is evident in both novels. For instance, in the first chapter of *The Great Gatsby*, Tom Buchanan thinks that civilisation is shattered and that the white race would be submerged. He emphasises the need for the dominance of the white race, declaring, 'Well, these books [referring to *The Rise of the Colored Empires* by a man called Goddard] are all scientific', and further states, "Well, it's a fine book, and everybody ought to read it. The idea is if we don't look out the white race will be—will be utterly submerged. It's all scientific stuff; it's been proved.' Daisy concurs, saying, 'We've got to beat them down', illustrating their belief in racial superiority and entitlement (11).

Similarly, in Aravind Adiga's *The White Tiger*, Balram reflects on the manipulative nature of political ideology. He states, 'Whatever was being done was being done for our own good. The great Socialist's enemies would try and steal the election from us, the poor, and take the power away from us … Did we understand?' (100). Here, the ideology of maintaining inequality and preserving the status quo is evident, as it keeps class divisions intact.

Another crucial issue that arises within this ideological framework is the desire for social mobility among the economically disadvantaged. This aspiration often manifests as a longing to emulate the lifestyles of the affluent—the wealthy white class in *The Great Gatsby* or the upper-class elite in urban settings in *The White Tiger* respectively. Additionally, within these rigid class structures, women frequently lack agency. In *The Great Gatsby*, characters like Myrtle Wilson are objectified and treated as commodities, while in *The White Tiger*, women are portrayed as trapped, unable to think freely or enrich their lives. A striking passage in Adiga's novel highlights this oppression and equates their life to those of animals such as monkeys that exhibit a social herd behaviour pattern: 'Once you walk into the house, you will see—if any of them are still living, after what I did—the women. ... At night, they sleep together, their legs falling one over the other, like one creature, a millipede' (21).

These entrenched class divisions are stark and resistant to change, ultimately undermining the confidence of the lower class.

As Wilson argues, the oppressed often lack credibility regarding their own identities, deferring to the inflated credibility of their oppressors. The influence of high-status individuals gradually erodes the lower class's self-esteem and understanding, leading them to accept detrimental myths perpetuated by the privileged class, which seeks to maintain the material inequalities that benefit them (57). Consequently, class struggle perpetuates systemic oppression, with the lower class entangled in a web of false aspirations.

In *The White Tiger*, Balram's attempt to learn driving highlights this struggle. The old driver explains to Balram that to be a driver one needs to 'to become a driver. Moreover, the road is a jungle, get it? A good driver must roar to get ahead on it' (57). Similarly, Gatsby's journey of self-reinvention reveals his desire to transcend his humble beginnings. An important move is his sense of self-assurance seen in Nick's description of his smile: 'He smiled understandingly—much more than understandingly. It was one of those rare smiles with a quality of eternal reassurance in it, that you may come across four or five times in life' (38). Fitzgerald endeavours to create the character Gatsby who can perform and imitate the role of the rich but in spite of his attempt to dress, act and behave as the elite it is evident that others in society recognise his inferior background.

It is also evident that class divisions are influenced by regional contexts. In *The Great Gatsby*, social stratification is marked by distinctions such as 'white trash' and economic disparities. In contrast, *The White Tiger* presents a more complex interplay of class, caste, religion, politics and economic structure. While Gatsby embodies a certain falseness in his pursuit of wealth, Balram grapples with his identity as a halwa-maker, navigating the intricacies of Indian politics, democracy and societal expectations. Adiga suggests that crime can serve as a path to social ascent, a point that has sparked debate among critics. Balram points out the pervasive corruption within the political landscape, asserting, 'You see, a total of ninety-three criminal cases—for murder, rape, grand larceny, gun smuggling, pimping, and many other such minor offences—are pending against the Great Socialist and his ministers at the present moment' (97–98).

This critique underscores the systemic injustices that continue to plague society, revealing the challenges faced by those at the bottom of the social hierarchy.

Through Balram's journey and the exploration of class dynamics, *The White Tiger* reveals the complexities of Indian society and the lengths to which individuals may go to break free from the chains of economic oppression. Adiga's narrative serves as both a reflection on the socio-economic landscape of contemporary India and a critique of the systemic inequalities that persist within it. Even though *The Great Gatsby*, on the other hand, may not reveal exploitation openly, it still addresses the common man's desire to belong and be part of the American Dream. While Fitzgerald discusses the predicament of life and the instability of the desire for social mobility, Adiga delves into the precariousness of life and the endeavour to turn the tables of misfortune. If Gatsby is unable to erase the past and move into the future, Balram Halwai is quite successful in attempting to throw away the past, grasp the present and create a future. In conclusion one can say that Fitzgerald presents a dual message about life in America and life itself. Although the essence of life is to gain wealth, attaining it is elusive. An individual like Gatsby is stuck in this duality and ultimately is vanquished as this is beyond his reach. On the other hand, Adiga delineates the duality in India is regarding action and inaction. Therefore, Balram resorts to action so that he can secure the agency to change his fate even though his action may be morally and ethically a sinful one. He, eventually, must resort to this because the affluent have means of eating up the not-so-affluent as it happens in *The Great Gatsby* and therefore what matters is life and survival and not morals.

Works Cited

Adiga, Aravind. 2008. *The White Tiger*. Harper Collins India.

Adiga, Aravind. 2008. Interview by Stuart Jeffries. 'Roars of Anger'. *The Guardian*, 16 October 2008. https://www.theguardian.com/books/2008/oct/16/booker-prize.

Aiyar, Swaminathan S. A. 2009. 'India weathers 12 months of financial crisis.' *The Economic Times*, 13 September 2009. https://economictimes.indiatimes.com/swaminathan-s-a-aiyar/india-weathers-12-months-of-financial-crisis/articleshow/5005007.cms?from=mdr.

Cambridge Learner's Dictionary. 'Class.' https://dictionary.cambridge.org/dictionary/learner-english/class.

Collins Dictionary. 'Class.' https://www.collinsdictionary.com/dictionary/english/class.

Das, Raju. 2015. 'Critical Observations on Neo-liberalism and India's New Economic Policy'. *Journal of Contemporary Asia*, 45(4): 715–726.

Fitzgerald, F. Scott. *A Life in Letters*, ed. Matthew J. Bruccoli. New York: Scribners, 1994.

Fitzgerald, F. Scott. 1981. *The Great Gatsby*. India: Oxford University Press.

Klikauer, Thomas. 2017. 'Business Ethics as Ideology.' *Critique*, 45 (1–2): 81–100.

Martinez, Julia. 2024. 'The Great Gatsby.' *Encyclopedia Britannica*, 21 October 2024, https://www.britannica.com/topic/The-Great-Gatsby.

Merriam Webster Dictionary. 'The American dream.' https://www.merriam-webster.com/dictionary/the%20American%20dream.

Murtoff, Jennifer. 2025. 'The American Dream.' *Encyclopedia Britannica*. https://www.britannica.com/topic/American-Dream.

Oxford English Dictionary. 'The American dream.' https://www.oed.com/dictionary/american-dream_n?tab=factsheet#5337887100.

Picketty, Thomas. 2020. *Capital and Ideology*, trans. Arthur Goldhammer. Cambridge, Massachusetts: Harvard University Press.

Wilson, Lee. 2021. 'Why They Know Not What They Do: A Social Constructionist Approach to the Explanatory Problem of False Consciousness'. *Journal of Social Ontology*, 7(1): 45–72.

9

Of the American Dream and a Delusional Love: Ambition and Obsession in *The Great Gatsby*

Amit Shankar Saha

The tipping point at which Jay Gatsby's obsession topples his ambition is crucial to the understanding of how the dynamics between chasing the American Dream and pursuing a delusional love works. But it is this very point that eludes the reader much like the elusive point exactly when Doctor Faustus was damned in Christopher Marlowe's eponymous play. It is the point from which there is no coming back. It is this point that many critics have been in search of as if on a quest for the Holy Grail. *The Great Gatsby* was published in the year 1925 and since then critics have been on a proverbial wild goose chase but so too has Gatsby—his pursuit of love is also unattainable. However, there is a difference between the two—for the critics it is an attempt to crack some kind of code but for Gatsby it is a kind of calling, a vision, an all-consuming ambition and a delusional obsession with no possibility of achieving the goals.

Early reception of the novel concentrated on the moral issues in it—focusing on the decadence and hedonism of the Jazz Age. In the 1920s and 1930s, despite the appreciation of its prose style, the novel was not regarded by some critics as a major work, let alone a potential classic. The theme of obsessive love and romance was often overshadowed by discussions critiquing the Jazz Age and its superficial nature. Edwin Clark writing in *The New York Times* (1925), admired the novel's craft:

> Of the many new writers that sprang into notice with the advent of the post-war period, Scott Fitzgerald has remained the steadiest performer and the most

> entertaining. … this is a book of potent overtones—the decay of souls is more tragic. With sensitive insight and keen psychological observation, Fitzgerald discloses in these people a meanness of spirit, carelessness and absence of loyalties. He cannot hate them, for they are dumb in their insensate selfishness, and only to be pitied. The philosopher of the flapper has escaped the mordant, but he has turned grave. A curious book, a mystical, glamorous story of today. It takes a deeper cut at life than hitherto has been enjoyed by Mr Fitzgerald. He writes well—he always has—for he writes naturally, and his sense of form is becoming perfected.

But H. L. Mencken in *The Baltimore Evening Sun* (10 April 1925), reprinted in the *Chicago Sunday Tribune* (3 May 1925) writes:

> Scott Fitzgerald's new novel, *The Great Gatsby*, is in form no more than a glorified anecdote, and not too probable at that. … This clown Fitzgerald rushes to his death in nine short chapters. The other performers in the Toten Tanz are of a like, or even worse quality. One of them is a rich man who carries on a grotesque intrigue with the wife of a garage keeper. Another is a woman golfer who wins championships by cheating. A third, a sort of chorus to the tragic farce, is a bond salesman—symbol of the New America! Fitzgerald clears them all off at last by a triple butchery.

But, despite these contrasting early reviews, it should be noted that the book at least caught the attention of the public and the critics alike and did not pass off unnoticed.

Later on after Fitzgerald's death and with the advent of New Criticism, Existentialism and Psychoanalytical Criticism the greatness of *The Great Gatsby* was established. It was considered a great American novel due to its symbolic depth, structure and prose style, and by examining characters like Jay Gatsby in terms of existential angst or through Freudian lenses. The relationship between Gatsby and Daisy began to come into focus and the ideas of obsessive love, singular ambition and the American Dream started intersecting into a tragic dimension, emblematic of the larger American ethos. Lionel Trilling writing about Fitzgerald in 1950 says,

> *The Great Gatsby*, for example, after a quarter-century is still as fresh as when it first appeared; it has even gained in weight and relevance, which can be said of very few American books of its time. This, I think, is to be attributed to the specifically intellectual courage with which it was conceived and executed, a courage which implies Fitzgerald's grasp—both in the sense of awareness and of appropriation—of the traditional resources available to him. (251)

Marius Bewley, writing four years later, gives an affirmation of the stature of *The Great Gatsby*. More importantly, he extricates *The Great Gatsby* from the shadow of the Jazz Age and explains that apart from its exploration of the Jazz Age, the novel has an artistic form that itself marks its greatness.

> Critics of Scott Fitzgerald tend to agree that *The Great Gatsby* is somehow a commentary on that elusive phrase, the American dream. The assumption seems to be that Fitzgerald approved. On the contrary, it can be shown that *The Great Gatsby* offers some of the severest and closest criticism of the American dream that our literature affords. Read in this way, Fitzgerald's masterpiece ceases to be a pastoral documentary of the Jazz Age and takes its distinguished place among those great national novels whose profound corrective insights into the nature of American experience are not separable from the artistic form of the novel itself. (1954)

Robert Ornstein in 1956 states that 'in *Gatsby* Fitzgerald did create a myth with the imaginative sweep of America's historical adventure across an untamed continent. But his fable of East and West is little concerned with twentieth century' (139). Ornstein delves into the novel's mythic and psychological dimensions, positioning Gatsby's pursuit of the American Dream within a deeper context of individual ambition and longing. But this was not to be the definitive trend as with the revival of Cultural and Historical Studies the idea of the Jazz Age and the American

Dream resurfaced with renewed force although this time, with the novel already established as a classic, the treatment was different.

The novel started being situated more firmly within the cultural and social milieu of the 1920s offering critiques of American materialism and decadence. Gatsby's embodiment of the American Dream and its promises and failures once again started being explored. The disillusionment after World War I and the societal ramifications of the subsequent economic boom were the focus of the critics. Daisy's character again started being seen as symbolic and Gatsby's infatuation with her was seen as analogous to the nation's enthralment with success and materialism. Thomas A. Hanzo in 1957 brings the narrator Nick Carraway into focus, commenting that his voice introduces and concludes the action and he acts as a foil to Gatsby. And yet there were still critics like Gary J. Scrimgeour who, in 1966, questioned the classic status of *The Great Gatsby* after comparing it with Joseph Conrad's *The Heart of Darkness*. Thomas E. Boyle in 1969 comments on the multiplicity of critical perspectives on the novel and writes:

> This novel, for example, has been interpreted as if it were metaphysics, sociology, and intellectual history. One would never know from much that is written on *Gatsby* that it is an aesthetic object (or better—process) standing, as Eliot said of the poem, somewhere between the author and the reader. The more critics I read the more convinced I become that standards are to literary criticism what faith is to religion. My argument, however, is neither a lament over the diversity of critical frames of reference, nor a plea for critical ecumenicalism. The warring factions among critics are, to me, a testament to the depth and the differences of human perception. (21)

Once a kind of reconciliation was reached about the status of *The Great Gatsby,* other approaches to the novel were engaged with by researchers. Nick Carraway's subjectivity and the stability of the narrative were questioned. In fact, whether Gatsby loved Daisy or was it just his love of the idea of being in love also came into the domain of criticism. Then there was the deconstructionist turn where the unreliability of love was studied. There was the feminist turn where the women characters of the novel were investigated by Lois Tyson and Betty Friedan, among others. The object of Gatsby's obsession, Daisy Buchanan's, role and agency in the story were re-evaluated in terms of her position in a patriarchal society. And the queer turn even said that perhaps it was Nick who was in love with Gatsby and to escape this predicament, Gatsby pursued an unattainable goal. Some scholars like Bryant Mangum and Ruth Prigozy examined racial undertones in Gatsby's ambition (consider, for example, his association with Wolfsheim and the criminal underworld). Also class struggles, as seen in the differences between East Egg and West Egg or Tom Buchanan's disdain for Gatsby's 'new money', were further brought into focus. There are elements of ecological concerns, too, in the novel like the depiction of the industrial dumping ground called the Valley of Ashes. Psychoanalytically, Gatsby's ambition and obsessive love were analysed not just as an economic or societal drive in capitalist America but as a core component of his identity construction and his desires and downfall were given a universal dimension. Critics like Richard Lehan delved deeper into the character of Gatsby to understand his motivations.

Despite all these opinions and criticism the character of Jay Gatsby remains an enigma. Everywhere in the novel lurks a mystery. The Gothic mansion where Gatsby lives is mysterious; the green light at the end of the dock, across the bay from Tom Buchanan's place, is mysterious. There is a mystery in Nick's coming to the newly-rich West Egg part of Long Island and his interest in the bond business even though he is Yale-educated and is well-connected in the more fashionable East Egg part of Long Island. The character of Jordan Baker, whom Nick loves, is also shrouded in a bit of mystery. Even when a minor character like Gatsby's friend Wolfsheim is introduced, it is done in an enigmatic way: 'A small, flat-nosed Jew raised his large head and regarded me with two fine growths of hair which luxuriated in either nostril. After a moment I discovered his tiny eyes in the half darkness' (Fitzgerald 1993, 73). There is ominousness in the landscape too as is evident in the depiction of the 'solemn dumping ground':

> But above the gray land and the spasms of bleak dust which drift endlessly over it, you perceive, after a moment, the eyes of Doctor T. J. Eckleburg. The eyes of Doctor T. J. Eckleburg are blue and gigantic—their retinas are one yard high. They look out of no face, but, instead, from a pair of enormous yellow spectacles which pass over a non-existent nose. Evidently some wag of an oculist set them there to fatten his practice in the borough of Queens, and then sank down himself into eternal blindness, or forgot them and moved away. (Fitzgerald 1993, 36)

So it is quite understandable that the duality of the pursuit of the American Dream and the pursuit of an obsessive love will be enigmatic. There is a sort of ominousness in the dynamics of ambition and delusion. The simultaneity and intersection of the two quests make them indistinguishable from each other. By achieving the American Dream Gatsby will win over Daisy and by winning over Daisy he will be fulfilling the American Dream. It is a Möbius strip kind of situation. Gatsby seems to be progressing towards his goal but for an outsider-observer, like Nick Carraway, he is doing so in a Sisyphean manner without reaching any destination because there is no target.

The exploration of how ambition and obsession mix to create a simulated reality in the mind of the protagonist is something that is seated deep in human psychology, as well as has outward symbolic significance. Karl Marx, Frantz Fanon and other theorists have shown how the mind and the material condition, social circumstances and political situation are interdependent. Hence, it is quite understandable that such will be the case with Jay Gatsby—a character whose real name was James Gatz who rose from modest origins, as revealed by Gatsby's father at the end of the novel. How the American Dream shapes human psychology, especially for one who is willing to indulge in its lure, is something that has been quite a common theme in the literature of the period. Critics have discussed the rise of the individual amidst the cacophony of the Jazz Age that is symbolic of decadence and delusion. But the angle of love queers the pitch further and produces a dilemma about whether the individual is propelled by mere ambition or there is an obsession acting as a subterranean spirit that is making the individual pursue a goal that is apparently unattainable. The connotation of 'Dream' in the American Dream is of attainable success but the connotation of delusional dreaming is not of success, of achievement or the attainment of any goal but a state of stasis, a dream state, where the pursuit itself becomes the goal and there is no reaching but just being.

Gatsby is sucked into a world of delusion, where he is pursuing a Sisyphus-like goal of winning over Daisy without ever attaining success. Although he does impress Daisy and she starts having a sort of affair with him after being brought in touch with each other once again by Nick Carraway. Nick creates the possibility of success but it is evident that Daisy is carried away by Gatsby's new life. Despite his doubts of things being otherwise, Gatsby keeps on thinking that Daisy loves him wholeheartedly. He never doubts this fact or he chooses not to doubt it. Starting from this premise, whatever he does seems both logical and justified. But the premise itself is untenable. According to Milton R. Stern, 'Gatsby knew full well that when he made Daisy the receptacle of his dreams he would be forever wedded to her. It would henceforth be emotionally and spiritually—if I may say so, *nationally*—insupportable to find the basket broken and shabby after he had put all his East and West Eggs in it' (Bloom 2006, 102, italics in original).

Does Daisy really love him? Gatsby's mind would not answer that question in the negative. Any evidence that comes to the contrary he can argue against. He has reasons for everything. He removes the plausibility of anything negative. He has developed his psychology to always be positive. He thinks everything is possible if only the chance, the scope, the spark is kept alive. He gets such confidence to believe that he has the power to change his destiny from nowhere else but the pursuit of the American Dream—the world of possibility does not exclude the possibility of winning over love. The American

Dream asserts that if anyone has merit then that person can rise in life socially and economically and Gatsby believes in it just like many others do and have proved it too. Gatsby's success is also one such proof. But he wants to apply the same process to love. He wants to make his love for Daisy so outstanding that success will be ensured. What he does not understand, or rather chooses not to understand, is that the pursuit of wealth is one thing and the pursuit of a human being another—the former does not have a will of its own but the latter does. The very individuality with which he can change the will of the world is the same individuality that becomes an impediment when he tries to change the will of another individual. For Daisy, all parameters of a person's life like origin, wealth, social status and moral standards matter alongside love. She will carefully make her choice—step by step in a calculated manner. Obviously, the question remains: what if the car accident had not happened? But even then Gatsby remains calm because he is ready for all circumstances—he sees here another opportunity to foreground the uniqueness of his love by taking the blame upon himself. If the accident had not happened, would Gatsby have won over Daisy? Remember that Daisy was driving the car; she was in the driver's seat. Long before the accident takes place, in a conversation with Gatsby after Daisy leaves his mansion, Nick observes:

> He wanted nothing less of Daisy than that she should go to Tom and say: 'I never loved you'. After she had obliterated four years with that sentence they could decide upon the more practical measures to be taken. One of them was that, after she was free, they were to go back to Louisville and be married from her house—just as if it were five years ago. (Fitzgerald 1993, 105–06)

Gatsby tells Nick, 'I'm going to fix everything, just the way it was before' (Fitzgerald 1993, 106) as if the married woman Daisy Buchanan can be restored to the unmarried Daisy Fay once again. This is Gatsby's confidence emanating from his grounding or essential belief in the pursuit of the American Dream. He even tries to do this, with as much confidence, when the big confrontation takes place. Daisy had invited Nick for lunch at the Buchanan house along with Jordan Baker and Gatsby. Daisy sends Tom to make a cold drink and once Tom leaves, Daisy kisses Gatsby and tells him that she loves him.

> Jordan reproaches her for it, and Daisy displays a range of emotion in a remarkably short amount of time. Jordan's remark makes Daisy look around 'doubtfully,' but then Daisy counters, attempts a dance to show she doesn't care a whit for convention, but as her daughter comes into the room, reverts to an overblown affectation of motherly love. The child has a different effect on Gatsby, making real Daisy's bond to Tom in ways that his willful denial could no longer overcome. (Bloom 2006, 60)

Tom wants to ask Gatsby one more question before they disperse, a parting that will lead to the incident in which Daisy, while driving a car, fatally hits Tom's mistress Myrtle, which in turn will drive Myrtle's husband, Wilson, to take revenge and kill Gatsby in the belief that he was the one driving the car. Tom accuses Gatsby of causing a row in his house and Daisy comes quickly in defense of Gatsby by saying that it is not Gatsby but Tom who is causing the row and asks him to control himself. And Tom in reply says, 'I suppose the latest thing is to sit back and let Mr Nobody from Nowhere make love to your wife.' (Fitzgerald 1993, 121). That was all Gatsby needed to put it all in the open despite Daisy's intervention:

> 'Your wife doesn't love you,' said Gatsby. She's never loved you. She loves me'.
>
> 'You must be crazy!' exclaimed Tom automatically.
>
> Gatsby sprang to his feet, vivid with excitement.
>
> 'She never loved you, do you hear?' he cried. 'She only married you because I was poor and she was tired of waiting for me. It was a terrible mistake, but in her heart she never loved anyone except me!' (Fitzgerald 1993, 122)

Both Gatsby and Tom argue and they want Daisy to vouch in their favour. Daisy is put in a spot. In the end, she confesses:

> 'Oh, you want too much!' she cried to Gatsby. 'I love you now—isn't that enough? I can't help what's past.'

> She began to sob helplessly. 'I did love him once—but I loved you too.'
>
> Gatsby's eyes opened and closed.
>
> 'You loved me too?' he repeated.
>
> 'Even that's a lie,' said Tom savagely. 'She didn't know you were alive. Why—there're things between Daisy and me that you'll never know, things that neither of us can ever forget.'
>
> The words seemed to bite physically into Gatsby. (Fitzgerald 1993, 124)

Tom is jealous that his wife loves another man and he shows that in his speech. But Gatsby speaks as if it was impossible for Daisy to love another man once she had loved him. It is too idealistic to think that love can be felt for only one person. Daisy would be happy to love both of them for different reasons and would not like any further precipitation of the situation. Even after this Gatsby does not believe that it is possible for Daisy to love another man and he insists that he will talk to her alone. Remember, Gatsby loves Daisy but he lost her because he was poor. He addressed his poverty, the reason for the loss and became rich. Now he sees that the cause of his loss is no longer there so he should gain what he has lost, although the original object sought is no longer available because it has been taken by someone else. But he believes that this object, being a person of volition, can return by exercising her will. He cannot see any reason for why it cannot happen. His mind is stuck at this point. Is this the point of no return? Is this the point from where Gatsby cannot escape his obsession just like Marlowe's Doctor Faustus cannot escape his damnation despite being asked to seek forgiveness from God who is all merciful and will forgive. Doctor Faustus assumes that he is past redemption and that the only path left for him is damnation. Gatsby, too, imagines that there is no alternative for him in his life but to pursue his love obsessively. If Doctor Faustus is deluded into believing that he is beyond redemption then Gatsby is deluded into believing that he is beyond any alternative ambition in life. His pursuit of the American Dream has Daisy as its goal. Gatsby finds no valid reason to abandon his pursuit or take up an alternative one because in both cases his love will be demeaned in some way. He chooses not to demean his love and keep it on the highest pedestal. For some this will sound delusional, for some it will be idealistic, but for Gatsby it is the only reality, albeit simulated. He will not permit any other. Ambition and obsession become one for Gatsby and even a hundred years after the publication of this novel the character of Gatsby still generates enigma because of this very fact.

Works Cited

Bewley, Marius. 1954. 'Scott Fitzgerald's Criticism of America.' *The Sewanee Review*, 62(2): 223–246. https://fitzgerald.narod.ru/critics-eng/bewley-criticism.html

Bloom, Harold, ed.2006 .*F. Scott Fitzgerald's 'The Great Gatsby'*. New York: Chelsea House.

Boyle, Thomas E. 1969. 'Unreliable Narration in *The Great Gatsby*.' *Bulletin of the Rocky Mountain Modern Language Association*, 23(1):21–26. https://muse.jhu.edu/pub/143/article/457930/

Clark, Edwin. 1925. 'Scott Fitzgerald Looks Into Middle Age.' *The New York Times*. 12 April 1925. https://archive.nytimes.com/www.nytimes.com/books/00/12/24/specials/fitzgerald-gatsby.html

Fitzgerald, F. Scott. 1993. *The Great Gatsby*. Hertfordshire: Wordsworth Classics.

Friedan, Betty. 1963. *The Feminine Mystique*. New York: Norton. https://nationalhumanitiescenter.org/ows/seminars/tcentury/FeminineMystique.pdf

Hanzo, Thomas A. 1957. 'The theme and the narrator of *The Great Gatsby*.' *Modern Fiction Studies*, 2(4):183–190. The Johns Hopkins University Press. https://www.jstor.org/stable/26273109

Lehan, Richard. 1990. *The Great Gatsby: The Limits of Wonder*. Boston: Twayne Publishers. https://books.google.co.in/books/about/The_Great_Gatsby.html?id=TR1oQgAACAAJ

Mangum, Bryant. 2014. 'An Affair of Youth: In Search of Flappers, Belles, and the Legendary Fitzgeralds.' *Broad Street Magazine*,

Spring 2014. https://broadstreet.medium.com/an-affair-of-youth-3f699ead9f0a

Mencken, H.L. 1925. '*The Great Gatsby*.' *The Baltimore Evening Sun*, 10 April 1925. https://fitzgerald.narod.ru/critics-eng/mencken-gg.html Also in the *Chicago Sunday Tribune*, 3 May 1925. https://www.chicagotribune.com/entertainment/books/ct-prj-great-gatsby-f-scott-fitzgerald-hl-mencken-20141010-story.html

Ornstein, Robert. (1959) 'Scott Fitzgerald's Fable of East and West.' *College English*, 18(3): 139–143. http://www.jstor.org/stable/372321

Prigozy, Ruth, ed.2002. *The Cambridge Companion to F. Scott Fitzgerald*. Cambridge: Cambridge University Press.

Scrimgeour, Gary J. (1966) 'Against *The Great Gatsby*.' *Criticism*, 8(1): 75–86. https://www.jstor.org/stable/23094241

Trilling, Lionel. 1950. 'F. Scott Fitzgerald.' In *The Liberal Imagination*, edited by Lionel Trilling, 243–254. New York: The Viking Press, Inc. https://fitzgerald.narod.ru/critics-eng/trilling-fsf.html

Tyson, Lois. 1996. 'Criticism by Lois Tyson.' *The Great Gatsby*, edited by Harold Bloom, 61–79. Philadelphia: Chelsea House Publishers.

10

The Real, the Surreal and the Dream in Jay Gatsby's World

Neeraj Pizar

This essay explores the religious implications and symbolism in F. Scott Fitzgerald's novel, *The Great Gatsby*, focusing on the character of Jay Gatsby. It begins by discussing the concept of the American Dream and its various interpretations through American literature. Fitzgerald's portrayal of the American Dream in Gatsby lacks the optimism and fulfilment found in his earlier works. The author describes Gatsby as a self-appointed prophet and the embodiment of the corrupted American Dream representing materialistic love, dedicated to the pursuit of wealth and status. His existence is built on lies and delusions and he is portrayed as a fraud, a product of the hedonistic 1920s.

In setting the stage for the exploration of the thematic interplay between Gatsby and the American Dream, it is prudent to commence with an examination of the elusive yet enduring concept of the American Dream itself. This enduring motif, often referred to as a 'myth', has recurrently found its place in American literature, tracing its roots to the earliest colonial writings. It is, in essence, a belief held close to the American ethos: the conviction that every individual, regardless of their social origins, possesses the agency to pursue and ultimately attain their cherished aspirations, whether those aspirations are of a political, pecuniary or social nature. The American Dream thus stands as a literary manifestation of the very essence of America—a land of boundless opportunities.

A kaleidoscope of literary figures, including luminaries like William Bradford, Walt Whitman, St Jean de Crevecoeur, Ralph Waldo Emerson, Thomas Jefferson and Benjamin

Franklin, have, through their distinct voices, woven intricate facets of this theme into the fabric of American literature. Their interpretations, diverse and multifaceted, bear testimony to the manifold forms assumed by the American Dream. For Bradford and his puritan contemporaries, it was a spiritual quest, a journey toward transcendence. Jefferson, on the other hand, conceived it as the flowering of political fulfilment, an ideal stemming from the innate perfectibility of humanity. Meanwhile, de Crevecoeur and Franklin were champions of the self-made man—a doctrine that preached self-reliance and industriousness. Emerson envisioned the American Dream as an opportunity to pose the profound questions for which humans were designed. For Whitman, it was an embodiment of democratic ideals, the embodiment of 'en masse'.

Among these literary titans, F. Scott Fitzgerald emerged as a pre-eminent figure in the twentieth century, inextricably linked to the American Dream. While the American Dream had been a foundational element for many writers, for Fitzgerald, it became more than just a theme; it was the fulcrum upon which much of his work pivoted. Fitzgerald approached the American Dream with a unique perspective that contrasted with the optimism and fulfilment prevailing in the views of his predecessors.

Embracing a metaphorical framework, the earlier proponents of the American Dream could be likened to Old Testament prophets who prophesied the advent of a golden age. They envisioned a utopia, complete with a messianic figure who would personify the quintessential 'American'. In the oeuvre of F. Scott Fitzgerald, Jay Gatsby becomes this much-anticipated embodiment. For Fitzgerald, the American Dream reached its zenith during the 'orgiastic' post-World War I era, often referred to as the Roaring Twenties. He not only positioned himself as the herald of the Jazz Age but also ascribed to it the title of the arch-high priest. In his magnum opus, *The Great Gatsby*, Fitzgerald introduced Jay Gatsby, who played the dual role of high priest and unwitting prophet of an era marked by hedonism. Gatsby, both in persona and practice, embodied the ethos of this period. He inadvertently became a harbinger: his tragic downfall serving as an omen foretelling the eclipse of the American Dream and the twilight of an era. Gatsby became a prophetic archetype, the voice of a generation.

This essay delves into the religious imagery present in the novel. Gatsby is compared to an inverted or perverted Christ, with other characters representing various biblical figures. The description of Gatsby's mansion, with its opulence, and the chaotic scenes during his parties, is likened to Babel and Milton's Pandemonium, symbolising Gatsby's decadent world. The valley of ashes, a desolate wasteland, is seen as a spiritual wasteland, representing the materialistic and mortal nature of Gatsby's world.

Fitzgerald's *The Great Gatsby* is deeply entrenched in the critique of the American Dream, which forms the fulcrum of much of his literary exploration. At its core, the novel critiques the materialistic distortion of this dream, using Jay Gatsby as a central figure who embodies both its allure and its ultimate corruption.

In *The Great Gatsby*, Fitzgerald portrays Gatsby as a prophet of the Jazz Age, an era marked by hedonism and material excess. Gatsby's dream is not rooted in spiritual or moral fulfilment but is, instead, a pursuit of wealth, status and a materialistic ideal of love, epitomised by Daisy Buchanan. As the narrative progresses, it becomes evident that Gatsby's existence is built on illusions and lies, making him a tragic figure ensnared in the false promises of a corrupted American Dream.

Fitzgerald employs religious imagery to deepen the critique of materialism. Bernard Tanner's interpretation, presented in 'The Gospel of Gatsby', likens Gatsby to an 'inverted Christ' and draws parallels between biblical figures and the novel's characters. Tanner's analysis, while imaginative, forces a rigid allegorical framework onto the narrative, reducing its complexity. On the other hand, A. E. Dyson's minimalist view, which isolates Dr T. J. Eckleburg as the sole religious reference, is equally limiting.

Instead, Fitzgerald's use of symbolism is cumulative, creating a tapestry of religious motifs that are both nuanced and subversive. Nick Carraway's description of Gatsby as a 'son of God' encapsulates this subversion. Gatsby is not a divine figure but a disciple of Mammon, the biblical symbol of material wealth. His opulent mansion, with its towering architecture and lavish parties, mirrors the Tower of Babel—a monument to human hubris and disconnection. The chaotic revelries within this 'temple of excess' reflect the moral and spiritual decay of the 1920s.

Gatsby's dedication to his fabricated identity underscores his estrangement from authenticity. His carefully constructed persona, marked by grandiose tales of wealth and heroism, is ultimately unsustainable. As Nick unravels the layers of Gatsby's deception, the tragic futility of his pursuits becomes apparent. Gatsby's association with figures like Meyer Wolfsheim, a symbol of corruption and moral turpitude, further emphasises his descent into materialistic despair.

The valley of ashes serves as a powerful symbol of the spiritual desolation underpinning Gatsby's world. This desolate wasteland, overshadowed by the brooding eyes of Dr T. J. Eckleburg, represents the moral void created by the relentless pursuit of material wealth. The 'dust' of the valley signifies the disintegration of the American Dream into a perverted vision, stripped of its original moral and spiritual aspirations.

Fitzgerald's religious imagery, including the parallels between Gatsby and biblical archetypes, critiques the hollowness of a society obsessed with material gain. By positioning Gatsby as a tragic figure ensnared by his devotion to an unattainable ideal, Fitzgerald underscores the futility of the corrupted American Dream.

The symbolic richness of *The Great Gatsby* gains further depth through the juxtaposition of its contrasting landscapes and their associated values. The valley of ashes, with its bleak and desolate imagery, serves as a stark counterpoint to the hedonistic opulence of West Egg and the pulsating vitality of New York City. This barren expanse is not merely a physical space but also a powerful metaphor for the spiritual vacuum and moral decay that underpin the pursuit of materialism.

The omnipresence of Dr. T J. Eckleburg's watchful eyes looming over the valley provides a theological dimension to the narrative. These unblinking eyes, set against a dilapidated billboard, embody a form of detached divinity—a deity rendered impotent and reduced to a commercialised symbol in a world obsessed with wealth and status. George Wilson's anguished cry, referring to the eyes as 'the eyes of God', underscores the characters' desperate search for meaning and accountability in a society that has abandoned traditional moral and spiritual values.

Moreover, the link between the valley of ashes and Gatsby's own rise and fall is significant. Gatsby's dream, built on the allure of material success and the promise of Daisy's love, is irrevocably tied to the corrupt foundations of his wealth. The valley stands as a grim reminder of the cost of such pursuits—both in terms of human exploitation, represented by the gray figures toiling in obscurity, and the spiritual emptiness that materialism begets. Gatsby's connection to the valley is not direct but symbolic; his lavish mansion, extravagant parties, and carefully curated persona are all financed by the moral compromise and societal decay that the valley epitomises.

The spectral presence of figures such as Owl Eyes within the narrative further enriches the theme of observation and truth. Owl Eyes, encountered first in Gatsby's library, marvels at the tangible authenticity of Gatsby's books, despite their unread pages revealing the hollowness beneath the facade. His later appearance at Gatsby's funeral, in stark contrast to the absence of the many who frequented Gatsby's parties, positions him as a witness to the tragedy of Gatsby's life—a life consumed by artifice and unfulfilled aspiration.

Fitzgerald's exploration of these interconnected symbols highlights a broader critique of 1920s America, of a society grappling with the disintegration of traditional values amidst an era of unprecedented prosperity and moral ambiguity. The valley of ashes, Dr Eckleburg's eyes and the green light on Daisy's dock collectively weave a narrative tapestry that interrogates the tension between aspiration and reality, materialism and spirituality, and illusion and truth.

Through Nick Carraway's narration, the reader is invited to dissect these symbols and grapple with their layered meanings. The green light, which Gatsby stretches toward in a moment of almost religious fervour, becomes a recurring motif of unattainable desire—a beacon of hope that simultaneously underscores the futility of his quest. This imagery mirrors the American Dream itself: an ideal that, in its pursuit, often distances the dreamer from genuine fulfilment.

As the narrative unfolds, it becomes evident that the green light is not a symbol of love or reunion but a projection of Gatsby's idealised vision of Daisy—a vision that cannot withstand the reality of her flawed humanity. Daisy, in turn, embodies the dissonance between perception and reality, her voice filled with a charm that mesmerises yet ultimately betrays her selfishness and vacuity.

By the time of Gatsby's death, the interplay between the green light, the valley of ashes and the haunting gaze of Dr Eckleburg culminates in a poignant commentary on the cost of pursuing dreams that are grounded in materialism. Fitzgerald masterfully constructs a narrative that, while ostensibly a tale of romantic tragedy, unfolds as a profound exploration of the human condition and the existential crises of modernity.

Gatsby's death not only signifies the collapse of his personal dream but also epitomises the broader disintegration of the American Dream as portrayed by Fitzgerald. The Dream, once a beacon of hope, idealism and boundless possibility, has been perverted into a pursuit of wealth and superficial success. Gatsby's wealth, amassed through morally ambiguous means, serves as both the instrument of his ascent and the root of his demise. His opulent lifestyle, designed to captivate Daisy and restore a romanticised past, becomes an empty spectacle—a hollow testament to the futility of achieving fulfilment through materialism.

Nick Carraway, as the novel's reflective narrator, offers a lens through which Gatsby's tragedy is both mourned and critiqued. While Nick is captivated by Gatsby's boundless optimism and unwavering faith in the dream, he remains painfully aware of the societal forces and moral decay that doom Gatsby's pursuit. The final chapters highlight Nick's growing disillusionment with the East, its inhabitants, and its values. Characters like Tom and Daisy Buchanan, emblematic of privilege and entitlement, retreat into their 'vast carelessness', leaving destruction in their wake. Their indifference starkly contrasts Gatsby's relentless hope and underscores the moral vacuum at the heart of the novel's social critique.

The green light, introduced as a symbol of Gatsby's aspirations, takes on a deeper resonance following his death. It shifts from a representation of personal longing to a broader metaphor for the unattainable ideals that drive human ambition. Just as Gatsby reaches for the green light across the bay, believing it to be within his grasp, so too do countless individuals who chase after dreams that ultimately elude them. This motif is poignantly encapsulated in the novel's closing lines, where Nick reflects on the endless struggle of humanity, 'borne back ceaselessly into the past', striving for a future that remains perpetually out of reach.

Fitzgerald's portrayal of Gatsby as a modern tragic hero imbues the narrative with profound emotional depth and universal appeal. Gatsby's flaws—his naivety, his inability to distinguish between reality and illusion, and his blind devotion to an idealised past—render him both relatable and pitiable. His downfall, orchestrated by his unyielding belief in the dream and the machinations of a morally bankrupt society, evokes a sense of inevitability that aligns him with the great tragic figures of literature. Yet, unlike traditional tragic heroes whose fates are often sealed by personal hubris or divine will, Gatsby's tragedy is intricately tied to the systemic flaws of the world he inhabits.

The recurring biblical and mythological allusions surrounding Gatsby's character further enrich the narrative. His messianic qualities, underscored by his rejection, sacrifice, and eventual demise, frame him as a Christ-like figure whose death serves as a commentary on the moral failures of his society. However, unlike the redemption typically associated with such figures, Gatsby's death offers no salvation—only a grim reflection of the era's values and the inherent contradictions of the American Dream.

In *The Great Gatsby*, Fitzgerald masterfully intertwines personal tragedy with social critique, crafting a narrative that resonates with both the specific anxieties of the Jazz Age and the timeless struggle of human aspiration. Through Gatsby's rise and fall, the novel interrogates the delicate balance between ambition and morality, the allure of wealth and its corrosive effects and the enduring tension between hope and disillusionment. As the final chapters fade into the solemn image of a man alone in death, gazing toward a dream forever out of reach, Gatsby's story remains a poignant testament to the complexities of human desire and the inexorable passage of time.

Works Cited

Dyson, A. E. 1962. '*The Great Gatsby*: Thirty-Six Years After.' In *Twentieth Century Views: F. Scott Fitzgerald*, edited by Arthur Mizener, 113. Englewood Cliffs: Prentice-Hall.

Fitzgerald, F. Scott, and Maxwell Perkins. 1997. *Dear Scott/Dear Max: The Fitzgerald-Perkins Correspondence*, edited by Matthew J. Bruccoli and Judith Baughman. New York: Scribner.

———. 1924. 'Absolution.' *The American Mercury* 2(6): 336–338.

———. 1925. 'Echoes of the Jazz Age.' *The American Mercury* 25(100): 243–251.

———. 1953. *The Great Gatsby*, 65–66. New York: Scribner's Sons.

Goldhurst, William. 1963. *F. Scott Fitzgerald and His Contemporaries*, 37. Cleveland: The World Publishing Company.

Kane, Patricia. 1964. 'Place of Abominations: A Reading of the Valley of Ashes.' *English Language Notes* 1(4): 291–295.

11

A Kaleidoscope of Tragic Hues in F. Scott Fitzgerald's *The Great Gatsby*

Suchandana Bhattacharyya

> So we beat on, boats against the current, borne back ceaselessly into the past.
>
> F. Scott Fitzgerald, *The Great Gatsby*

The interim period of the Great World Wars saw the flourish of the Jazz Age in the 1920s in America. This was the 'Age of the Roaring Twenties', the 'Aspirin Age', the age of unbounded living, flashy lifestyles, and the bohemian expansiveness of 'Dreams'. Scott Fitzgerald used this socio-economic context to create his enigmatic novel *The Great Gatsby* which highlighted these tendencies of extravagant lifestyles that was the norm of the Twenties. The world in the wake of the First World War was responding to the great American Dream that tempted, lured and eventually destroyed. Fitzgerald has depicted, in his novel, how the hues of grey and black permeate the extravagant glitz and glamour of the blue and gold that pivot the world of Jay Gatsby. This permeation of alternate colours problematises the concept of the American Dream and ushers in considerations of friction between myth and reality.

The American Dream defines an attitude of hope and faith that proposes the fulfilment of human desires—desires related to spiritual and material improvement. With the beginning of the American civilisation and its first generation of settlers, the New World represented a new life of freedom and the promise of spiritual and material bliss. Material prosperity and progress maintained pace with religious and spiritual growth because both the Puritans and the Quakers were supportive of industry and material advancement. Thus, to look beyond the immediate present with an inordinate belief in the future, soon became a national characteristic that fed the rapid development and advancement of American society. The democratic system first voiced in Jefferson's Declaration of Independence in 1776, can be traced to this attitude of hope and faith.

What is intriguing to note is that the material aspect of the Dream was rapidly achieved, and it soon outgrew and even obliterated the initial spiritual ideals. What evolved, therefore, was a lifestyle of material well-being gravely lacking in spiritual purpose. However, another critical point of view maintained that the advancement attained by the American society was superficial and the Dream did not lead to any fulfilment, whether spiritual or material. Caught between these alternate perspectives, values and morality grew complex and diffused, creating a breach between one end of the social spectrum and another. F. Scott Fitzgerald's *The Great Gatsby* exists as a testimony to this diffused reality in which the character of Jay Gatsby remains forever suspended. The novel renders the great American Dream not only as illusory but also unmasks the hollow sham of hypocrisy, discrimination and exploitation that the Dream entailed. This clearly leads to the feelings of disenchantment with the Dream in the common masses. However, this disenchantment is preceded by a sense of surreal enchantment weaved by the scintillating world of Jay Gatsby.

Indeed, Fitzgerald's narrative can be compared to the movement of colours in a kaleidoscope. And these colours in the narrative are all deeply tragic. This is because these colours—white, black, blue, grey, green and gold—which imbue the fabric of this narrative are metaphors of emotions and sentiments that rise and fall incessantly in the characters like Jay Gatsby, Daisy and Nick Carraway. These human emotions of love, hope, bliss, fear, envy and loss take on the hues of black, white, blue, grey, green and gold. For instance, while blue and gold signify a love for opulence, green suggests envy yet hope for true love, grey symbolises loss and abandonment. This eclectic interplay of colours has an intrinsic connection to the tragic overtones of this narrative. This tragic overtone is an integral part of the social ambience of the novel and, gradually, it consumes the personal emotions of the primary characters.

Jay Gatsby finds himself caught within this catapult of social attitudes and personal emotions. Amidst such social and personal chaos of ambition and self-aggrandisement, he soars towards the pinnacle of success but loses his love, Daisy, in the process. The colours that revolve around his life and his world conglomerate, therefore, into an intensely tragic hue that becomes a metaphor for Gatsby's own personality. Just like the constant movement of colours in a kaleidoscope, there is, in his life, the constant flux of hope, pain, grief and loss that reminds him that having lost Daisy, he has lost his soul. What remains is the social carcass that is trapped within the gyre of tragic hues.

The only respite from this tremendous claustrophobia is the undying hope that he would reconnect with Daisy at some point in time when he can convince her that the opulence in the world of Jay Gatsby she witnessed was nothing but a sham. His desire for her is that of a moth for the star, yet he continues to aspire. To quote Shelley:

> The desire of the moth for the star,
> Of the night for the morrow,
> The devotion to something afar
> From the sphere of our sorrow?
>
> ('One Word is Too Often Profaned', lines 13–16)

These lines breathe life into Gatsby's love for Daisy that remains unfulfilled, unsatiated, trapped within the tragic lines of the gyre of his sorrow. This Modernist principle that explores love as an emotion that is sacrificed at the altar of ambition and economic and social success, is almost like a reiteration of the pangs of unrequited love explored and expressed by the Romantic poets.

In *The Great Gatsby*, Fitzgerald uses much of contemporary historical material. As critic Ronald Berman observes, 'The choice of place and subject, for example, was itself a statement' (Prigozy 2001, 81). Life in post-war New York City was 'monied, vulgar, noisy, chaotic and immoral'. In 1924, American critic H. E. Mencken wrote about the 'frenzied life of Manhattan' a 'spectacle, lush and barbaric in its every detail…' (Prigozy 2001, 81). Hence, through the use of potent symbols of colour, Fitzgerald was perhaps trying to create the new American novel, thereby, replacing the moralistic Victorian conscience with Modernist subjectivity. The result was a novel titled *The Great Gatsby*, the story of a Modernist hero who began life as Jimmy Gatz, moving steadily upward and making it big in America. In the process, he loved and lost Daisy Fay and trapped within the kaleidoscope of his unipolar world, he understands that in order to get her back, he would need a good deal of money. When we meet him, he is a story of 'success', a personification of the grand American motif. However, this world of social glitter is based upon ambiguities. In the words of critic Berman, 'One begins to expect that "after having been everywhere, and seen everything and done everything…", it is a world of broken relationships, false relationships; a world of money and success rather than social responsibility; a world in which individuals are all too free to determine their moral destinies' (Prigozy 2001, 83). This is the kaleidoscopic world of Jay Gatsby.

The persona of Jay Gatsby is at the vortex of this world. In the essay by David Parker titled '*The Great Gatsby*: Two Versions of the Hero', an idea is developed that the figure of Jay Gatsby is a curious admixture of both the first who is a, 'prototype, we find in medieval romance and ancient epic, and idealist, loyal to transcending object, and relentless in his quest for it. He seeks honour, love or the surreal, and he affects the reader with all the potency of myth. The second kind, though doubtless developed from the first, is in sharp contrast. If he has a quest, it is essentially an inward one. Circumstances compel him to explore his own being, to discover, and to perhaps to modify, his own identity…. The achievement of *The Great Gatsby*…, is in the profoundly satisfying way Fitzgerald manages to include both versions of the hero in one version, balancing each against the other, and avoiding the blight of one-sidedness' (1973 5–6).

Hence, the American Dream and its illusions and Jay Gatsby and his quest for love together create a world of shimmering reality in which Gatsby coexists with his Dream. In fact, entrapped within this gyre of temporality, Jay Gatsby stands vis-à-vis the supreme dilemma of the American Dream. The Dream, however, reverts into a claustrophobic reality that stifles every hope of holistic success. In this friction between the capitalist and consumerist approaches to human existence, the Dream comes across as deeply flawed and vastly inadequate. So, while coexisting with this Dream, Jay Gatsby and his obsessive quest for love in Daisy, too, seem flawed and limited. On the veneer, like the Dream, Gatsby's love for Daisy appears to be unwavering. But again, just like the Dream this emotion, too, remains elusive, and beyond any possibility of fulfilment. Gatsby, however, is not less tenacious in any way in his love for Daisy which continues for five years despite their separation and her marriage to Tom Buchanan. He persists with the Dream of uniting with her despite its possibility being like a mirage. In the words of David Parker, 'Gatsby too is dauntless, but absurdly so. He cannot conceive failure, and in a sense fails less than the image he chose to embody his dreams' (1973, 8).

Almost as a foil to Jay Gatsby stands the character of Nick Carraway, who spirals in the margin of Gatsby's world and his Dream. Critics have drawn parallels between Nick Carraway, the narrator of this novel, and Mr Lockwood, the narrator of *Wuthering Heights*. It has been observed that both these characters have obvious deficiencies as narrators of their particular stories, but through the astonishing actions and strange passions of others, both are able to rectify those deficiencies. As a consequence, both these characters learn to contemplate with sympathy what they may not have comprehended before. Nick Carraway's mid-Western background gives his character both a secure sense of identity and a moral standpoint which allows him to retreat from the unfamiliar. Standing counter to Nick and his rigid inflexibilities is the eponymous character of Jay Gatsby who professes to be the architect of his own destiny.

The use of the superlative 'Great' in his profile and as the title of the narrative urges one to probe the complex irony that defined the man. Jay Gatsby was the epitome of capitalist idealism and yet he suffered from an extreme sense of inadequacy. His life gyrated around the 'green light', a beacon symbolising his ideal consummation through his union with Daisy, but hopelessly elusive. The colour symbolism in *The Great Gatsby* allows the juxtaposition of the alternate ways of life lived by Gatsby and the Buchanans. All through the narrative, Gatsby is associated with light and colours of shimmering silver. The images of the moonlight, starlight or artificial light is closely associated with him and the house he inhabited. In contrast, Daisy is immersed in images of darkness with only the lone 'green light' indicating her presence beyond Gatsby's reach. There are repeated references to 'twilight' in connection to Daisy. When Nick puts together the events of Daisy's life after Gatsby's departure five years prior to the time depicted in beginning of the novel, he writes: 'through this twilight universe Daisy began to move again with the seasons…' (Fitzgerald, 130). And references to her finally putting out the green light on her dock is a symbolic indication of the ultimate destruction of Jay Gatsby and his Dream.

The array of colours in the world of Jay Gatsby fails to dissipate the dark shroud of silence that threaten to advance and consume him at every step. It is as though he cannot disengage himself from the darkness within and without him. Jay Gatsby lives in his larger-than-life image immersed in hues of blue and gold, which however, cannot conceal the hues of grey and black that stain his mind from within. The colour green has been used in its conventional concept of desire, jealousy and wealth while the colour yellow symbolises depravity and crude baseness of the *noveau riche* wealth of Gatsby. Critics have opined that Fitzgerald uses colours in *The Great Gatsby* to synchronise pure innocence with moral decay and death. Hence, we have the coalition of colours: white, yellow and green. The predominant colour that emerges in the world of Jay Gatsby is gold, which serves to imply the materialistic stand of the protagonist. Gatsby's hope, or the lack of it, is symbolised by his 'white and pink suits'. Interestingly, he wears white when meeting Daisy which indicates the innocence and intensity of his passion for her.

Apart from the significance and synthesis of colours in the novel, the synchronisation of time is also noteworthy. Fitzgerald writes: 'Gatsby never understood that he was trapped by time and human history. Yet, even in the only moment he ever had his future—in the past, in his youthful imaginings—the dream light was punctuated by the sounds of time'

(Tredell 1997, 105). Further, Fitzgerald writes in the novel: 'a universe of ineffable gaudiness spun itself out in his brain while the clock ticked on the washstand and the moon soaked with wet light his tangled clothes upon the floor' (77). And in the moment that Gatsby meets Daisy in Nick's bungalow, he is tormented by time— dead time. He feels he can turn back time into the past but that clock does not work, that 'defunct mantlepiece clock' (68). It is observed that it is 'inevitable that Nick's premonitory warning about time should be fulfilled in Daisy's final announcement of her inability to fulfil Gatsby's dream…' (Tredell 1997, 106).

In the essay titled '*The Great Gatsby*: Apogee of Fitzgerald's Mythopoeia', critic Neila Seshachari writes, 'a close study of *The Great Gatsby* will reveal that there are basic generic differences between the traditional American Dream and Gatsby's own personal quest. The American Dream has been an affirmation of the romantic possibilities of the human imagination and a belief in man's inherent greatness. Gatsby's personal philosophy synchronises with this outlook. However, apart from this common faith, the actual direction that Gatsby's personal dream took does not follow the pattern of the American Dream' (2004, 28). However, since this personal quest or philosophy is a quest for the unattainable, we have to note the unmistakeable echo of the American Dream in Gatsby's quest of love for Daisy. This quest for the mythical ideal defines the American Dream although it is devoid of its realistic values. Jay Gatsby's one and only overwhelming and consuming passion, to which all other impulses are either subordinate or non-existent, is his hope of winning Daisy. In fact, his every effort including the accumulation of wealth and his nebulous parties are a shroud for his inherent desire to win back the object of his love, his passion, Daisy. Seshachari observes: 'His sense of worship—wonderment, anxiety, nervousness—are all obvious when he arranges to meet her at Nick Carraway's home for tea. The entire chapter in which he meets Daisy for the first time since their separation five years previously exudes Gatsby's sense of worship of Daisy. The preparation for the worship is itself very elaborate. Two whole days before their meeting—

in fact, on the day it is arranged—Gatsby's home is lit from tower to cellar in an unreal blaze' (Bloom, 30).

This 'unreal blaze' remains as a major symbol throughout the text enabling us to compare the impossibility of Gatsby's quest for Daisy to the unreality of the great American Dream. Yet another recurrent symbol in the narrative is water. It is extensively used as the point of connection between West Egg and East Egg. It is believed that Fitzgerald used the water symbol as a leitmotif. From Gatsby's swimming pool to the final rain at his funeral that gently purifies everything, water plays a crucial role in his life. In fact, Nick Carraway's first glimpse of Gatsby is that of him standing on the shore of the bay stretching his arms in an almost mystical contemplation towards the dark waters separating him from his Daisy. Water as a purifier is a mythic symbol. It purges, cleanses and heals the body from within. Therefore, his death in the water of his pool could be translated as a mythic symbol of his apotheosis. And the rain that incessantly falls at his funeral could be read as a fertility symbol which completes the restorative apotheosis of Gatsby. Rain translates into a metaphor of rejuvenation, indicating a deep sense of healing that Gatsby experiences through death. So as Joseph Campbell describes, Gatsby's life and death can be summed up through the process of 'separation—initiation—return' (Bloom, 33). Therefore, perhaps, it can be surmised that Jay Gatsby is a mythic figure as he functions both on the macrocosmic and the microcosmic levels.

Though the narrative is a critique of the materialistic dimension of the American Dream, this criticism does not affect the personality of Jay Gatsby and his overriding passion for Daisy, which was the sole focal point of his opulent lifestyle. Gatsby's wealth and his ostentatious display of it remain unblemished by the romantic idealism with which he pursues Daisy. All tensions, national, human and personal in colour synthesise in death, the death of Jay Gatsby. All conflicts are resolved and reconciled, too, in the end.

The synonymity between desire for Daisy and desire for wealth is reflected in Gatsby's dream and is corroborated in the words: 'her voice is full of money'. However, the critique of the materialistic outcomes of the American Dream continues through the eyes of Nick Carraway as he gradually learns the full extent of the Buchanans' corruption. Their failure is symbolic of the failure of an entire generation, a way of life directed by the American Dream. Critic Brian Way in his essay '*The Great Gatsby*' notes: 'Nick's disappointment has already been prefigured poetically in his first glimpse of the Buchanan household.... By the end of his first dinner party at the Buchanans', Nick Carraway is already disillusioned with the American rich' (Bloom, 43–45).

The motif of illusion and reality is carefully woven into the fabric of the narrative. Jay Gatsby had built his entire life around the notion that if he could get rich, Daisy would return to him. Therefore, critics claim that though Gatsby the dreamer dies, he dies believing in his dream, and so his dream continues to live on after him. So, if Jay Gatsby is an emblem of the world of illusion that he had created around him, Nick Carraway is the realistic narrator, the mouthpiece of the author, who keeps his part of the bargain by upholding the reality which counters Gatsby's web of illusion. Gatsby's philosophy of illusion is based on the principle that only incessant efforts will help to realise his Dream. The Dream is an illusion which continues to absorb and engulf individuals like Jay Gatsby who dare to step into its fold. So, caught up in the frenzy to reach this point of perfection and absolute consummation of his love, Jay Gatsby dwells in the world of illusion. So much so that even his conviction that Daisy loves him back is also fraught with delusion.

Fitzgerald writes: 'There must have been moments even that afternoon when Daisy tumbled short of his dreams—not through her own fault, but because of the colossal vitality of his illusions. It had gone beyond her, beyond everything' (Fitzgerald, 67). The colour that defines Gatsby's illusory world is blue and, ironically, that is also the colour of Nick Carraway's car, thereby connecting the domains of both illusion and reality. The pursuit of dream and personal desires amalgamate in the persona of Jay Gatsby. This fusion is reflected in the narrative every time Gatsby looks across the bay, desiring the presence and return of Daisy in his life. The challenge is to arrive at a point in which illusion and reality would coalesce and confirm the realisation of the Dream. That, however, is ultimately implied through Gatsby's death which heralds the ideas of apotheosis and a restorative growth of the dream, which remains larger than life. It embraces eternity with the promise of fulfilment beyond the precincts of human existence. This is what transforms Jay Gatsby into the 'Great Gatsby'.

However, critic Ronald Berman opines that Gatsby is imperfect despite his idealism. His idea of a good life revolved around wealth and property. His car, his prized possession, is described as 'a rich cream colour, bright with nickel swollen here and there in its monstrous length with triumphant hatboxes and supper-boxes and tool-boxes, and terraced with a labyrinth of wind-shields that mirrored a dozen suns' (Fitzgerald, 51). Therefore, his house, his car, his lifestyle all conglomerate to create a symbol of consumerism in a world driven by material needs. So, the only obstacle that appears to hinder Gatsby's dream and desire is dictated by human nature, time and chance. Gatsby does not want mere success, he desires to be a 'gentleman' for the object of his affection, Daisy. So then, the question that arises is that: is Daisy a symbol, objectifying the consummation of the desires of the Great Gatsby, the human individual who was living a larger-than-life reality? Or was Daisy that emblem of a simple, rare and pure love to which he aspired to revert back to from his role as the Great Gatsby?

This dilemma of desires enmeshes the life of Jay Gatsby, and we find him caught within this confusing whirlpool of his desperate thoughts and actions. We observe that Gatsby does not want to be praised for what he is but for what he is not. In this, he represents the tensions of the early Twenties. He is ascribed the labels of 'a perfect gentleman', 'a man of fine breeding', that indicate his integral position within the social class that he attained but had not been born into. When he says, 'here's another thing that I always carry' (Fitzgerald, 53), a photo of his 'Oxford days', it is his way of proving that he has always belonged among his peers and that his actual past had completely disappeared. Thus, we can proclaim that Jay Gatsby is not only the leading man of the Jazz Age but the last great figure of the 'gentleman hero'.

In the words of critic Ronald Berman, '...his character is thickened, made more intense, by obsolete qualities of courtesy, thoughtfulness and honour. Whether dealing with Nick Carraway or Daisy or with a girl who has torn her gown at his party, he has the nobility unknown to West Egg, forgotten by Eat Egg, and by our national memory. The irony of the novel is that he has become far more of a gentleman than his social adversaries....' (Berman 2007, 88). The language of the novel reflects the energy of the Twenties. The dynamism and the vitality that we observe in Jay Gatsby, in Myrtle Wilson and at times in Nick Carraway, suggests the ability to lead a life of feeling. It suggests an intensity and emotional commitment that display the vitality, energy and restlessness of the Twenties along with related national implications connecting the characters with the concept of the great American Dream. As in *The Wasteland* where Eliot was responding to a post-First World War Europe, a world morally coming apart, Fitzgerald depicts the world of the Twenties that was marked by radical changes, in which a generation was entrapped in sterile and purposeless lives gyrating towards an enigmatic light that beckoned and promised redemption.

Romantic fervour and echoes of Keatsian approach concerning pleasure and desire have been brilliantly fused with American materialism in *The Great Gatsby*. In his treatise *Beyond Culture* (1978), Trilling explains that the Keatsian conception of pleasure involves the principles of both reality and illusion. He cites from 'The Eve of St Agnes', where the moment of pleasure, erotic pleasure consummated through luxurious imagination, is the very essence of reality which when surrounded by darkness, becomes lifeless. It becomes transitory like a mere illusion. This trope can be observed in Fitzgerald's *The Great Gatsby*, where Daisy is not just a reflection of the magical, mythical world that Gatsby aspires to be the locus of, but the ultimate object in that world that is near yet so far, just like a Romantic illusion which has a real basis. This fusion of the real and the unreal is distinctly

Keatsian in motif and treatment allowing an apotheosis of this concept in Fitzgerald's narrative.

As Trilling further observes, that though Keats 'may be thought of as the poet who made the boldest affirmation of the principle of pleasure,', he may also be considered 'the poet who brought the principle of pleasure into the greatest and sincerest doubt' (1978, 58). So, this ambivalence in pleasure evolved as a principal trope for Fitzgerald and the American world which cloaked itself in an ambivalent luxury in the Twenties. And similarities between *Gatsby* and Keatsian thought in 'The Eve of St Agnes' is too stark. The description of refreshments at Gatsby's party replicates the feast Porphyro prepares for Madeline in the poem. Critic Harold Bloom in describing *The Great Gatsby*'s 'shirt scene' as the epitome of the novel, calls it 'an apotheosis of Fitzgerald's Keatsian art', and links the novel to 'The Eve of St Agnes' and the Keatsian concept of ambivalence in perfect pleasure. Keats writes in the poem:

> And still she slept an azure-lidded sleep,
> In blanched linen, smooth, and lavender'd,
> While he forth from the closet brought a heap
> Of candied apple, quince, and plum, and gourd;
> With jellies soother than the creamy curd,
> And lucent syrops, tinct with cinnamon;
> Manna and dates, in argosy transferr'd
> From Fez; and spiced dainties, every one,
> From silken Samarcand to cedar'd Lebanon.
>
> (1994, lines 262–70)

Similarly, in the novel when Gatsby presents before Daisy his own 'heap' of 'precious luxuries', Fitzgerald writes: 'He took out a pile of shirts and began throwing them one by one before us, shirts of sheer linin and thick silk and fine flannel which lost their folds as they fell and covered the table in many-colored disarray.... Suddenly with a strained sound Daisy bent her head into the shirts and began to cry stormily...' (Fitzgerald, 72–73). Both the poem and the novel, in this section, uses the term 'heap' to denote the excess that is available but never used. And Daisy's reaction in the 'shirt scene' is proof of the underlying erotic tension which bursts forth in the form of tears: a sign of consummation of desire in both these scenes of excesses. Perhaps this is what confirms the apotheosis of Keatsian art in Fitzgerald's novel.

Jay Gatsby, the symbol of excess, is never merely a symbol though. His pink suit, his repeated use of the phrase 'old sport', his collection of monogrammed shirts, his presentation of himself as an Oxford man, all individualise him enough to keep him from becoming a mere symbol or a type. It is believed that in creating Gatsby, Fitzgerald had drawn extensively from actual people around him. But in putting together the traits of some others he knew, Fitzgerald had created an enigma who could never be 'one of us'. Gatsby is an instance of complex contradictions. He has also been defined as the great American Everyman. He is, 'sinister and naïve, violent and soft-hearted, both a child of an American backwater and a would-be British aristocrat, an idealist and a predator… glamourous and banal in his efforts to recreate himself and his milieu according to a Platonic image of himself' (Roulston and Roulston 2007, 80–81).

The novel is, therefore, a kaleidoscope of tragic hues. Just as the myriad colourful images of a kaleidoscope are in a constant state of movement, changing and shifting patterns and formats, likewise the novel revolves through a maze of issues involving American life and its dilemma in the Twenties. It presents a blend of colloquial dialogue, a prose equivalent of Keats' poem, replete with nostalgia, suspense, violence, luxury, fashion and the social and personal experiences of the extravagant Twenties. Hence, the novel can be well acclaimed as a period novel. The agony and the ecstasy that Jay Gatsby experiences and takes his readers through, the gyre of his emotions that he allows his readers to witness, prove that he embodies the land of heart's desire, that multitudes aspire for and fail to achieve.

The consummation of these desires, as represented by Jay Gatsby, eventually moves towards a closure. However, this closure is only superficial since the conclusion of the narrative contains the idea that Gatsby continues to gyrate within the whirlpool of his emotions and desires. Even in the last moments of his life, he refuses to wake up from his Dream. His enigmatic life, caught in a swirl of tragic hues, meets an intriguing end as he reaches the point of culmination still yearning for a union with Daisy. *The Great Gatsby* is indeed a lament for a passing civilisation, in which a romantic egotist lives and dies in a Dream, with his life and death embodying a clarity and symmetry that remains unparalleled in American fiction.

Works Cited

Berman, Ronald. 2001. *Fitzgerald, Hemingway and the Twenties.* Tuscaloosa: University of Alabama Press.

Berman, Ronald. 2007. 'Individualism reconsidered'. In *F. Scott Fitzgerald's The Great Gatsby*, edited by Harold Bloom. New York: Chelsea House Publishers.

Bloom, Harold, ed. 2004. *Bloom's Major Literary Characters: Jay Gatsby.* New York: Chelsea House Publishers.

Bloom, Harold, ed.2007. *Viva Modern Critical Interpretations: F. Scott Fitzgerald's The Great Gatsby.* New York: Chelsea House Publishers.

Fitzgerald, F. Scott. 2020. *The Great Gatsby.* New Delhi: Fingerprint Publishing.

Keats, John. 1994. *The Complete Poems of John Keats.* New York: Random House.

Parker, David. 1973. '*The Great Gatsby*: Two Versions of the Hero'. *English* Studies 54(1): 37–51.

Prigozy, Ruth, ed. 2001. *The Cambridge Companion to F. Scott Fitzgerald.* Cambridge: Cambridge University Press.

Roulston, Robert and Helen H. Roulston. 2007. '*The Great Gatsby*: Fitzgerald's Opulent Synthesis (1925)'. In *F. Scott Fitzgerald's The Great Gatsby*, edited by Harold Bloom. New York: Chelsea House Publishers.

Seshachari, Neila. 2004. '*The Great Gatsby*: Apogee of Fitzgerald's Mythopoeia'. In *Bloom's Major Literary Characters: Jay Gatsby*, edited by Harold Bloom. New York: Chelsea House Publishers.

Tredell, Nicholas, ed. 1997. *F. Scott Fitzgerald: The Great Gatsby.* New York: Palgrave-Macmillan.

Trilling, Lionel. 1978. *Beyond Culture: Essays on Literature and Learning.* San Diego: Harcourt.

12

'A Quality of Distortion': Notes Toward a *Gatsby* Noir

Bennet Schaber

> You know, old sport, I've never used that pool all summer?
>
> F. Scott Fitzgerald, *The Great Gatsby*

> If that was true he must have felt that he had lost the old warm world, paid a high price for living too long with a single dream.
>
> F. Scott Fitzgerald, *The Great Gatsby*

> The poor dope! He always wanted a pool. Well, in the end, he got himself a pool, only the price turned out to be a little high.
>
> *Sunset Boulevard*

Deferred Vision

In 2003, Wheeler Winston Dixon published 'A Vision Deferred', what by now has to be considered the *locus classicus* of critical assessments of film adaptations of the novels of F. Scott Fitzgerald. Dixon, author of an earlier monograph devoted to Fitzgerald's career as a Hollywood screenwriter, deployed what were undoubtedly conservative, but also plausible and what have proven to be durable, criteria of judgment. Film and televisual versions of *Tender is the Night* and *The Last Tycoon* he dismissed in a sentence. And what were, at the time, the three film versions of *The Great Gatsby* (there are now many more) fared no better, although each received a more extensive historical and critical analysis. Nevertheless, Dixon made the verdict clear almost immediately: '[T]o date, not one of Fitzgerald's novels has been brought to the screen with a true sense of fidelity to the original source material' (2003, 287). With respect to *Gatsby* he wrote,

'This is a shame, inasmuch as the story structure of *Gatsby* in particular, is both suspenseful and highly visual…'. But the adaptations had apparently been botched because, 'screenwriters and directors… have taken excessive liberties with the work, which all but eliminate the intensity and power of the novel' (287). What 'suspenseful' can mean in this context is hard to say, given that the novel is a 'classic', which Dixon is quick to admit. But what it means to call the novel 'highly visual' also seems, at best, ambiguous. How exactly not only to adapt, but to remediate, what sometimes appears as a baffling synesthesia—those 'blue gardens', 'white girlhood', 'yellow cocktail music', 'a face with sad and bright things in it', 'unquiet darkness'—or as an even more baffling principle of erasure—'On the white steps an obscene word, scrawled by some boy with a piece of brick, stood out clearly in the moonlight, and I erased it', etc.? A passage like this, as Barbara Will (2005) argues, 'challenges its readers to question the terms through which 'presence' and 'visibility' can be signified' (126). How then to effect a remedial translation of a writing that retracts itself, leaving nothing but an afterimage, a negative figure or, in Fitzgerald's own words, 'a quality of distortion' associated with 'fantastic dreams' or the paintings of El Greco (2004, 176)?

Thus, even if Dixon's criteria of success, a remedial spectrum with fidelity on the positive end, excessive liberty on the negative, might continue to function for us, to what, exactly, are we being asked to be faithful? The 'source material' seems peculiarly unstable if not downright resistant; and prying apart—and then reassembling—suspense and visuality is hardly a simple matter. As Will's question about 'presence' and 'visibility' suggests, part of the difficulty here is that Fitzgerald's novel, with its attentiveness to its own heightened style (for example, the mock-epic 'curtains… like pale flags' that 'rippled over the wine-colored rug, making a shadow on it as wind does the sea' (2004, 8)), never ceases to insist upon itself precisely as style and self-reflexivity, as high-modernist writing. If a passage like this can be said to be visual, it is certainly not visual in any straightforward, naturalistic fashion that might comport with classical Hollywood realism. The same might be said for suspense, which the novel ceaselessly suggests is less narrative than hermeneutical, a suspension of meaning rather than narrative anticipation. What can it mean, for instance, to have asserted that 'Gatsby turned out all right' (2) after the cascading and catastrophic events of the final chapters?

In fact, many of these difficulties were made manifest in the very first adaptation of *Gatsby*, not a film but the theatrical version by Owen Davis (1926). Made less than a year after the novel's publication and just before the first film version (now considered lost), it would go on to form the basis of the second *Gatsby* film, released in 1949 and starring Alan Ladd. A highlight of the 1926 Broadway season, running for 171 performances, it received generally favourable notices. The reviewer in *The Bookman*, while praising the play's faithfulness to the 'spirit of the book', nevertheless noted, perspicaciously, that,

> For all its merits, the book still remains greater than the play, but this is unavoidable. Certain scenes, certain situations, do not lend themselves easily to stage production, and some of Fitzgerald's most glittering lines are better read than spoken. (216)

To read Davis's play today is to recognise the essential rightness of this evaluation. While keeping faith with the novel's moral core (Gatsby's fidelity to his 'incorruptible dream' does indeed make him 'worth the whole damn bunch put together'), the play makes no effort to grasp the novel as writing and, thus, as an experience of reading, instead transposing that narrative, hermeneutic process, which in the novel is more mental than extensive, into the naturalistic, objective and three-dimensional space of representation. And by filling out the *lacunae* of Fitzgerald's modern tragedy, it creates a psychological and sociological armature for its characters that is explanatory rather than probing. In short, the play, although in Dixon's terms faithful to 'the source material', nevertheless ignores the elements that make the novel a modernist and, sometimes, opaque artwork, instead turning it into a transparent depiction of people and events.

Transparency seems to have contributed to the play's popular success. According to the anonymous reviewer in *The Bookman*, the play was more popular than the novel itself. Nevertheless, the theatrical, representational and objective space of Davis' drama effectively negated the novel's very different commitments to a dramatisation of the time or process of reading and writing: a more dynamic and processual unfolding of both story and narration, often punctuated by phrases like, '*Reading* over what I have *written* so far, I *see* I have given the *impression*...' (55, my emphasis). Indeed, it may well be the epistemological uncertainty of this performative, discursive stereometry and recursiveness of reading, in which, often, writing and seeing are conjoined, that gives some real—albeit difficult and uncertain—meaning to what Dixon called 'suspense'. And perhaps the same can be said of 'visuality'.

The novel is almost certainly an instigator of vision, but it would also be an epistemologically and ontologically uncertain vision emerging from a dynamic process of perceptual and projective intensity, not given as an object reified in and as a material substance extended in space. These qualities of 'distortion', then, require quite different modes of suspense and visibility. And Fitzgerald was hardly the only modernist artist—Picasso, Benton, Beckman come immediately to mind—to recognise them in dreams and in the paintings of El Greco.

I would like to propose, therefore, that notions like fidelity or license, suspense or visuality, are not particularly helpful either as categories of judgment or remedial re-creation, at least where this novel is concerned, or unless we are willing to radically rethink their meanings. More forcefully, the categories suggest a fundamental misprision regarding the difficulties of simply adapting in a naturalistic modality the symbolism, expressionism and modernism that characterise the novel. Instead, I would like to entertain the notion that *The Great Gatsby* itself suggests, even models, the remedial processes and patterns it might require to emerge as a film, or a play for that matter, 'with the intensity and power of the novel'. What's more, I would propose that these processes—thematic and episodic, of course, but also and especially graphic and dynamic—often neglected in direct, film adaptations of the novel, have in fact found themselves dispersed and redistributed in films that make conspicuous reference to *Gatsby. Scarface* (1932), *Citizen Kane* (1941), and *Sunset Boulevard* (1950), function as registrations and highly stylised realisations of that modelling, including its symbolist and expressionist tendencies. To do this, I want to turn to an early, if somewhat obscure, theorisation of the modernist novel that already detected its affinities with the motion picture, and particularly the affinities between the formations of readerly and spectatorial consciousnesses, that might point, like the films of Hawks, Welles and Wilder, toward a film *Gatsby* yet to be achieved, the 'deferred vision' of Dixon's essay.

Novel, Movie and the Modern World

In May of 1919, Ralph Block (1889–1974) published 'The Novel in the Modern World' in *The Lotus Magazine*. A journalist, theatre critic, social theorist and, sometime poet, Block was enthusiastic about the naturalist, symbolist and expressionist directions of the advanced theatre in New York, writing encouraging reviews of early works by Eugene O'Neill, Susan Glaspell, Zona Gale and Wallace Stevens in the *New York Tribune*. He was also a prolific writer of essays on modern aesthetics and modern culture more generally, publishing in journals like *The Century, The Bookman, The Freeman, The Lotus, Vanity Fair, The New Republic* and *The Dial*, all associated with an emerging American modernism and in some of which Fitzgerald's prose also appeared. If Block is remembered today, it is less for those efforts, as interesting as they remain, than for subsequent essays on film theory and culture, and for his actual work in the film industry. He would become, in the 1920s and 1930s, an important producer, writer and editor, a founder and president of The Screenwriter's Guild and the recipient of an Academy Award in 1940. His writing about film would continue to be anthologised into the 1960s. For readers of this volume, it might also be of interest that Block spent the years of World War II in India working for the United States Office of War Information. Although he would continue to write about film, he never returned to the industry.

In 1919, Block had returned to New York from Washington DC where he had been the *New York Tribune's* Washington correspondent during World War I. Redirecting his energies,

Block entered the film industry, initially as publicity director for Samuel Goldwyn, before taking up duties more in harmony with his literary gifts at Famous Players-Lasky, Paramount, and later Fox and Pathé Exchange. Although he never seems to have met F. Scott Fitzgerald, he did know several prominent modernist writers, among them Marianne Moore and Eugene O'Neill, and had published in Harriet Monroe's influential little magazine, *Poetry*. 'The Novel in the Modern World' does not, then, address Fitzgerald directly (*This Side of Paradise*, Fitzgerald's first novel, and *Flappers and Philosophers*, his first story collection, would not appear until the next year), but it does make important—and early—claims on a notion of the modern, American novel, what it might be or become, and where its formal resources might lay.

Indeed, some of those claims, all of which we now associate with *Gatsby*—its embrace of the lyrical and narrative powers of modernist poetry as well as the economy and vitality of the American short story, and the importance of Conrad as a precursor and contemporary—dovetail quite nicely with similar claims made by Fitzgerald later in the 1920s (Mallios 2001).

In addition, Block linked the modern novel to the cinema, only just emerging from its transitional phase and beginning to consolidate into what would become a long-lasting institutional, industrial, cultural and narrative form. It is through this linkage that it becomes possible to reimagine *The Great Gatsby* as a meta-cinematic form, running ahead, like the film theory Block was himself constructing, of the actually existing state of cinema at the moment.

For Block, the novel was a crucially unstable aesthetic form, precisely because, to his mind at least, it was bound to time and, more directly, to its own time. Thus, Block asserted that, 'Dickens and Thackeray bulk in the eyes of so much of the world as great novelists of time, when they were only great novelists of their time' (1919, 232). The modern novel's success, then, depended upon its resonance with the temporal forms that conditioned its own emergence, the frequencies and wavelengths that, in Block's words, constituted the 'flux' of modern life.

The responsibility of and challenge to the contemporary novel, 'the conscious or unconscious demand the time is putting on [it]', was to address this 'constant flow of change... in an effort to adapt the mind and body to breaking and reforming rhythms of it' (1919, 233). Modern writers were doing this, in part, by 'emphasizing strange facts about form'. Block singled out Wyndham Lewis' *Tarr* (1918) and its 'new schemes of punctuation' as one example. But more crucially, speed and immediacy appeared to be the twin conditions of an emerging poetics. Of Joyce's *Portrait of the Artist as a Young Man* (1916), Block asserted that 'the narrative itself has a strange flavor of immediacy, as if it were all in process of happening at the very moment of its narration' (234). Dorothy Richardson, he contended, 'achieves this feeling of immediacy by the sharpness and great vividness of her subjective picturization. Her narrative conveys the feeling of a motion picture of a mind in action, as it works its way through the experience of living'. And indeed, as Laura Marcus has pointed out, consciousness in Richardson's novels 'is described primarily through shifting patterns of light and darkness' (1998, 154) that, later in her career, Richardson would explicitly compare to cinema, the registration and projection of, in her own words, 'light and shadow in movement'. In this respect, for both Block and Richardson, the successful modern novel needed to function like a sensitive and immediate recording device, very much like the seismograph with which Fitzgerald has his narrator, Nick Carraway, compare Gatsby: '... there was something gorgeous about him, some heightened sensitivity to the promises of life, as if he were related to one of those intricate machines that register earthquakes ten thousand miles away' (2004, 2). Later Nick will introduce the 'spectroscope' (44), among other apparatuses for detecting the sometimes finely grained, sometimes 'gaudy' range of modern sensations and their variable intensities that comprise the novel, the 'swirls and eddies' (42) of its sensory and discursive flux.

Those swirls and eddies appear to suggest a kind of Vorticist sympathy for what Ezra Pound called 'an intensive art' (1916, 104), or in Block's words, 'a prose [that] leaps more and more to the place of compression for the sake of intensity' (235). And if in 1925 very few American novels had attained this condition, even fewer films had risen to the challenge for which, as Block's text makes clear, 'the motion picture' itself supplied the relevant and representative metaphor.

What Block would eventually designate the movie's 'pragmatic sanction'(1927, 24), as opposed to a more straightforward, even if contested, aesthetic sanction, bound the movie to a set of temporal coordinates very much like those in his account of the modernist novel. 'The movies are implicit in modern life', he wrote in *The Dial.* 'They are in their very exaggerations—as a living art often may be—an essentialization of that which they reflect' (21). And he continued:

> The movie is in other words a new way to see life. It is a way born to meet the needs of a new life. It is a way of using the machine to see what the machine has done to human beings. [...] It requires a special kind of eye, a special kind of feeling about the relationship between things and things, events and events, and an intuitive as well as empirical knowledge of how to make the camera catch what that eye sees and that imagination feels. (23)

Crucially then, there was a dialectic between the complex, mechanical time of the apparatus and the equally complex, subjective time of the mind or brain with which it resonated. It was this same, or nearly the same, resonance that Block was detecting in the 'immediacy' with which the modern novel's varied forms of 'subjective picturization' created the impression that everything was 'happening at the moment of its narration'. And if, as I am attempting to develop here, there is a strong relation between what Block expressed as 'a motion picture of a mind in action', and what Fitzgerald expressed as, among other turns of phrase, 'fast movies' (4), or as the complex temporality of the 'beat' with which *The Great Gatsby* ends ('So we beat on... boats...borne back...'), it is thanks to this dialectic of modernity, of which the Vorticist intensification of images and the nascent cinema were both symptomatic.

A year after his essay on the modern novel, in an essay in *The Freeman*, Block would express it like this:

> [W]hat in the motion-picture is essential and unique is—above all things—motion. Every contribution to the general pattern—the setting, the acting, the lighting,

> the narrative itself—all are conditioned by the fact that they are composed and quickened to life and form only when there is added to them the vital principle of flux, of movement. As a static thing the motion-picture has no existence. But when once made to live it streams before the eye in a constant process of becoming.... It lives in a myriad of immediacies. (156)

In a period of less than a year, then, Block was now attributing to the movies qualities he had been detecting and indeed promoting in the modern novel. What in 1920 is claimed as 'essential and unique' to cinema, looks very much like the essential and unique characteristics Block had claimed a year earlier for the modern novel. As Sergei Eisenstein (1944) would point out some years later, what seemed intrinsic to the cinema was often and in fact a catalysation or dynamisation of processes already at work in other media, in this case the novel. The important thing was not to become enamored of claims of medium specificity, but to try to discern the actual lived, social processes and forces engineered into and at work across multiple media forms and the forms of thought and feeling with which they were implicated.

In an essay in *The New Republic*, Block did just that. 'The most distressing and fatiguing movies are those built upon highly complicated plot', he wrote. And he continued,

> The reason is as much philosophic as mechanical. The essence of plot is causal relationship—efforts impinging upon causes—and a successful illusion of life, especially in a time when the illusion of life is so completely a picture of accident and incoherence, can never be produced by a method which provides for accident only by such apparent design. (1924, 311)

It was not, then, an Aristotelian dramaturgy of causes that aligned the cinema with the modern novel, with 'the method of all modern art' (311), and with the modern antinomy of 'accident' and 'design', but what Block variously phrased as efficiency, compression, condensation, intensity, immediacy, continuity or continuousness. In the emerging cinema of the early 1920s,

> Scenes that pad the story, establish motives and background at great length, are conspicuously absent. Relations of scene to scene, continuity, is implicit in the material; the audience's imagination, stimulated by the condensation of meaning, is trusted to understand all that has gone before and will come after. (311)

This was not a simple question of technique but, as Block explained in *The Freeman*, something closer to 'what the moderns mean by significant form' (1920, 156). It was the ability to 'surprise humanity in the act of being itself, in all the illogic and absurdity of its varying patterns'; 'to rob appearance of its inanity, and to provide it with semblance and resemblance' (311). Joyce had done this in *Ulysses*, with 'words highly impregnated with meaning, the thousand attenuations and reverberations of human history'. But for cinema, it was not a question of words but of appearances themselves. And appearances would seem to 'lack the connotative power' of words, that is unless they were 'highly selected, condensed, organized and related to ideas' (311). As if in a modern novel.

Block thus characterised the emerging cinema as a distinct image practice and not some sort of vague visuality. But as distinct as it might seem, it shared essential features with the modernist novel, imagist poetry, and as Block would point out again and again, 'the drama of expressionism' (1920, 311). Indeed, the important trait seemed to lie in the adjective, modern. And in insisting upon this trait as it emerged from and within the contemporary world as aesthetic practice, the medial differences among novel, poem, story, film, drama, even painting and music, seemed to melt away into a shared, dynamic and crucially temporal process of reflection, expression and beholding. A dialectic that Block expressed through an appeal to Bergson (whom Fitzgerald had read in 1917): 'For the camera, movement must be living, warm, vital, and flowing rather than set and defined in an alphabet of traditional interpretation. Like Bergsonian time, it must seek to renew and recreate itself out of the crest of each present moment. It is in this sense that it resembles music' (1927, 20). Against that 'alphabet' of tradition, cinema held some of the same promises as the other modern, experimental arts: openness, innovation, immediacy and the potential subversion of normative accounts of space and time. 'There is therefore, a *continuousness* essential to the process which must be recognized', Block (1920, 157) argued, here again about the cinema, but with implications for all the modern arts, 'a flux that will determine the [...] artist's treatment. The mind of the audience alone can see the created thing as a unity; it never appears as such on the screen'.

It is in this insistence upon duration as renewal and recreation, but also at odds with traditional forms of aesthetic order, that Block's cinema resembles Fitzgerald's 'yellow cocktail music'. Temporalisation as novelisation. The experience of the modern novel, like that of the contemporary cinema, at least in its best moments, was an experience of time.

In its affinities with Bergsonian creative duration, filmic continuousness, like modernist prose, could wrest even nature from its 'traditional alphabet'. Fitzgerald does exactly this at the opening of *Gatsby*: 'And so with the sunshine and the great bursts of leaves growing on the trees, *just as things grow in fast movies*, I had the familiar conviction that life was beginning over again with the summer' (2004, 4, italics added for emphasis).

The outside world and interior consciousness find themselves correlated and condensed through an appeal to cinematic dynamism. An old trope becomes new in the time of accelerated film. Passages like this form a recurring motif across the length of the novel. 'I began to like New York, the racy, adventurous feel of it at night', writes Nick, 'and the satisfaction that the *constant flicker of men and women and machines* gives to the *restless eye*' (2004, 56, italics added for emphasis). This was exactly what Block asserted as the promise of both modern cinema and the modern novel: 'a new way to see life... born to meet the needs of a new life. A way of using the machine to see what the machine has done to human beings'.

Examples could be easily multiplied. I will adduce one more because it both contrasts with and complements the 'fast movies' of the novel's opening. In one of the novel's most terrible moments of misrecognition, Nick steals a view of Myrtle at her window above Wilson's garage: '... and one emotion after another crept into her face *like objects into a slowly developing picture.* Her *expression* was curiously familiar—it was an *expression* I had often seen on women's faces, but on Myrtle Wilson's face *it seemed purposeless and inexplicable until I realized* that her eyes, wide with jealous terror, were not on Tom, but on Jordan Baker, whom she took to be his wife' (124–25, italics added for emphasis). A dynamic process is at work here. In Block's words, 'relations implicit in the material', not an external chain of causes, are responsible for the formation of the picture Fitzgerald creates: an immanent, 'slowly developing' and distorted figure in close-up, a literal expressionism, as the repeated use of the word, 'expression', emphasises. But it is also an expression built up out of the development of what appears to be a form of cinematic or photographic continuity, 'one emotion after another', what Block called the 'flavour of immediacy, as if it were all in process of happening at the very moment of its narration'.

We might say that Fitzgerald's novel, like the movies, develops its continuities from series of discontinuous states, punctuated by accidents or catastrophes. As Block had surmised, 'a [moving] picture of accident and incoherence', in Fitzgerlad's words, 'purposeless and inexplicable until' raised to a significant, formal totality in the mind that synthesises them, here Nick Carraway's. 'I was doing what the cinema was doing', wrote Gertrude Stein in 'Portraits and Repetition' (1934), 'I was making a continuous statement of what that person was until I had not many things but one thing' (294). Fitzgerald was doing it too. 'If personality is an unbroken series of successful gestures', we read on the novel's second page, 'then there was something gorgeous about him' (2004). The 'unbroken series', like Stein's 'continuous statement', or the 'constant flicker of men and women and machines', indicates an essential affiliation between modernist method and cinematic continuity. But more importantly, what was being revealed here was not just that the modern novel and the cinema were, as Block initially argued, of their time, but that they were also deployments, analyses and experiments with modern temporalities, indeed with readerly and spectatorial consciousness as temporalisation: 'a new way to see life... born to meet the needs of a new life'. The vocabulary of speed, compression, acceleration, intensity, but also expression, series, rhythm and continuousness, implied at least that much.

'How about the movies?'

Movies, movie stars, directors, movie magazines, the homes of movie stars to the west of Central Park, even the 'big, cool' movie houses on 'Fiftieth Street' (2004, 125) suffuse *Gatsby*. And movies form, as well, a kind of allusive texture of the novel's prose. When Gatsby styles himself as an erstwhile 'young rajah', Fitzgerald may mean us to think of the 1922 film of the same name, written by June Mathis and starring Rudolph Valentino as the titular hero (who, like Gatsby, also collects rubies).

'After that I lived like a young rajah in all the capitals of Europe'. The Maharajah of Dharmagar (Rudolph Valentino) embraces Molly Cabot (Wanda Hawley) in *The Young Rajah* (1922). Paramount Pictures. Wikimedia Commons.

We are told that Jay Gatsby is 'a regular Belasco', thus likening him to the Broadway producer who, in 1912, reconstructed an authentic Childs Cafeteria on the stage of the Republic Theatre, thus blurring the line between the real and its representation, an approach that would become increasingly associated, not with the stage, but with the movies (Essin 2009).

'This fella's a regular Belasco'. Cinematic realism in David Belasco's staging of the Childs Restaurant Scene in *The Governor's Lady* (1912). *The Theatre Magazine*, 16: ix. Wikimedia Commons.

But if *Gatsby* has been curiously resistant to adaptation by those same movies, it may be, paradoxically, because Fitzgerald was already adapting a range of meta-cinematic procedures and phenomena (like the colour-music of Gatsby's parties or 'the constant flicker of men and women and machines' on Fifth Avenue or 'the ecstatic patron of recurrent light' of Gatsby's first meeting with Daisy) that the really existing cinema of his time (and even after) was not able to register with any sort of clarity, but only in fragments and in the absence of a coherent theory of the kind Block was trying to construct. But it is odd that the intense engagement with movies that characterised Fitzgerald's entire career should be so absent from those same movies' engagement with Fitzgerald.

The now lost 1926 film apparently aimed for mass spectacle, with plenty of bathing beauties and Daisy, played by Lois Wilson, drinking absinthe. Only a fragment of the film is extant, but we know that Fitzgerald and Zelda went to see it and were anything but impressed: 'We saw "The Great Gatsby' in the movies', Zelda wrote to her daughter. 'It's ROTTEN and awful and terrible and we left' (Daniel 2013). The 1949 version, based upon the Davis stage play, cast Alan Ladd as Gatsby, a gangster who attempts, too late, to reform, in an effort to be worthy of the magnitude of his romantic dream. He spends a good deal of time in bathing trunks, modelling his manly physique to Nick, played by Macdonald Carey. In this version, it is Jordan Baker who turns out all right, even attending Gatsby's funeral.

The 1974 version, no doubt the most famous, took Fitzgerald's vocabulary of gaudy, gauzy and gorgeous and translated it directly into star power; Robert Redford and Mia Farrow are nothing if not radiant. A made-for-television version from 2000, along with two film versions from 2002 and 2013, all attempted to make use of the novel's framing through Nick's retrospective narration. In the first, Nick, played by Paul Rudd, narrates in voice-over. In the second, Nick is transformed into the music journalist, Tre (Andre Royo), with Gatsby transformed into the hip-hop mogul Summer G (Richard T. Jones) and Daisy become Sky (Chenoa Maxwell), his lost college sweetheart. It is she who dies at the hands of a jealous husband, with G resigned to a 'heartless' life as a businessman.

Baz Luhrman's 2013 film in 3D was also hip-hop inspired, and notable not just for its stars, Leonardo DiCaprio and Carey Mulligan, music and frenetic energy, but for the portrayal of a convalescent Nick (Tobey Maguire), who types the novel in a therapeutic effort to cure his alcoholism. All of this is, as it were, 'in' the original novel; and thus each of the films has something to recommend it. And yet, as so many critics and reviewers like Dixon have remarked, each seems to miss the target.

What the films seem to lack are the very qualities Block proposed—and Fitzgerald realised—in his argument for the modern novel: epigrammatic and penetrating brevity, concision and sharpness of characterisation, stylistic compression and intensification, and a narrative form 'that has the strange flavor of immediacy, as if it were all in a process of happening at the very moment of its narration' (234). In other words, the problem seems to stem not from a lack of fidelity to the 'source material', but from a commitment to overly classical forms of the narrative realism characteristic of Hollywood, forms that were only just coming into focus when Block was writing and Fitzgerald composing the novel. What is lost is the inscription of the movies as a modern force interacting with and interrogating and interrogated by the formal processes of modernist prose.

In short, the very temporalising processes that haunt Fitzgerald's novel (writing and reading as creative duration) and which the cinema as an experience of time, in and as vision, both enacted and metaphorised. The challenge, immense, or so it seems to me, is to find a cinematographic correlative for Fitzgerald's prose, for his sentences, their graphic materiality and the time of their unfolding, and to articulate that with the novel's insistence upon the co-presence of Gatsby's many pasts as constitutive of his overdetermined present, those multiple 'states' (Fitzgerald 2004, 91) through which he passes and which lead to 'an inconceivable pitch of intensity' (92). Like his house, with its Restoration salons, Merton College Library, period bedrooms, etc., Gatsby is simultaneously the soldier who arrives in Louisville, the gangster confederate of Wolfsheim, Dan Cody's friend and apprentice, the Oxford man, perhaps a nephew of the Kaiser, the boy, Jimmy Gatz, who inscribes his schedule on the flyleaf of *Hopalong Cassidy*, etc. One can only look for him in one past at a time, which only flavors or tinges the immediacy of the present in which, nevertheless, all the pasts continue to coexist, like a slowly developing picture or as in a fast movie. But each search, each sequence, series or continuous statement, leads only to a suspension, to a hesitation or mute opening of duration. 'It's the funniest thing, old sport', he said hilariously. 'I can't—when I try to—' (91). Or again: 'For a moment a phrase tried to take shape in my mouth and my lips parted like a dumb man's.... But they made no sound, and what I had almost remembered was uncommunicable forever' (111). These suspensions, like the repetitions that are their corollaries ('Gatsby... Gatsby... Gatsby... Gatsby' we read on the novel's second page) are the traces of a temporalisation in which every plunge into the past opens a fissure in the present.

Gatsby's Noir Afterlives

I hope the previous sections have made clear that what I would consider the basis for a film adaptation of Gatsby has far less to do with suspense, visuality or fidelity to the source material than with an attentiveness to the novel as an experience of time, a flux or continuum of creative duration, to use Block's vocabulary, that crucially includes the time of writing, reading and, yes, seeing. What is required, I believe, is an engagement with forms of cinema that are less classical, more expressionist, and with stronger affinities with aesthetic modernism. And a successful adaptation may require as well an *auteurist* presence commensurate with the novel's reserve, its stuttering, hesitations, lack of transparency and, for lack of a better word, style, a graphic work or dimension irreducible to plot, character or story, but distributed across the surface of the text.

This dimension, what Block called 'appearances', 'highly selected, condensed, organised and related to ideas', would supply an indirect but necessary link to the modernist novel, its forms of reflexivity and recursiveness, as well as its ambivalent claims on aesthetic autonomy (Block's 'new way of seeing'). In short, a successful adaptation of *Gatsby* cannot be a film that seems to have been made by no one in particular. It will require material traces of an ideal or virtual authorial presence in excess of any narrative vehicle or contrivance: Fitzgerald ≠ Nick ≠ *Gatsby*.

As the epigraphs to this essay indicate, part of what I want to consider here as a potential fund for a yet-to-be-realised film *Gatsby*, derives from an uncanny resemblance between the ending of Fitzgerald's novel and the opening of Billy Wilder's *Sunset Boulevard*, a film that fulfills, I believe, all the requirements I've listed above. The words of the film's opening voiceover, spoken by fictional screenwriter, Joe Gillis (William Holden)—'The poor dope! He always wanted a pool. Well, in the end, he got himself a pool, only the price turned out to be a little high.'—closely echo those of Jay Gatsby and Nick Carraway near the conclusion of *The Great Gatsby*. Spoken from the quintessential and indeed impossible place of noir subjectivity—Holden's character is dead even before he begins to narrate—the lines also echo, in the split between a living voice and a dead body floating in a swimming pool, the split between Gatsby's auto-narration ('I've never used that pool...') and Nick's interior reconstruction of that experience ('If that was true... he paid a high price...').

The similarities don't end there. The novel and the film both record the collapse of a dream that, through a series of perspectival shifts, seems either enormous or remarkably trivial (in the idiom of the film: 'I am big. It's the pictures that got small'); both relentlessly reckon with the difficulties of narrating that dream that those shifts imply; and finally, both end with the hero murdered in a swimming pool. The flashback, voiceover narration of *Sunset Boulevard*, through which Wilder condenses Gatsby and Nick, or what we might call the indicative and conditional moods, allows the film to begin precisely where the novel ends. Meanwhile, Joe Gillis, the film's protagonist, is both a social striver and a writer, very much like Nick Carraway or Fitzgerald himself. What I want to suggest, then, is that *Sunset Boulevard* might well be considered a kind of loose or meta-adaptation of *Gatsby* precisely through its efforts to grasp, in their aftermath, the hopes and disappointments of the movies and of Hollywood of the 1920s, according to the style and procedures, the model, constructed by Fitzgerald's devastated and diminished narrator who, by the novel's end, seems to have grown into the 'hard-boiled painting' (Fitzgerald 2004, 3) he is said, at the novel's opening, to resemble.

In this respect, Fitzgerald's Nick Carraway can be understood to inaugurate a series of distinctively American, 'hard-boiled' narrators characteristic not just of crime fiction (Hammett, Chandler and their epigones), but of an enduring and still vibrant strain of expressionist or neo-expressionist filmmaking with origins in the 1920s and of which *Sunset Boulevard* is an exemplary instance. But, if Gillis can narrate from beyond the grave, it is because the film gestures towards a shaping, authorial force in excess of that narration and with no proper place (its locus is temporal rather than spatial, virtual rather than real). In Block's words, 'a motion picture of a mind in action'. In Will's parlance, a challenge to 'the terms through which "presence" and "visibility" can be signified'. How exactly do we 'see' the film; and 'who' shows it to us? This is what I will call '*Gatsby* noir'.

Sunset Boulevard tells the story of Joe Gillis, an unsuccessful screenwriter who, in an attempt to elude bill collectors, finds himself hiding out in the home of former silent film star, Norma Desmond. He is convinced to help her write a film adaptation of *Salome* as a vehicle for her return, after many, many years, to the screen. Drawn progressively deeper into her psychoses, he becomes her (much younger) lover, thus thwarting his budding romance with the young writer, Betty Schaefer. When he finally finds the courage to leave Norma for Betty, he is gunned down, portable typewriter in hand, and falls into the swimming pool. The film is thus, like *Gatsby*, an extended flashback narrated by a young man with literary, financial and erotic ambitions, as if knotting together Nick, Gatsby and Fitzgerald.

Billy Wilder and Charles Brackett, the film's screenwriter, both knew Fitzgerald from his time in Hollywood and both admired him intensely. Brackett and Fitzgerald were good friends, both Ivy-educated novelists who would end their careers as screenwriters. Wilder met Fitzgerald in 1937 while the novelist was living at The Garden of Allah bungalow colony on, where else, Sunset Boulevard. Fitzgerald had also known, from a previous sojourn in Hollywood during the 1920s, Gloria Swanson, who created *Sunset Boulevard*'s most memorable rôle, Norma Desmond, forgotten star of the silent cinema, whose operatic name (Bellini's *Norma* meets Verdi's *Otello*) emphasised her outsized and psychotic character.

The fatalistic and tragic tenor of the film is also consonant with the temporalising forms of *Gatsby* that Block theorised as critical aspects of both the modern novel and cinema. This is thematised by the film's dual poles of female attraction and the function of Joe's writing in relation to each (he is initially depicted at his typewriter, a pencil in his mouth, an image the film continuously develops until the point of his death).

Joe Gillis (William Holden), Norma Desmond (Gloria Swanson), and Betty Schaefer (Nancy Olson) at the typewriter in *Sunset Boulevard* (1950). Directed by Billy Wilder. Paramount Pictures.

Joe is progressively drawn into a past characterised by vampirism and incest in, what amounts to, Norma's mausoleum, suggestively described in the screenplay (Wilder 1994) as, 'one of those abortions of silent-picture days' (24), as if to emphasise its reproductive dead end.

Through writing, he is expected both to exhume and to copulate with, and thus resurrect, the dead. The other pole is occupied by Betty, the young screenwriter, where writing is also phrased as copulative, but in the service of a living present, possible futurity and a non-perverse pleasure, what might be called the film's thwarted, 'orgastic future'. The film seems to make clear, however, that what we are presented with is less a choice and more a representation of a lethal, self-destructive subjectivity for which the attraction of one pole requires the repulsion of the other which sustains it.

As in *Gatsby*, the attempt to revivify the past, which also requires a series of transgressions, turns out to be fatal to the present. As Nick observes in the novel: '[Gatsby] looked around him wildly, as if the past were lurking here in the shadow of his house, just out of reach of his hand' (Fitzgerald 2004, 110). And the past, as well as the future it is thought to promise, remain just out of reach for Joe as well, who also dies in the shadow of Norma's house, built with, according to the screenplay, 'beams imported from Italy, with California termites at work on them' (Wilder 1994, 24). Thus, as in Gatsby, is connoted the corruption or 'foul dust' (Fitzgerald 2004, 2) that will float in the wake of his dreams. Norma plays the 'grotesque… ashen fantastic figure gliding towards him' (161) at the film's end, a condensation of Wilson, Mabel and something unshowable (an erased word) or unspeakable ('what I had almost remembered was uncommunicable'). The sublime El Greco effect.

Wilder's film meets all of the requirements for a compelling *Gatsby* adaptation. Most importantly, by emphasising the time of seeing—vision as an experience of time and memory irreducible to space and extension—the film takes shape through the conflicted and conflicting subjectivities of the characters whose words and gazes shape or deform it, and through a more unlocalisable, authorial force that gives it 'what the moderns mean by significant form'. Wilder, however, was not the first filmmaker to use *The Great Gatsby* as a kind of generative matrix and then transform it into something nearly unrecognisable. Nor was *Sunset Boulevard* the first film of major ambition to set its sights on *Gatsby* and also deploy a noir or neo-expressionist aesthetic.

Citizen Kane (1941), what Gilles Deleuze called 'the first great film of a cinema of time' (1985, 99), is more than resonant with the great American novel of time. Greg Toland's high-contrast cinematography, deep focus, canted angles and breathtaking close-ups, and Welles's direction, laden with the expressionist elements he knew so well from a life in the advanced theatre, made of the film a kind of noir biography of the Gilded Age and modernising America. Herman Mankiewicz, responsible for the first draft of the film, originally titled *American*, knew Fitzgerald's novel well, while his brother Joe knew and worked with Fitzgerald himself (the two were hardly fond of one another).

As in the Wilder film, there are many echoes of *Gatsby* in *Kane*, some quite distinct, others barely audible. Both tell the stories of young, idealistic men from the American West who encounter the corruption of the East and who remain fixated on an image or object from a past they would desperately like to retrieve. And both protagonists see their dreams, in the words of the novel, 'broken up like glass' (Fitzgerald 2004, 148), Kane's more literally when his prized glass ball rolls from his dead hand at the film's conclusion. And again, both novel and film maintain their density and complexity by means of reconstructive, participant narrations. Finally, those narrators, according to Robert Carringer, find that no 'significant incident, detail, or object can provide a unifying or definitive perspective on a man's life' (1975, 314).

Gilles Deleuze has suggested that what makes *Citizen Kane* a crucial reference for any attempt to think rigorously about modern cinema is its temporalising dynamics, the ways it complicates not only representations of time and the past (flashbacks, for instance), but the ways in which it frees time from its subordination to movement and the very forms of causality or design against which Block argued.

Like *Sunset Boulevard, Citizen Kane* is also, in effect, narrated from beyond the grave, from the place of a pure, temporalising subjectivity (who exactly sees, and who exactly shows us, Rosebud consumed by the flames, like a word erased at the film's conclusion?). Like Block (and perhaps Fitzgerald), Deleuze makes recourse to Bergson in order to elaborate *Kane*'s 'figures of temporalization' (110). Both recall *Gatsby*. In the first, an image from the past is recalled but can no longer be made to function in the present, just as, for example, Gatsby's attempts to draw the image of Daisy *out of the past* and to relive it in the present are thwarted by Daisy's 'carelessness' and 'the hard malice' (Fitzgerald 2004, 148) of Tom Buchanan's world, with shattering consequences. In the second, the image eludes recollection, hovers on the edge of memory (perhaps it never existed?), and so casts a *shadow of a doubt* across every other image. This is the time, of which Dixon had a presentiment, of a vision endlessly deferred, 'borne back ceaselessly into the past'. This is also the time—alliterative, allusive, anaphoric, rhythmic—of authorial inscription.

Citizen Kane, therefore, also fulfils the requirements for a successful film *Gatsby*. But it was Howard Hawks and Ben Hecht's *Scarface* (1932) that set the table for the appearance of *Gatsby* on screen as a kind of uncanny guest. Like *Gatsby, Scarface,* a gangster's rise-and-fall story modelled on the career of Al Capone, tells the tale of a 'colorful character'—romanticised and sentimentalised in the mind of the public—who has 'everything he wants BUT what he really wants', and that's Poppy, a woman with a flower's name, like Daisy Buchanan, who 'belongs' to another man. Like Fitzgerald's and Welles's eponymous heroes and *Sunset Boulevard's* Joe Gillis, *Scarface*'s Tony Camonte (Raymond Massey) is invariably 'reaching out my hand to snatch something' that consistently eludes him. And like his literary progenitor, he invites Poppy to his new and extravagant home. 'How do you like this place?' he asks her. 'Kind of gaudy, isn't it?' she replies. 'Gaudy?' says Tony, 'well come here; I'll show you something'. Of course he proceeds to show her his collection of shirts (Roberts 2006). Replacing the green light on Daisy's dock is an illuminated sign, visible through Tony's window, that announces: 'The World Is Yours'. Finally, and in another filmic conflation of Gatsby and Nick as twin narrators, Tony claims authorship of his own fable: he compares his machine gun to a typewriter with which he will 'write his name in the sky'. Like screenwriter Joe Gillis, newspaperman Charles Foster Kane, and editorialist-for-the-*Yale News* Nick Carraway, he too is a writer.

Unlike the fractured and multiplied narrators of *Citizen Kane* or the hard-boiled, morally compromised, but desperate-to-be-understood narrator of *Sunset Boulevard, Scarface* seems to lack any form of a sustained, narrational voice. There are occasional scenes in which newspapermen discuss their coverage of Tony's criminal activities, which they simultaneously condemn and yet patently sensationalise in a drive to sell papers. There are also images of the headlines from those same papers, which reflect the images of fascination through which the public both romanticises and speculates about the origins of Tony, much in the way the guests at Gatsby's parties do about him. But it is Lee Garmes and L. William O'Connell's remarkably fluid cinematography and chiaroscuro lighting effects that make of the film's camerawork a compelling visual correlative of Fitzgerald's justly celebrated sentences, as well as of the participant-observer narrator who characterises the novel. *Scarface*'s heightened visual style, then, powerfully augments its claims on *Gatsby*.

Scarface also offers its spectator another, and crucially unlocalised, dimension through which to experience the film's temporalising dynamics; and one that also, like *Sunset Boulevard*, entertains an uncanny relation with *Gatsby*. The scar in *Scarface* is a mark forming a letter, an X, on Tony's left cheek. An identifying mark, it nevertheless detaches itself from its bodily support to enter the film's visual economy as a form of writing, an inscription that tears every form away from its own identity.

It appears as a shadow cast across a variety of figures by street signs, buildings and windows. Its form is revealed in girders of warehouse interiors and in the trestles of Chicago's elevated, urban railway. And it appears, more than once, as writing, most famously as a mark penciled into a bowling score sheet just before the death of a rival gangster (Boris Karloff). In its cruciform shape it signifies a crossing, a transgression and, finally, death. A figure of both inscription and erasure, simultaneously a mark and its crossing out, the X is the immanent trace of a material continuity that can only exist for the film's spectator, a graphic match that links image to image and propels the spectator into time, precisely in the absence of the kinds of causal chains against which Block argued. In Block's terminology, the X is 'implicit in the material'.

Indeed, the development of the X-form, as motif and as material presence, is probably closer to what Block had in mind apropos of continuity or continuousness than the more complex temporalisations of *Sunset Boulevard* and *Citizen Kane*, staged as they are in depth and within the image itself, an exploration of time within the image that would have been foreign to Block's own film experience.

A scar becomes a letter. Transformations of the X in *Scarface* (1932). Directed by Howard Hawks. United Artists.

As deployed by Hawks, the X-form subjectifies the entirety of the film's visual environment, producing a sense of a virtual, authorial, shaping force, a motion picture of a mind in action, in much the same way Fitzgerald's sentences function for a reader.

Indeed, there exists a kind of intra-graphic work within the texture of Fitzgerald's prose with an uncanny premonition of the film's similar deployment of the letter X. Readers attentive to that texture have always recognised Fitzgerald's fondness for alliteration (Nicholas 1976). Less remarked is the persistent presence, often doubled, sometimes multiplied beyond that, of the letter G, not only in the novel's title, 'Great Gatsby', but also in the almost unvarying way in which the appearance of the word, Gatsby, finds itself nearly immediately repeated, as in, 'Only Gatsby, the man… Gatsby who represented…' (Fitzgerald 2004, 2).

This graphic, infra-stylistic work extends beyond names and alliteration proper into the doubled G of the word egg, repeated no less than five times on page 5 alone (and accompanied by another doubled Gatsby: 'It was Gatsby's mansion. Or, rather, as I didn't know Mr Gatsby…'), to the doubled G of 'Oggsford', also doubled ('He went to Oggsford College. You know Oggsford College?'), to that other Wolfsheim neologism, 'gonnegtion' (Fitzgerlad 2004, 70). It is more than tempting to see in the X of the film-work of *Scarface* the legacy of the G in the text-work of *Gatsby*. But even in the absence of any empirical filiation, these infra-visual and infra-graphic devices appear to be critical to the temporalisations through which the aesthetic objects form in the minds of spectators and readers. They unfold, in Block's words, as a 'myriad of immediacies'. The 'mind' or thought they reveal remains virtual.

As in Fitzgerald's novel, *Sunset Boulevard*, *Citizen Kane* and *Scarface* all end with their protagonists dead in some version of what, in *Gatsby*, Nick calls 'that huge incoherent failure of a house' (Fitzgerald 2004, 179–80), their dreams finally incapable of protecting them from, indeed even provoking, a murderous outside world that resonates with and even doubles a delusional and equally self-destructive interior.

Norma Desmond's decaying mansion, Kane's Xanadu, and Tony's steel-shuttered penthouse, all echo the architectural and aspirational excesses of West Egg, including European and other exotic trappings barely camouflaging otherwise dubiously acquired wealth. But what is most striking, beyond narrative, episodic, rhetorical and character similarities, is the choice all three films make to inscribe those borrowings within the visible forms and co-ordinates of the expressionism that characterises noir visuality. It is as if the creators of the films had all detected, in the very first, penumbral appearance of Gatsby to the man who would narrate his story, the novel's spectral, noir afterlives.

> I saw that I was not alone—fifty feet away a figure had emerged from the shadow of my neighbor's mansion and was standing with his hands in his pockets.... When I looked once more for Gatsby he had vanished, and I was alone again in the unquiet darkness. (Fitzgerald 2004, 20–21)

What all three films seem to register, therefore, is an affinity between Fitzgerald's remarkable contribution to a uniquely American form of the modern novel and noir or neo-expressionist aesthetics as a commensurate but also uniquely American form of modern cinema. If *The Great Gatsby* was, in Block's words, 'proposing a new way to see life', so too was the American film noir.

The noir or expressionist elements of the films are thus indicative of a response or even debt to the novel that has at least three dimensions. First, the exaggerated mannerisms or affectations of the protagonists—Tony's whistling or hand gestures, Kane's bombast and impressive stride, Joe's cynical wisecracking or the pencil he keeps in his mouth—establish character with the same kind of efficiency, concision and continuity as Fitzgerald deployed in the creation of his and as Block had asserted in his analyses of the modern novel and film. Second, the filmic images are insistently subjectivised, perception and representation fully immixed to yield 'a motion picture of a mind in action'. We might call this the El Greco effect: a distortion of the image field that gives to it a quality of thought or expression and so subjectifies it. By blurring the distinction between the objective and subjective, the real of perception and the real of representation, the film and the modernist novel discover their expressive affinities.

These are crucially linked to time and memory: Tony's ties to his mother and his violent, even incestuous relation to his sister; Kane's fixation on his childhood, maternal home, and the transitional objects (Rosebud, the glass ball) that make possible the coexistence of past and present; Joe's Oedipal catastrophe as Norma's young lover. And third, a graphic impulse that undermines and deforms deformation itself, what in Fitzgerald is neither story nor style, although often indicated by anaphora and alliteration, but writing as the literal or graphic work of letters, an automatism of inscription that, like the El Greco effect, also signals an affiliation between modernist writing and the cinematic machine, a 'beat' that transforms 'continuousness' into a complex experience of time and duration. A successful film *Gatsby,* noir or otherwise, will have to rise to that.

Works Cited

Block, Ralph. 1919. 'The Novel in the Modern World'. *The Lotus Magazine* 10(5, May): 232–35.

———. 1920. 'Motion'. *The Freeman* (27 October): 156–57.

———. 1921. 'The Movies versus Motion Pictures'. *The Century Magazine* 102 (October): 889–92.

———. 1924. 'The Ghost of Art in the Movies'. *The New Republic* (14May): 310–12.

———. 1926. 'Review of *The Great Gatsby,* Stage Play by Owen Davis'. *The Bookman* 63(2, April): 216.

———. 1927. 'Not Theatre, Not Literature, Not Painting'. *The Dial* 82(1, January): 20–25.

Carringer, Robert L. 1975. 'Citizen Kane, the Great Gatsby, and Some Conventions of American Narrative'. *Critical Inquiry.* 2(2): 307–25.

Daniel, Ann Margaret. 2013. 'What Did F. Scott Fitzgerald Think of *The Great Gatsby*, the Movie, in 1926? He Walked Out'. *Huffpost.* https://www.huffpost.com/entry/the-great-gatsby-movie-1926_b_3024329.

Davis, Owen. 1926. *The Great Gatsby, from F. Scott Fitzgerald's novel.* Irvin Department of Rare Books and Special Collections, University of South Carolina Libraries, Columbia.

Deleuze, Gilles. 1989 [1985]. *Cinema 2: The Time Image*. Minneapolis: The University of Minnesota Press.

Dixon, Wheeler Winston. 2003. 'The Three Versions of *The Great Gatsby*: A Vision Deferred'. *Literature/Film Quarterly*. 31(4): 287–94.

Eisenstein, Sergei. 1949 [1944]. 'Dickens, Griffith, and the Film Today'. In *Film Form*. New York: Harcourt.

Essin, Christin. 2009. 'Designing American Modernity: David Belasco's *The Governor's Lady* and Robert Edmond Jones's *The Man Who Married a Dumb Wife'*. *Theatre History Studies* 29: 32–51.

Fitzgerald, F. Scott. 2004 [1925]. *The Great Gatsby*. New York: Scribner.

Mallios, Peter. 2001. 'Undiscovering the Country: Conrad, Fitzgerald, and the Meta-National Form'. *Modern Fiction Studies* 47(2): 356–90.

Marcus, Laura. 1998. 'Introduction. Continuous Performance: Dorothy Richardson'. In *Close Up, 1927–1933: Cinema and Modernism*, 150–59. Princeton: Princeton University Press.

Nicholas, Charles. 1976. 'The G-G-Great Gatsby'. *CEA Critic* 38(2): 8–10.

Pound, Ezra. 1970 [1916]. *A Memoir of Gaudier-Brzeska*. New York: New Directions.

Roberts, Marilyn. 2006. '*Scarface, The Great Gatsby* and the American Dream'. *Literature/Film Quarterly* 34(1): 71–78.

Stein, Gertrude. 1967 [1934]. 'Portraits and Repetition'. In *Writings and Lectures 1911–1945*. London: Peter Owen.

Wilder, Billy. 1999. *Sunset Boulevard. The Complete Screenplay*. Berkeley: University of California Press.

Will, Barbara. 2005. '*The Great Gatsby* and the Obscene Word'. College Literature 32(4): 125–144.

Editor and Contributors

Sanjukta Dasgupta, Professor and Former Head, Department of English and Former Dean, Faculty of Arts, Calcutta University, is a critic, editor, poet, short story writer and translator. A recipient of several international fellowships, including the Fulbright postdoctoral fellowship, she has also served as Chairperson of the Commonwealth Writers Prize jury, as Convenor of the English Language Board, Sahitya Akademi and is currently member of the Advisory Committee of the Jnanpith Award. Her honours include major literary and lifetime achievement awards and is currently a ScoTs Edinburgh Research Affiliate.

Sachidananda Mohanty was formerly the Vice-Chancellor of the Central University of Odisha, and Professor and Head of the Department of English, University of Hyderabad. Currently, he serves as member of the University Grants Commission and as National Fellow at the Indian Institute of Advanced Study. Recipient of many national and international awards, such as Katha, British Council, Fulbright, Charles Wallace, and the Salzburg awards, he has published extensively in the fields of British and American literatures, gender studies, translation studies and post-colonial studies.

Somdatta Mandal is former Professor of English at Visva-Bharati University. A recipient of several prestigious fellowships like the Fulbright Research and Teaching Fellowships, the Charles Wallace Trust Fellowship, the Rockefeller Residency, and the Salzburg Seminar, she has been published widely both nationally and internationally. Her publications include monographs, edited volumes and translated volumes. Her areas of interest are American literature, contemporary fiction, film and culture studies, diaspora studies and translation.

Manju Jaidka, former Professor and Chairperson at Panjab University, Chandigarh, is a Fulbright fellow and two-time

Rockefeller fellow. She has published nearly thirty books and over a hundred research papers in reputable journals, and authored volumes of poetry, drama, and fiction. Her work on disability management, *The Next Milestone*, was commissioned by the World Health Organisation. She has compiled the encyclopedias of Indian Writing in English and Diasporic Indian English Writing.

Tania Chakravertty, academic-turned-administrator, critic, author, translator and reviewer, is currently Principal, Shri Shikshayatan College, Kolkata. Selected in 2010 for the prestigious International Visitor Leadership Program (IVLP) funded by the US Department of State's Bureau of Educational and Cultural Affairs, she has published various monographs and contributed articles in several national and international anthologies and journals. Her areas of academic interest include gender studies, American literature, literature of the diaspora and translation studies.

Avishek Parui is Associate Professor of English and Memory Studies at IIT Madras and Associate Fellow of the UK Higher Education Academy. He serves as the faculty coordinator of Centre for Memory Studies at IIT Madras, member of the advisory board of Memory Studies Association, and the co-founding chairperson of the Indian Network for Memory Studies. He has authored *Postmodern Literatures* and *Culture and the Literary: Matter, Metaphor, Memory*, and is co-editor of *Memory Studies in India: Texts and Contexts*.

Madhuchhanda Ray Choudhury is Associate Professor of English at Sister Nivedita University and former Head, Department of English. Her articles and book chapters have appeared in publications of national and international repute. She contributed a chapter on Daphne du Maurier in *Posthumanism and Literary Insights* (2025). She has previously worked with Amity University, St Xavier's University, Visva-Bharati University and Osmania University. Her research interests are gothic literature, the eighteenth-century British novel, monsters and monstrosity.

Richard A. Courage holds the rank of Distinguished Teaching Professor at the State University of New York. He researches, teaches and writes about American and African American literature and cultural history, composition and rhetoric, and online learning and has published extensively on these subjects. *Roots of the Black Chicago Renaissance: New Negro Writers, Artists, and Intellectuals, 1893 to 1930* is his most recent publication.

Amritjit Singh is Langston Hughes Professor Emeritus of English and African American Studies at Ohio University. Singh has authored, edited and coedited over fifteen books, including *The Novels of the Harlem Renaissance* (1976, 1994); *Postcolonial Theory and the United States* (2000); *The Collected Writings of Wallace Thurman* (2003); *Interviews with Edward Said* (2004); *Revisiting India's Partition: Essays on Culture, Memory, and Politics* (2016); and *Critical Perspectives on Chitra Divakaruni: Feminism and Diaspora* (2022).

H. Kalpana Rao, former Professor of English at Pondicherry University, is a scholar of critical theory, cultural studies and feminist literature. She has received numerous awards and international fellowships, including the Fulbright fellowship in 2022. She has authored *Quilting Relationships: A Cruise through Comparative Literary Studies* (2009) and co-edited *Kala Pani Crossings, Gender and Diaspora* (2023). She contributed to *A Companion to World Literature* (2019) and serves as literary editor for *Muse India*.

Amit Shankar Saha is Associate Professor and Head of the Department of English at Seacom Skills University. He has authored *Transitions: Indian Diaspora and Four Women Writers, A Portrait of the Artist as a Young Essayist*, along with five collections of poems. He is editor-in-chief of *EKL*

Review and Assistant Secretary of the Intercultural Poetry and Performance Library. He has contributed articles and chapters on diaspora studies, Indian Writing in English, gender studies and culture studies.

Neeraj Pizar is Associate Professor of English and Communication Skills and the Controller of Examinations at the Centre for Distance and Online Education, Chitkara University, Punjab. With over thirteen years of academic experience, his areas of interest include drama, linguistics and English literature. His publications include his doctoral book *The Enigma of Amleth: A Study of Selected Versions of Hamlet* and contributions to the *Encyclopedia of Indian Writing in English* in collaboration with Professor Manju Jaidka.

Suchandana Bhattacharyya is Associate Professor at the Department of English, St Xavier's College, Kolkata. She has presented research papers at various national and international conferences worldwide and published extensively on race, gender and identity in noted academic journals and anthologies. Her research interests include American fiction and African American literature, particularly the works of canonical authors, Maya Angelou and Alice Walker.

Bennet Schaber is Professor and Chair, Department of Cinema and Screen Studies School of Communication, Media and the Arts State University of New York, Oswego. A former Luce Foundation–University of Pennsylvania Japan Fellow (2006–07), he is also Visiting Professor of Film at the University of Kairouan, Tunisia. He has participated in the NEH North Africa Institute (Oregon State University, 2014) and NEH Modernism Institute (Newberry Library, Chicago, 2022).